The **Struggle Within**

a novel

The **Struggle Within**

a novel

Sarah Whelan

Author Photograph by Joyful Reflections Photography

Any people depicted in stock imagery provided by Getty Images are models, and such images are being used for illustrative purposes only. Certain stock imagery © Getty Images.

ISBN: 978-1-4834-8427-3 (sc)
ISBN: 978-1-4834-8426-6 (e)

Library of Congress Control Number: 2018904550

Lulu Publishing Services rev. date: 04/23/2018

ACKNOWLEDGEMENTS

Each of us must be our own hero, but it helps to be surrounded by people with superpowers. I am grateful to those with the gifts of compassion, tolerance, and generosity. Some of you were the first readers of this book, and I hope you know how much I trust and admire you. Others knew that I had undertaken this challenge and repeatedly offered words of encouragement. I needed them, and you made a difference. Still others helped me simply by being positive elements in my life. I gained energy and motivation from sharing our stories and challenging ourselves to be better every day.

To my beautiful family, thank you for supporting me while I wrote this book. You are the heart of my story, and I could not do life without you.

I also want to acknowledge the editors who helped shape this book. Sione Aeschliman, thank you for your insightful and honest critique. It enabled me to strengthen both the content and style of the book. Caroline Connick, I appreciate your professional copyediting work. I can't wait to see where your own writing journey takes you.

CHAPTER ONE

Inside

He had to stop the injustice, and his fight started now. José issued his command before the guards entered the cellblock. "Vámanos, brothers," he told his fellow prisoners.

Heavy footsteps, dangling keys, and the slamming of the cellblock door announced the arrival of four prison guards. The forty-eight cell doors in A-Block unbolted and slid open, as they did every morning at the Arnone State Correctional Institution. José and his team were ready.

The sound of a hundred men starting their daily routines should have greeted the guards in A-Block. But this day, the prisoners remained in their cells, an unnerving stillness replacing the usual activity. A flash of confusion washed over the guards' faces, and in an instant, eight of José's soldiers rushed at the guards, kicking and punching them until they were pinned to the floor. They stripped the guards of their duty belts and collected their flashlights, pepper spray cans, batons, handcuffs, and radios.

Within minutes, José had seized control of A-Block.

1

"Tie 'em up and throw 'em in a cell," he ordered. "Everybody else, stay put!"

José turned to one of his supporters, nicknamed "Fido" because the guards assigned him a variety of chores and he obeyed like a well-trained dog. All of his fetching and rolling over had earned him favor with the prison staff, and José would exploit those privileges to execute the next phase of his plan. "It's your turn, mi amigo."

José opened the cellblock door and waved Fido through. Fido bolted to the control room a few yards away in the prison's central corridor and knocked frantically on the thick glass. "It's Officer Rodriguez, man! He's having a heart attack or somethin'. You gotta hurry!"

The guards in the control room jolted upright. "What? Rodriguez?" one shouted, vaulting from his chair and sending his breakfast tray flying. "Is he okay? Fido, get back in the block and make sure nobody hurts him. We'll get an ambulance."

"But he's dying in there, man! We need that shocker thing! You know what I'm talkin' about!" Fido yelled.

José had propped open the cellblock door to allow the control room guards to hear the simulated sounds of commotion going on inside. His soldiers staged the scene that was supposed to be playing out in A-Block. "He ain't breathing!" one shouted. "No pulse either. Open his shirt. We're starting CPR," said another. "I don't think he's gonna make it! Fido, where's the help?"

"You just gonna let him die?" Fido pleaded. "Help him!"

"We'll take care of him, Fido, but we can't do shit till you go back in the block and slam the door shut behind you. Now go!"

Fido did as he was told, and José's plan moved one step forward. Using Fido's hysterics as a diversion, two members of his crew had already crawled through the cellblock door by the time the guards issued a lockdown order over the prison's loudspeakers. Thick, clear panels on all four walls of the control room gave the guards a 360-degree view of the central corridor. But the panes started at waist height and José's soldiers had snuck on hands and knees to a hidden position just outside. The instant a guard opened the control room door with the defibrillator in his hand, they burst in and knocked him to the floor.

José's men beat the two guards into unconsciousness and dragged them out of the control room, across the central corridor, and through the cellblock door that José held open for them. When one of the guards let out a moan, José's soldier answered it with a kick to the head. They disappeared into A-Block, letting the door shut behind them.

It was not by coincidence but by clever planning that José started the prison riot on this August morning. On any other day, a supervising correctional officer or the warden himself might have witnessed the control room attack and sounded the alarm. Normally, higher-ranking officers would have been conducting patrols, paying particular attention to the central corridor that held the control room and connected the cellblocks to the prison's cafeteria and administrative wing. But not today. Today, the warden and his senior command staff were miles away at the state capitol building, so the prison was at minimal staffing in terms of both the number and seniority of the guards on duty.

A triumphant José entered the control room with his best friend Mateo by his side. He adjusted the red and blue bandana on his shaved head, stroked his goatee, and nodded with satisfaction as he scanned the many screens showing live surveillance video from cameras positioned throughout the building. Amused at the incompetence of the control room guards, he grinned and patted Mateo on the back.

José had put in place several diversions to make sure the guards would not witness the attack in A-Block. First, he had arranged for the kitchen workers to deliver breakfast to the control room only seconds before the attack took place. The guards were too busy taking in the food trays and settling down to eat their breakfasts to pay attention to the surveillance screens. He also made sure the attack in A-Block happened fast, and his soldiers moved the guards out of sight of the surveillance cameras as soon as they were overtaken. Still, if the control room guards had been diligent, they might have seen what was happening, but they were lazy and stupid. They got what they deserved.

José would not make the same mistakes. He would use the control room's technology to operate the prison's door locks and security cameras, its radios and the intercom system to communicate with his fellow prisoners on the inside, and its phone to connect him to both enemies and allies on the outside. But all of that would come later.

So far, José had only taken control of A-Block, which was the smallest in the Arnone prison and closest to the control room. The remaining cellblocks were his next targets, and these might pose more of a challenge. Cellblocks B through G each held about 250 men, and H-Block, which was farthest from the control room, held ninety protective custody prisoners.

"First thing is to call off the ambulance," José said. "Say it was a false alarm. If we're lucky, nobody on the outside knows anything yet. Hacker, you ready?"

"Yep," he replied, patting a tiny notebook in his shirt pocket. Hacker was weak and awkward—not the kind of person who would normally thrive in a maximum security prison. But José had taken note of his intelligence and computer skills early on and protected him from the otherwise inevitable abuse he would have suffered at the hands of his fellow prisoners. Now, José would put Hacker's expertise to good use and cash in on the loyalty he had earned.

With José looking over his shoulder, Hacker called the emergency dispatchers and, using a guard's name and ID number, canceled the ambulance. He pressed the keyboard combinations to lock the cell doors in A-Block, so the prisoners who were not part of the plot were confined to their cells. The injured guards were locked in with them. Only José's men were free, and Hacker opened the cellblock access door to let them into the central corridor.

The radio in the control room awakened with a guard's voice. "Hey, this is Monroe in B-Block," it said. "What's going on?"

4

Hacker's eyes widened, and he looked up at José.

"Just be calm and answer like you're a guard," José said, nodding and pointing to the radio.

Hacker cleared his throat and pressed the talk button on the portable radio. "We have a medical emergency in A-Block, so sit tight. It's gonna be a while."

"Who's hurt?" the voice continued.

"Just a sick inmate," Hacker replied. "That's all. Everybody's okay."

"All right. Tell 'em to hurry it up. My shift's almost over."

José shook his head and sighed. "Damn, that Monroe's a real dick. But it sounds like he believed it. We have to start moving on the other cellblocks now!"

In the months leading up to this day, José had enlisted supporters throughout the prison to help overthrow the guards and take control of the building. These soldiers knew the plan in advance and were prepared to strike, but the four or five guards assigned to each cellblock had no idea anything out of the ordinary was happening. The prison was in lockdown because of the supposed emergency, so the guards in the cellblocks were simply standing watch, waiting for an announcement to resume the daily routine, while the individual cell doors remained closed.

Hacker sat at the computer console and straightened his black-rimmed glasses. He pulled the notebook from his pocket and placed it next to the keyboard. Printed on the first page were letter-number combinations starting with, "B-2, B-3, B-6, B-29, B-46." Dozens more followed, each pair representing one of the cellblocks B through H and the number of the individual cell within them. Hacker leaned forward and started typing the series of codes to unlock the cells that held José's men.

He had to work fast. The cell doors would open as soon as he typed each code, so too much of a delay might allow the guards to hear commotion from an adjacent cellblock and take precautions to defend themselves. Or worse, one of them might activate his radio or hit his personal distress alarm and alert the rest of the facility to the danger.

While Hacker typed, José's eyes darted from one surveillance screen to the next. He held his breath and traced the scar on his collarbone with his fingers. The success of his plan hinged on these next few minutes. Five cell doors opened in B-Block, and ten of his soldiers charged out, overpowering the guards with punches, kicks, and strikes with handmade weapons. Similar scenes were playing out in the other cellblocks. Several victims activated their radios, as evidenced by the clicking sounds they made when the talk buttons were pressed. One or two of them managed to transmit a grunt or scuffling sounds, but to José's relief they did not succeed in communicating coherent warnings to their colleagues. The near-simultaneous timing of the cellblock attacks meant that the guards were unable to save themselves.

The remaining cellblocks fell as easily as the first. José confirmed through the surveillance video that all guards were incapacitated, and he spoke through the open door of the control room to his crew from A-Block who were gathered into the central corridor. These were some of his most loyal soldiers and fellow members of his Los Solidos gang. He could trust them with this assignment.

"Go to the chow hall and the administrative wing," José told them. "Make sure nobody's roaming the halls, and barricade the outside doors."

In the control room, José watched with exhilaration as his plot came to fruition. By 7:59 a.m., less than thirty minutes after his "Vámanos, brothers" command, the Arnone State Correctional Institution was completely under his control.

"Hacker, give me the microphone."

This was his chance to make his brothers understand that they deserved justice. He would be the one to lead their fight for freedom. All of the effort he'd spent studying and developing an understanding of social justice was paying off now.

Holding the microphone in one hand and his printed speech in the other, José spoke to everyone in the prison through the loudspeakers. "My brothers," he began, "this is our revolution, and I, José Ayala, am its leader. The government took away our hope and any chance we had for redemption, and today we show them that oppression is over. We are the men who will fight for freedom."

The sounds of prisoners screaming and rattling objects against the bars of their cells reached the control room, but José could not make out the exact words. He imagined, or rather hoped, that they were shouts of agreement and cheers of encouragement. He did not need their support to be successful, but he yearned for them to have faith in him as a leader and to believe in his cause.

José continued reading from his script. "What we have to do won't be easy, but we are righteous, and we will win this fight. This is a critical time. We have to put aside our differences and stop being our own worst enemies. We need to focus our anger against the people who deserve it—the ones who are keeping us down. For now, the doors stay locked. I'll make sure you're fed, but the rest is up to you. If you start a fire, then you will choke and burn. If you clog your toilet, then you will live with the stink."

The racket from the cellblocks was louder than before. José switched off the microphone and turned to his supporters in the control room. "This part's probably not applause, but fuck them. They have to wait." He raised the microphone again, channeling his inner preacher-activist. "You are an important part of this revolution, and I promise you'll have your chance to fight. Right now, my brothers, I need you to be patient. It won't be long before you're free. We will win this fight. Trust me in that. For now, I will leave you to think on the words of another great man who fought for his freedom and won it. They're our words now. 'If there is no struggle, there is no progress. Those who say they want freedom, but do not want to fight for it, these are men who want crops without plowing up the ground. They want rain without thunder and lightning. They want the ocean without the awful roar of its waters. This struggle may be a moral one; or it may be a physical one; or it may be both moral and physical; but it must be a struggle. Power concedes nothing without a demand. It never did and it never will.'"

José released the microphone switch and heaved a sigh.

"That was some fancy speech. I was getting all choked up over here," Mateo said, wiping away an invisible tear.

"Our special friend helped me write it. We've been practicing my public speaking skills too. Not bad, huh?" José said. He turned to Hacker and Fido, who were seated at the computer consoles. "You two are in charge of the control room now. You're the only ones allowed in here. If you need me," José said, grinning and bowing at the waist, "I'll be in my office."

José left the control room with Mateo by his side and flanked in the front and rear by four soldiers who served as his bodyguards. Krueger, Coop, and two brothers nicknamed "Big G" and "Baby G," or just "the G's," all wore duty belts stolen from the prison guards.

Of the men sworn to protect José, one was strikingly more menacing than the others. Krueger's towering height and muscular body, coupled with the feral look in his bright blue eyes, instilled fear in everyone in the prison—guards and prisoners alike—even in José. His shaved head accentuated his most distinctive physical feature: a wrinkled, red scar that covered the right side of his otherwise pale face. The sleeves torn off his shirt exposed a picture of his namesake, villain Freddy Krueger, tattooed over his bicep.

Krueger's scars, bald head, and scowling expression contrasted with Coop's smooth skin and neatly combed blond hair. Although the differences in their appearance were striking, both were among José's most formidable soldiers.

José led Mateo and the bodyguards to the administrative wing, which held the lobby, visiting rooms, chapel, and management offices. His soldiers had cleared this area in the initial stages of the prison takeover, and the main entrance was secured with a metal bar that spanned the double-doors. Two soldiers stood guard by the entrance, but the lobby was otherwise empty. José headed straight for the door marked, "Ronald Hayward, Warden."

"Open it," he ordered, and Coop stepped forward to shuffle through a set of keys he had taken from a guard. "You won't get in that way." José pointed at his feet and smirked. "Just bust it open!"

Coop's first kick was unsuccessful in breaking the door's lock, but it elicited a high-pitched scream from an adjacent office. The men turned in unison toward the sound.

"Looks like they missed someone," José said through clenched teeth. Rage swept over him at the thought that his soldiers had already made a mistake.

"I got it," Krueger volunteered, storming toward the inhabited room and kicking open the door.

"No! Please!" A shrill voice echoed through the lobby.

Krueger returned, dragging a wriggling woman behind him. He hoisted her up with a tug to the bun in her hair. "Can I kill her?"

"No!" she cried.

José stared into the woman's hazel eyes, and she gradually quieted and turned her face toward the floor.

"You're the warden's secretary," he deduced. A conspicuous silence told him that the group was eager to have an answer to Krueger's question.

The woman straightened, patted the creamy brown skin of her face, and smoothed her calf-length skirt. Her efforts to assume a dignified pose were awkward, however, and truly pointless, since Krueger still held a fistful of her grey hair in his hand.

"Y-Yes," she stammered and cleared her throat. "My name is Mrs. Williams. Please let me go."

José shook his head. "Well, I can't do that, but I'll let you live for now. I've heard some rumors about you, and I think you might be useful in more ways than one." He winked and held out his hand to shake hers. "My name is José Ayala. I am the leader of this revolution."

The portable radio tucked into José waistband awakened with Hacker's voice. "Hey, boss. I got the warden on the phone. He says he's calling to check in, but I don't think he knows what's going on yet. What do you want me to say?"

"Tell the asshole he ain't in charge anymore," José replied. "Tell him he better not try to come in here, or else people will die. And then tell him to fuck off."

"He's not in charge. Don't try to break in. Fuck off," Hacker repeated. "Got it."

"And send some H-Block bitches to my office," José said. He released the talk button on the radio and turned to Mateo. "Start organizing stuff in the chow hall and make sure everybody's where they're supposed to be. It's gonna be a busy day."

A second, well-placed kick to the warden's office door achieved its goal, and José rushed inside. The first thing he needed do was find the gun. Rifling through the warden's file cabinet, he yelled over his shoulder, "Follow me."

Chapter Two

Outside

Beth Sharpe had always believed she would change the world. It had caused her ridicule and cost her relationships, but she had willingly accepted those consequences. She was determined. It's why she became a prison counselor, why she got out of bed and drove to work every day.

It wasn't until she passed the first "Correctional Facility Area. Do Not Stop!" sign and a police car sped by her with its sirens blaring that she realized something was wrong.

A long line of cars clogged the road ahead, and it took her twenty minutes to drive the last half mile to the prison. When she reached the parking lot entrance, a police officer held up his hand to signal her to stop, and she rolled down her window.

"No visitors today, Miss." The blue-uniformed officer leaned over and slid his sunglasses down his nose to look at her. "You'll have to come back another time."

"I work here," Beth said. "What's going on?"

"Some kind of riot, I guess. It's probably nothin' major," he replied, pushing his sunglasses back into place and wiping the sweat

11

from his forehead. "You wanna turn around and go home, or you wanna wait it out here?"

"Here. I'll definitely wait here." The fluttering in Beth's stomach told her it wasn't "nothin'," as the officer had predicted. If there was a riot going on in the prison, it was definitely something. She was worried.

She ignored the road sign's prohibition and parked alongside the curb. She left her car there and rushed across the street, past the officer, and onto the field that served as a buffer between the road and the prison's perimeter fence. She approached a group of men talking near a state police cruiser.

"What's going on?"

"Who the hell are you?" a police officer replied. He crossed his arms in front of his chest and made no effort to hide a head-to-toe inspection of Beth.

"Beth Sharpe. I'm the counselor here." The officer's ogling repulsed her and, under normal circumstances, she would have pointed out the location of her eyes and told him to keep his own focused there. But, she was desperate to know what was happening in the prison, and she decided not to fight that particular battle today.

"Well, I didn't know prisons had such pretty counselors," the officer chuckled. "I just might—"

Beth interrupted before he finished his thought, assuming she would not appreciate whatever came out of his mouth next. "Please. Just tell me what's happening."

Another man stepped forward, frowning at the police officer as he pushed past him. Beth identified him as a prison guard, based on the uniform he was wearing, but she had never met him before.

"I've heard about you," he said, pursing his lips and lifting his chin. Beth didn't know if this was a good or bad thing, but at least he was acknowledging her. "There's a riot going on in there," he said, gesturing over his shoulder toward the prison. "None of the higher ups were around when it started. They were all in a meeting at the state capitol this morning. Did you know about that?"

Beth shook her head.

"Hmm," he said, raising an eyebrow. "Apparently, the warden was warning the governor about the mess her new policy is causing and trying to convince her to bring back parole."

"Really? Did she agree to it? How did the riot start? And what do we know about what's going on inside? Has anyone been hurt?"

The guard sighed as if answering her questions was proving too exhausting for him. "My guess is the governor didn't agree to anything. The warden called the control room to check in when the meeting ended, and an inmate answered. You realize what that means, right? If the inmates are in the control room, then they have the whole prison. They said not to come near the building, or else they would kill hostages."

"Oh my god," Beth breathed.

"Yeah," the guard said. He frowned and turned his back to her.

Realizing that she would get no more information from this group, Beth walked away. News of the riot spread, and the media arrived to chronicle the events. So too did the prison guards who were lucky enough to be off-duty when the riot began and the families of the hostages locked inside. Beth's colleagues leaned against the growing number of police cars assembling in the field. All they could do was watch and wait, becoming increasingly anxious as the hours passed.

Beth searched the crowd in the field for familiar faces, recognizing many of the guards who worked the day shift. They were the ones who escorted inmates from the cellblocks to the group counseling sessions she held in her office in the administrative wing. There was one person in particular she hoped to find. Dan Cooney was a guard at the Arnone prison and a close friend of Beth's. In truth, he was more than just a friend. She had last seen him two nights before when he had stayed overnight at her apartment, but she couldn't remember what his work schedule was for the week.

"Think," Beth told herself, tapping her thigh. "Was Dan supposed to work last night?" She reached for her cell phone to call him. No answer. She waited a few minutes and called again, but he still didn't pick up.

Dan would answer if he could. She knew it. He must have been inside when the riot started. She hoped that he had found a hiding place somewhere with the other guards, maybe in the infirmary or the administrative wing. But she couldn't stop herself from fearing that the worst-case scenario was true.

Beth was determined to find out about Dan, but the sound of voices broadcasting over portable radios interrupted her search. Many of the guards gathered in the field had tuned their own radios to the frequency used inside the prison, and they were listening for communication from their coworkers inside.

"This is Warden Ronald Hayward." The sound came simultaneously from a dozen radios turned to their highest volume. "I need to know that my people are safe, and I am willing to listen to whatever you have to say. What do you want?"

"I'll tell you what to do and when to do it," an unidentified voice replied. "But I promise you this. If I see a cop move to attack us, I kill hostages. If you piss me off, even a little, I kill hostages. Now, shut up and wait for my instructions." A click and then silence followed, and Beth thought that was the end of the prisoner's instructions, but the voice resumed. "Oh, and by the way, your secretary says, 'Hello.'"

"What? Who is this?" The warden continued to speak into his radio, but his subsequent broadcasts went unanswered. Beth wasn't entirely sure, but she thought she recognized the voice from the other end of the radio exchange. No one asked for her input, though, so she kept her thoughts to herself and waited in the field with her colleagues for most of the day.

She overheard the guards and police officers grumbling about the lack of a fast and decisive response to end the riot. They were outraged over the threats of violence from inside the prison, and they envisioned a police raid to retake it that would include SWAT teams and automatic weapons. Beth cringed at their proposals. Any such response would end in massive bloodshed. She had studied prison riots in college, and if history did in fact repeat itself, a police raid to retake the prison would cost the lives of many inmates and hostages. She knew the stakes were high, even if the bullish police officers did not. Surely, the warden understood the risks as well and, at least for now, the threat of violence against the hostages outweighed the government's interests in ending the riot quickly.

A guard—the same one who hold told her about the riot that morning—walked up to her. He no longer wore his uniform shirt, leaving only a white, sweat-soaked t-shirt covering his chest. "They're not gonna need any counselors here today, kid. Why don't you just get out of here?"

"Thank you, but I'll—" Beth started her reply, but a collective gasp from the crowd drew her attention to movement at the prison's main entrance. The door opened and a man emerged to begin a slow, unsteady walk toward the perimeter fence where everyone waited impatiently for him to arrive. He wore a yellow jumpsuit rather than the standard light blue shirt and pants worn by most inmates. This was a bad sign. Yellow meant that this man belonged in the prison's protective custody unit, which housed the inmates who would be in danger among the general population—those who were young, weak, transgender, or those who had earned the most undesirable labels of "snitch" and "baby rapist." Most of the men in protective custody were there because others wanted to hurt them, and the appearance of this man meant the riot had breached that section of the prison, putting the most vulnerable at risk.

It took several excruciating minutes for the inmate to reach the fence. Warden Hayward stepped forward to meet him, and they spoke in hushed tones through the metal fence links. Beth crept closer, straining to listen. The warden motioned toward a folded piece of paper the inmate held in his hands. In response, the inmate shook his head, mumbled a few words, and backed away from the fence.

The warden jerked his head and scanned the faces behind him. He locked eyes with Beth, and his glare spoke simultaneously of confusion and anger. In what Beth could only attribute to an involuntary reaction, she pointed to her chest and rounded her shoulders. *Me?*

She was, indeed, the target of the warden's stare. His creased forehead and scowl stirred in her stomach the same fluttering she had felt earlier that day when she'd first learned about the riot. She had initially identified the feeling as concern for the welfare of everyone involved, but it was now, unmistakably, dread. Sweat seeped from the warden's reddened face and tousled grey hair, and he hurried toward her in his rumpled business suit. She stumbled backwards, and a whisper escaped her throat. "Shit."

Beth felt a hundred eyes converge on her. She smoothed back the dark brown curl that had sprung from her hair elastic and squared her shoulders in preparation for whatever came next. In her role as prison counselor, Beth interacted with the inmates every day, but the administrators mostly ignored her, and they certainly never asked for her opinion. Indeed, most of the guards considered her attitude naïve and her role in the prison unimportant. One of them had reminded her of this fact only minutes before this, telling her to go home and let the professionals deal with the riot. Beth had shrugged off his comment as the insult it was intended to be, but now she wished she had followed his advice.

The warden reached her in a few long strides. "This inmate insists he will only deliver his message to you, Ms. Sharpe. Do you have any idea why that is?"

"No." Beth shrugged. "I can come over there, though, if you want."

"No. That won't be necessary. What the hell is going on?" he said, more to himself than to her, and turned to head back to the fence.

Beth shook her head and shrugged a second time. She had no explanation—at least not one she was willing to offer at the moment. Beth felt her colleagues close in on her as they all tried to get closer to the action.

The warden confronted the prisoner again, and the ensuing discussion continued longer than anyone expected. At one point,

Captain Sullivan, second-in-command at the Arnone prison and commander of the prison guards, joined in the argument, but he quickly threw up his hands and walked away.

The yellow-suited inmate remained standing on the other side of the fence with his shoulders slumped, eyes pointed at the ground, and paper clenched in his hand. Beth knew the warden would not allow any prisoner to bypass his authority, and she suspected that his patience was nearing its limit.

"Guards, open the gate!" The warden called to the men standing outside the gatehouse.

The inmate shook his head and took three backward steps. He thrust his arm into the air with the piece of paper in his hand and pressed his eyes tightly closed. One popping sound, like a muffled firework, resounded. Then came another.

Someone screamed, "Shots fired! Shots fired!"

Many of the police officers around Beth dropped to the ground. Everyone else ducked and covered their heads. Beth had followed the lead of the police officers around her. *But how could there be shots fired when there are no guns allowed inside the prison?* She managed to stand and began wiping the dirt from her clothes when she saw the prison door open.

Two men dressed in light blue emerged with their heads wrapped in torn white sheets that left only their eyes exposed. They strained to carry a body, one man holding its arms and the other its feet.

"No! Oh no!" the warden shouted.

Beth could see that the body wore a guard's uniform, and she could tell from its limpness and the way the head bobbed that there was no life left in it. The hair on the misshapen head was many shades darker than Dan's, and she felt momentary relief, followed by guilt that someone else would be grieving this death. Holding onto the limbs, the two men swung the body back and forth, building up more speed and height with each pass. She imagined they were counting, "One, two, three," and they tossed it away from the door.

"Here, Beth, take it," the protective custody inmate waiting on the other side of the fence yelled to her. He stepped closer and pushed the folded paper through the metal links.

Beth looked to the warden for instructions, but his hands covered his face and he shook his head gently from side to side. This was her chance to act, and she rushed to the fence. Her eyes met those of the inmate, and she felt sympathy for him. Before that day, Beth had believed that this was her best attribute as a prison counselor—that she could disregard a person's violent criminal history and, instead, focus only on his humanity. Now, she wasn't sure of anything. She took the paper and, without another word, the inmate turned to start a slow trek back to the prison.

Beth unfolded the paper and read its message. "Oh no," she whispered to herself. She felt the blood drain from her face as she refolded the paper, held it tightly against her chest, and walked away.

"Ms. Sharpe, come back here! Ms. Sharpe, what does it say?"

She heard the warden calling, but every cell in her body told her that retreat was the only option.

"Ms. Sharpe, for Christ's sake, stop!" the warden shouted.

The urgency in the warden's voice compelled her to obey, and Beth willed her legs to reverse course. She realized that her mouth was agape, and she snapped it shut, causing her teeth to whack together and her lower lip to jut out in a temporary under bite. She took a deep breath and held it as she shuffled back toward him.

The warden's arms twitched. "Give it to me," he ordered, snatching the paper from her hand.

Beth squeezed her eyes shut and made a solemn wish that somehow the words written on the paper had changed, or better yet, disappeared entirely. She opened them again to witness the warden's bewildered expression when he read them.

She did not wait for his confusion to turn to accusation. With her courage fully consumed, she turned and ran away from the prison fence, from the gawking crowd, and from him. She pushed through the obstacles in the field as quickly as she could, and she thought for a moment that she might escape before anyone stopped her.

"Ms. Sharpe, where are you going?" The warden yelled after her. "Come back! That's an order!"

There was nothing, short of being tackled by one of the scowling police officers, that could have forced Beth's legs to stop this time. Her harried walk became a full sprint, and she was breathless when she reached her car. She managed to start the engine and turn the wheel by the time the warden caught up with her. He planted both hands on the hood of her car and glared up at her through narrowed eyes. Clinging to the car with one hand, partly to steady himself and partly to prevent her from driving away, he slid along to the driver's side window and motioned for her to open it.

"What are you doing?" he said between heaving breaths. "You can't leave. You need to explain this."

"I need to go home," Beth said. "I'll be back in a few hours, and I'll explain everything. I'll make this right. I promise."

"You'll explain it now." The warden's voice was low and dangerous. He waved the paper in her face through the open car window. "'It must be a struggle.' That's all it says here. What the hell is this supposed to mean?"

Beth looked past the waving paper and up into the warden's eyes. She acknowledged that they shared the same emotions at that moment, despite their conflicting roles. They were overwhelmed with the weight of what had already happened and with dread for the tragedies they had yet to suffer. Despite her actions and because of them, lives could be lost, careers ruined, relationships tainted, and futures destroyed.

She'd never meant to change the world like this.

Beth lifted her chin and made her confession. "It means, Warden, that this is all happening because of me. It's my fault."

CHAPTER THREE

Inside

4:05 PM

With the gun he had found hidden in the warden's office, José solidified his status as the most powerful man in the Arnone prison. Plus, he had definitely gotten the attention of the cops outside when he used it to kill a guard and force the warden to follow his directions. Finally, José had delivered his message to Beth, and he knew that she would understand its meaning and do whatever she could to help him. Now, he would start making real progress.

José's soldiers laughed out loud as they walked through the main doors into the prison lobby, returning from their trip to toss the guard's body onto the prison's front sidewalk. "Sucks to be them," one of them said as he unraveled the strips of sheet wrapped mummy-like around his face.

"You should've seen those pigs out there," the other soldier said as a greeting to José. "They were staring with their mouths open like fucking dead fish."

"Well, that's how I want them," José said, tucking the gun into the waistband of his pants. "They'll take me serious from now on. When I say Beth gets a message, they damn well better give it to her."

One of the soldiers turned to his body-dumping partner and tapped his shoulder. "Hey, let's do another guard."

José's face contorted and rage swept over him. This soldier was not part of his core group of supporters, and his assumption that he had any decision-making power infuriated José. He was not a member of the discussion group that had worked together for years to understand the values of justice, freedom, and the role of activism in changing the system. He was not involved in planning the revolution, and he did not truly appreciate the reason for it. He was of no use to José other than as a soldier in his army.

Without any other warning, José bounded at the man and knocked him into the wall. Krueger and the other bodyguards scrambled to back up their leader. Spit sprayed from José's mouth as he shouted, "You don't do anything unless I say so! You don't get to kill whoever you want."

José punched him hard in the face. "That guard died because I needed it done. I'm in charge. I'm the goddamn leader, and you're nothing!" José punched him again, unleashing a stream of blood from his nose. "You got that, asshole?"

"Yeah," he sputtered. "I got it."

Mrs. Williams hugged herself tightly.

"What's next?" Mateo asked.

José let go of the soldier and turned to Coop, who jumped backward and held his hands up in front of his face. But José was not bent on attack. Instead, he grabbed the radio from Coop's belt and activated it. "Let that be a warning to you, warden. The hole in that guard's head will remind you to follow my directions from now on. Do not come near this building."

A current of hot air reached him. José crooked his neck to glower at the protective custody bitch as he limped through the door, finally returning from his mission to deliver the message to Beth at the fence. "Did she say anything?"

"No. I just gave her the paper and turned around to come back, like you told me to."

José felt a pang of disappointment—a reaction he had not expected. He was aching for some sign that Beth understood his message and that she was going to stand beside him in this struggle. His messenger hadn't given her a chance to say or do anything to encourage him to continue, but he assured himself that there would be plenty of time for that later. "Clean up that mess over there," he ordered, pointing to a pool of blood on the floor and shoving the man toward it.

José instructed the soldiers to replace the pole that secured the main door handles and stand guard in the lobby, and he and his entourage returned to the warden's office. He was pleased with himself for choosing the warden's office as his headquarters. It was close to the main entrance, and his bodyguards outside the office door could monitor most of the lobby from their post. If the police attacked, his soldiers would see it coming and warn José right away. They also had a clear view of the office doors and easy access to the visitor's area and the chapel. José had propped open the door that separated the lobby from the central corridor, which led to the cafeteria on one end and the control room and cellblocks on the other.

When José had first entered the warden's office, he was singularly focused on finding the gun. This time, he could enjoy it, and when he stepped onto the office's beige carpet, he took in the layout of the room. Dark wood paneling covered the bottom third of the walls, and the rest was maroon in color. The wall opposite the office door, behind the warden's desk, was the only exception. A large window covered by a semitransparent curtain took this spot, allowing the afternoon sunlight to seep through. A large flat-screen TV hung on the wall to right of the door, visible from the table as well as the warden's desk.

"Pretty nice, amigos, don't you think?" José sat in the warden's chair, tossed his bandana onto the desk, leaned back with his hands clasped behind his head, and crossed his feet on top of the desk. Mateo stood between him and the window, and a scowling Krueger propped himself the right corner of the office in front of the door to the private bathroom. Mrs. Williams teetered on the edge of one of the chairs that surrounded the oval conference table, and Coop stood with his back against the closed door to the lobby.

José placed a portable radio on the desk and turned the sound to its maximum volume. Other than some static, it was silent. "Perfect," he said, nodding. He smirked and lifted his chin to direct his next remark to Mrs. Williams. "What other surprises do you think we'll find in here?"

He ran his hands along the inlaid leather surface of the warden's antique wooden desk and stroked the crown brass handles that adorned every drawer. For the moment, he ignored the computer on the desk and began rifling through the drawers.

In the top drawer, he found a pair of binoculars. "For you, mi major amigo," he said, spinning around in his chair and handing them to Mateo. In another, José discovered a master set of keys and a silver letter opener with "RTH" engraved on the handle. He turned it over and read aloud the inscription, "With love always, Nancy."

"Aww. How sweet. It's yours now," he said, tossing it to Coop. "You can sharpen it up and make a good knife."

José leaned over to grope the underside of the desk. "There's something else I'm looking for. Ah, here it is." He pulled at an object that was taped to the wood. In one dramatic movement, he yanked against the adhesive and held up a replacement clip for the gun.

Krueger snorted, and Mrs. Williams lowered her head.

"You didn't know these were here, did you, Mrs. Williams?" José chuckled. "Just like you didn't know about the gun the warden had hidden in his cabinet. We all know guns aren't allowed, but it looks like the warden can't follow his own goddamn rules." He reached further under the desk and plucked off two more replacement clips.

"Okay, Mrs. Williams, now it's your turn. Come get this computer started, and put the surveillance video on the big screen."

Mrs. Williams did not move. Not an inch. She remained seated in the chair where Krueger had shoved her. One second passed, and then another. Krueger growled and started toward her, but José held up his hand to signal him to stop. *Was this woman actively defying him, or was she paralyzed by fear?* José wasn't sure.

"Mrs. Williams." Coop stepped away from his post at the door, leaned over, and clapped his hand on the conference table. "Mrs. Williams, you have to do what you're told."

The woman's entire body shook, and she awakened from her trance. She staggered over to the desk and followed José's instructions. Soon, images from the surveillance cameras appeared on the screen above the conference table, and she showed him how to control the video feed and toggle between different cameras. Mateo, always José's right-hand man, looked over his shoulder.

José listened closely and soaked in the information. "Can I zoom in?" he asked.

"Yes." Mrs. Williams nodded and pointed to the screen. "You click here to do that."

From his seat at the warden's desk, José could watch everything happening in the cellblocks, the common areas, and even the prison yard and guard towers outside.

"I got it," José said, exploring the different camera views. He was satisfied with his progress so far, but there was still plenty to do. "Mateo, you get things moving. I'll check in with the team leaders in the cellblocks."

Soon, the prison was operational again, and terrified men in yellow jumpsuits, whom José had nicknamed "worker bees," were doing the grunt work needed to keep things running smoothly.

After they had both finished their tasks, José met up with Mateo in the lobby.

"I put a bunch of the guards in the chapel," Mateo said, pointing toward the door. "Two soldiers are watching them. The rest are spread around the cellblocks, just like we planned."

"Good. Let's put all the dogs back in their cribs and meet back here in an hour."

By midnight on the first day of his revolution, the prisoners had been fed a hot meal, lights were out in the cellblocks, and soldiers were standing watch throughout the prison. José and his crew settled in for the night. Whatever challenges came the next day, he would not waste this opportunity for justice.

CHAPTER FOUR

Outside

Beth was already awake when her cell phone rang. She rolled off her couch, where she had collapsed from exhaustion the night before, to grab it.

The death of her colleague and the revelation of her role in inspiring the prison riot were heavy weights on her chest. Not to mention that Dan—her friend and lover—was locked inside. *It must be a struggle. Jesus, what was I thinking? How did I not understand that inmates would interpret that differently than I do?* Beth pushed her thoughts aside and answered her phone.

"Ms. Sharpe, where are you? You were supposed to come back first thing this morning."

She identified the irritated voice as that of Warden Hayward, but all she managed was an unintelligible, "Uh," before he continued.

"Be here in thirty minutes."

Beth hit the red button on her phone, even though the warden had already ended the call. She fastened her hair into a ponytail and donned her standard black pants and short-sleeved shirt. She carried a blazer of the same color over her arm as she descended the stairs from her apartment.

"Morning, Bob," she called out from her building's parking lot and waved to the repair shop owner next door. Bearded Bob, as she jokingly called him, was already working hard—and sweating profusely—under the hood of a grey minivan.

He straightened his back, wiped his head with an already dirty rag, and held up one hand in a partial wave. "It's gonna be another hot one. Stay cool out there," he yelled and went back to work.

Beth had lived in that apartment above the Chinese restaurant for three years. It still amazed her that Bearded Bob and everyone else in town went about their quiet suburban lives in blissful ignorance of the fact that they shared their community with several prisons and thousands of convicted criminals.

Beth backed out of her assigned parking spot. Most days, she chuckled at the sign, "Reserved. Tenant Parking." There was never more than a car or two vying for the restaurant's ten parking spaces, so designating a spot for her was completely unnecessary. This day, she didn't find any humor in it.

Beth drove the same route that she took to work each day along five miles of winding country roads, but it struck her for the first time that the houses and yards became smaller as she came closer to the prison. Eventually, the residential neighborhoods morphed into a stark landscape. Ahead was the state's largest prison compound, which included several low- and medium-security facilities that resembled schools, except that they were surrounded by tall fences edged with razor wire. The Arnone State Correctional Institution, a two-story maximum-security prison, was set farther back from the road than the others. It had the same perimeter fencing, but it was also overlooked by two tall guard towers and had a larger field separating it from the road.

Overnight, this field had transformed into a staging area for the many agencies responding to the riot. The employee and visitor parking lots were full, so Beth parked on the street between two news vans. She walked onto the field and past dozens of police cars, their engines running incessantly to keep the air conditioning going inside. Police officers chatted with one another in small groups. A few officers fiddled with their shotguns. Others stood with their arms crossed and expressions severe, looking somehow more intimidating than the ones holding the weapons. Armored trucks and National Guard soldiers in camouflage uniforms added to the spectacle. Huge portable lights towered above with their individual generators humming, ready to illuminate the scene after the sun went down.

Beth headed for the shiny black coach bus parked close to the prison gate. It was labeled "State Police Mobile Incident Command Center" and had satellite antennae, tinted black windows, and folded-down stairs leading to the door. An armored police truck, with "SWAT" emblazoned on every exposed surface, was parked beside it.

A group of prison guards greeted Beth with silent stares as she approached. She scanned the men's aggravated faces and eventually recognized one of Dan's friends. Despite the obvious annoyance of the other prison guards, she stopped to speak with him.

"Hey, do you know where Dan is? I haven't been able to reach him, and I'm worried."

"I don't know if he was working yesterday," he replied. "The captain has a list of guys who were on the schedule, so he can tell you for sure."

Another guard—this one Beth did not recognize—stepped up to her. "What the hell, lady? How dare you come back here? Haven't you done enough already?"

Beth stood motionless, unable to counter his allegations. Apparently everyone knew about the content of the message the inmates had sent her the day before, and public opinion was that Beth had played a role in starting the riot. Perhaps someone had leaked the information, or maybe they had overheard Beth's conversation with the warden and circulated some version of the story. Either way, the rumor mill seemed to be working at maximum efficiency.

"Come with me, Ms. Sharpe," a state police officer said, leading her by the arm away from the conflict.

He escorted her to the mobile command center and held the door open for her as she ascended the stairs. Once inside, Beth blinked while her eyes adjusted to the dim lighting, and she welcomed the air conditioned coolness. Four faces turned toward her—Warden Hayward, Captain Sullivan, a state police officer, and a civilian about Beth's age who was seated at a computer workstation. He turned away from the screen only long enough to glance at her when she walked in.

"Good morning, Ms. Sharpe," the warden said.

"Yeah. I hope you're well rested," Captain Sullivan added, making no effort to mask his sarcasm.

"This is Lieutenant Colonel Thomas Mitchell," the warden said, gesturing toward the tall police officer. "He's second-in-command at the State Police Department."

"It's a pleasure to meet you, colonel." Beth held out her hand to shake his.

Beth instantly liked the colonel. He had smooth, dark brown skin and eyes, and he stood with perfect posture in the Class A uniform of the Connecticut State Police—navy blue jacket, collared shirt and tie, grey uniform pants, and various patches and pins. The Stetson-style hat covering his salt and pepper hair completed the uniform. Colonel Mitchell could have been an intimidating presence, but as he shook Beth's hand she sensed genuine kindness.

Beth turned to Captain Sullivan. She needed to know what Dan's situation was. "I have a question for you," she said. "The guards told me you have a list of people who were working yesterday. Would you check that list for me please? I need to know if Dan Cooney is on it."

"What's it matter to you? Cooney a friend of yours or something?" Captain Sullivan shuffled through his pages-long list of names.

Beth held her breath.

"Yeah. Cooney's name's here. There are a lot of people in danger now because of you." He glared at her and did not give her enough time to recover before he continued. "I notice you haven't asked about the officer who was killed last night. We identified him—thank you very much for your concern—only because we read his name tag with binoculars. His body is still lying out there on the sidewalk in front of the prison, and he still has a hole blown out of his head. And today, in this heat, he's going to start rotting before his family can even claim him."

"That's enough, Captain." The warden collapsed into one of the chairs around the conference table. Beth and the others followed his lead. "Let me update Ms. Sharpe on what has transpired since she left so abruptly yesterday. We already cut off the phone lines and the internet connection to the prison, but the inmates have been using the guards' radios to communicate. Not much went on overnight, but the activity has picked up this morning. We overheard someone, who I assume is the inmate leader, address a 'Mateo.' Do you know who that is?"

"I do know a Mateo. Mateo Ray," Beth said, adding, "but there's more than one prisoner with that first name."

"True." The warden paused for a second. "But we should gather any information we can about that one anyway, just in case." He turned his head toward the information specialist's workstation. "Young man, search our databases for a Mateo Ray."

"My name's Andrew," he called back without removing his gaze from the screen. "I'm on it."

"So, what's the plan?" Beth scanned her surroundings, noting the multiple video screens positioned around them and the radios and speaker phone system in the center of the table.

"You don't worry about what the plan is," Captain Sullivan said, his eyes narrowing. "You do what we tell you, and that's it."

"Right now, we need to gather as much information as we can." Colonel Mitchell ignored Captain Sullivan and substituted his own response. "If you would, Ms. Sharpe, please explain the meaning of the note the inmate delivered to you yesterday."

"Yes, Ms. Sharpe." The warden placed the paper, now sealed in a clear plastic evidence bag, on the table. "You said 'it must be a struggle' means the riot is your fault. How so?"

"I think," Beth said, taking a deep breath and letting it out slowly in a futile effort to calm her nerves. "I'm pretty sure it's related to a lesson I gave in one of my counseling groups. It's a quote from Frederick Douglass from a speech about how people need to fight if they want to free themselves. He said those in power will never give it up on their own. And so, there must be a struggle to force the power to shift."

"Who the fuck is Frederick Douglass?" Captain Sullivan's normally-flushed face turned a darker red, and Beth thought he was on the verge of climbing over the table to strangle her.

"Oh. I figured you would know that," Beth said, instantly regretting blurting that out. *But, seriously, how could he not know about such an important historical figure?* "I'm sorry, captain. Frederick Douglass was a slave who escaped to freedom before the Civil War. He was an abolitionist, the Father of the Civil Rights Movement, and he worked for justice for all groups that were enslaved in one way or another—blacks, women, and other minorities." None of the men at the table interrupted her, so she continued. "He was an amazing public speaker, and he inspired slaves and others to rise up against their oppressors."

"Of course he did," Captain Sullivan mocked. "And you thought it was a good idea to teach inmates in a maximum-security prison about a slave who fought against his masters? Do you see any similarities there? It sounds to me like you were trying to start a riot."

"Captain Sullivan," Colonel Mitchell began, "you're out of line. I don't believe Ms. Sharpe intentionally provoked the inmates to violence."

"Absolutely not," Beth said. "I was trying to inspire them, of course, but I didn't mean for them to start a riot. My goal was to motivate them to change." The pitch of her voice rose and her speech quickened as she spoke about her work. "As you would know if you had any understanding of correctional theory, positive behavioral change is a promising strategy for reducing recidivism, and motivation is the key to future success. You, Captain, only care about forcing the inmates to obey your rules, and you do that through punishments that crush their spirit. That won't result in long-term change. When they get out of prison, they'll go right back to being criminals because you've treated them that way all along. I'm trying to help them find the motivation within themselves and empower them to change."

The men sat in stunned silence. Even Andrew stopped typing for the first time since Beth entered the command center. She pushed her shoulders back and fixed her expression. She was certain that her assertions would enrage Captain Sullivan, but he needed to hear this. They all did. She had to make them understand the reality of the injustice the inmates faced and the underlying reasons for their actions. She had to convince them that inmates were worthy of being saved, and she braced herself for the next move in the confrontation.

Captain Sullivan shook his head and threw up his hands. "I don't even know what to say to that! You provoked convicts into starting a riot, and you have absolutely no idea the kind of violence they'll inflict on my men. Not to mention what they'll do to each other. Your stupidity makes you just as dangerous as they are—and just as guilty."

"Enough." The warden stood and planted both hands on the table. "Ms. Sharpe, tell me. Why would the inmates expend the time and effort to write a note and hand deliver it to you? I don't understand. What's the point?"

"I think they want to show that they're doing this for a specific reason. They're telling us this isn't about cruelty or violence—that their actions are meaningful. They want everyone to know they're trying to accomplish something important. Maybe they think I can help explain that. Maybe they want me to advocate for them."

Before the warden could reply, the door to the command center opened, and two men entered and introduced themselves. The first was the governor's chief of staff, Artie Fitzroy. Short and thickset with a receding hairline and perpetual scowl, he carried himself with an arrogance that made Beth—and she predicted everyone else in the room—instantly dislike him. The second newcomer was a member of the FBI's Critical Incident Response Crisis Negotiation Unit who introduced himself as Special Agent Dean. Dressed in khaki pants and a dark blue polo shirt with "FBI" embroidered on the left breast, he promised that he was there for support and not to run the show. He smiled and exaggerated his relaxed stance, but Beth found him to be more phony than sincere. He reminded her of the many other men she had met in her short career who acted like they were doing everyone else a favor just by being in the room. When he quoted the Negotiation Unit's motto, *Pax Per Conloquium*, meaning resolution through dialogue, in the first few sentences he spoke, both Beth and Captain Sullivan rolled their eyes.

The door to the command center opened again, and a state police officer leaned in. "Sirs," she said, "the TV reporters out here are asking for an update. Actually, they're demanding it, and they're being real pains in the ass. Thought you should know."

"Thank you, officer," the warden said. "Colonel Mitchell, you're with me. Captain Sullivan, please stay here and brief the new arrivals." He motioned toward Fitzroy and Agent Dean. "Ms. Sharpe, you can wait outside. But stay close."

Beth exited the mobile command center and walked onto the field outside. Her colleagues turned their backs when she approached, so she found a spot closer to the road and sat in exile on the grass. Beth would use her banishment as an opportunity to regroup and plan her next move. She refused to become just another spectator, unable to influence the course of events and powerless to help the people she cared about.

CHAPTER FIVE

Inside

DAY TWO
7:45 AM

This was a real achievement—something no one had ever accomplished before him. Not the uprising itself—those had happened before. José had looked it up. Prison riots were always bloody and chaotic with men running amok and beating on guards and each other. He had even memorized the official definition of a riot: "A large group of people behaving in a violent and uncontrolled way. Noisy, violent, or wild disorder or confusion."

This was different. The actions José led at the Arnone prison did not constitute a riot. They were neither wild nor uncontrolled, and there was no disorder either. At the moment, they didn't even qualify as violent. This was no riot. This was a well-organized, politically-motivated revolution.

The morning after he took over the prison, José felt refreshed and eager to continue his thus-far successful plan. He stretched his arms over his head and crooked his head from side to side to crack his neck. "Wake up, Mrs. Williams," he ordered.

The warden's secretary awakened with a start, gulped a breath of air, and sat up. With flattened hair as evidence of a night spent sleeping with her head on the table, she scanned her surroundings with bleary eyes. José watched from behind the warden's desk as Mrs. Williams eyed Big G and Baby G sleeping beside her and then looked warily at him.

"Go ahead and use the bathroom," José told her. "Amigos, time to wake up!"

He turned to the computer and shuffled through the surveillance camera feeds, confirming that everything was calm in the cellblocks and the facility was intact. He lifted the radio from its charger on the desk to address his team leaders supervising the cellblocks. "Good morning, my brothers. I need status updates from all of you, starting with A-Block."

"All clear in A." "B-Block's good." "Nothin' happening in C." The orderly replies came all the way through, "H is good too, boss."

"All's well in the control room," Hacker added to complete the reports.

"Hold tight everyone," José said. "We'll make good progress today, I promise."

Mateo, Coop, and Krueger entered the room. "Sleep well?" José asked.

"Yeah. The couch in the captain's office was great," Mateo said. "We all set to go?"

"Ready. You get things moving in the blocks. I'm gonna work on negotiating," José said. "You want me to get anything for you?"

"Let's see, a new car, some beautiful women to keep me company. I have a long list," Mateo joked. "I'll head to the control room now to let the worker bees out of their cells and start giving out the jobs for today."

José noticed that Krueger had attached his own handmade weapons to the duty belt he wore around his waist, and he cringed for a split second at the sight of them. While his namesake Freddy Krueger had used razor fingernails to slash his victims, the prisoner Krueger had chosen a whip and club for his weapons. The whip's handle looked to be made of rope and electrical tape, and some thin strings at the end had double-sided razor blades hanging from them. The club was a solid piece of wood with a jagged chunk of metal fastened to it by tightly wrapped electrical cords.

At the sound of a door opening in the corner of the office, Krueger lurched forward and grabbed both of these weapons from their pouches on his belt. Mrs. Williams emerged from the bathroom to find a monster bearing down on her. She fell to the floor, curled into the fetal position, and covered her face with her hands.

"Stand down, Krueger," José ordered, rushing to lift up the woman and stop Krueger's attack.

"I don't want to die," she sobbed.

"You're not gonna die. Don't be dramatic. You're okay." José tried his best to calm her. "Krueger, go wait outside. In fact, all of you can leave us alone for a while."

José knew all too well that Krueger was a brutal, even sadistic, fighter. He had no reservations about using Krueger and his weapons for protection, but he did not want to be on the receiving end of them. Likewise, Krueger's temper and taste for violence were assets as long as they were directed at José's enemies. José would need to keep a close eye on him to make sure that he remained loyal and content.

"Thank you for that," Mrs. Williams said after the others had left the room. "I promise I'll be of more use to you alive than dead."

"I know you will," José said. He smiled in an attempt to put her at ease.

"Oh please," she whispered, eyes widening. "Don't hurt me. I'm an old woman, and I have a husband at home. Please don't."

At first, José didn't understand what she meant. "I'm not...You think..." His confusion lifted, and he tasted bile in his throat. *I am no sexual predator!* "I'm not gonna touch you. Yuck. No! But now I'm losing my patience. Come here and sit down," he said, pushing her into the warden's chair. "I need your help to explain why I'm doing this and make my demands. I'll tell you what to say, and you type it in a letter and make it sound good. Can I count on you for this, Mrs. Williams?"

"Absolutely," she said, her body still shaking. "I'll do whatever you say. Just please don't hurt me."

"I swear," José said, placing his hand over his heart to show the sincerity of his promise.

He waited while Mrs. Williams settled into the warden's chair and adjusted the keyboard and computer screen. "Okay. I'm ready," she said. "Should we start with the date? It's August eleventh, I believe."

"Yeah. I want to address it to the warden, but there's a whole mess of people out there," José said, flipping his hand toward the window. "Should we put them too?"

"Whatever you think, but we can start with Ronald T. Hayward comma Warden." Mrs. Williams spoke as she typed. "Not knowing exactly what your goals are yet, I would assume you'll want to include Governor Julie Webb and Commissioner of Corrections Joshua Holmes. The state police too, although I'm not sure the name of the person in charge there."

"Just put 'state police,' and that's enough," José said.

"Alright. Next, you'll need the greeting."

"Dear shitheads sounds about right." José chuckled.

"You could say, 'Dear Sirs and Madams' or the classic 'To Whom It May Concern,'" Mrs. Williams suggested. "Maybe just 'Dear Warden Hayward' would work, since you will be directing your concerns to him."

José nodded and shrugged his shoulders. His interaction with Mrs. Williams felt oddly familiar. It reminded him of the casual conversation he and Beth fell into when they were talking about issues or writing up their essays. In any case, he felt it was safe to stop looking over Mrs. Williams' shoulder, and he took a seat on the other side of the desk.

"Now onto the body of letter," Mrs. Williams said. "What do you want it to say?"

"We have no hope in here. None. I want to say that it's not fair to lock us up forever. We deserve a chance at parole. I want justice for us and a way to get freedom." José removed the paper he kept in his shirt pocket and unfolded it. "Here, let me read you the speech I gave yesterday, so you know where I'm coming from."

"You don't need to do that," Mrs. Williams said in a soft voice. "I'm sorry. I didn't mean to interrupt you, but I heard your speech already."

"What do you mean you heard it already?" José leaned forward and put his hand on the desk. Only one other person knew the content of his speech. "How? Who told you?"

"No one told me. I came in early yesterday to get some work done while Warden Hayward was out, so I was in the copy room. I didn't even realize anything was happening until you started speaking over the intercom. By that time, I couldn't escape or do anything to save myself. I heard yelling, and I was too afraid to run out. There's no phone or computer in that room, so I just hid in there until I heard you banging on the door." She paused. "So, I've heard you give that speech already. If you have it there on paper, why don't I just use that?"

José let out a sigh and relaxed back into his chair, regretting his doubts about Beth's allegiance.

"There's something at the end that might be good," he offered. He handed over the paper and watched Mrs. Williams closely as she read it.

"I see it," she said. "Yes. I think this quotation is very appropriate. Let me see what I can do using the speech as a template."

Again, Mrs. Williams spoke as she typed. "The government has taken away our hope and the opportunity to earn back our freedom. We as a people have been wronged, and today we stand up against those who are holding us unjustly. We are the men who will fight for freedom."

"Good so far," José said, waving his hand to encourage her to continue.

"Now, we'll add this passage that starts with 'If there is no struggle.'" She typed quickly. "It ends with 'Power concedes nothing without demand.'"

"That's powerful stuff," José said. "Now put this: 'So far, we've put up with the injustice, but we have to draw the line. This is our revolution. We won't take it anymore, and we'll do whatever it takes to win this fight.'"

"Alright. I have all of that typed in here," Mrs. Williams said. "If you don't have any more justifications, the next part should list your demands. What is it that you want? What are you hoping to accomplish, specifically?"

"Specifically, I want Beth Sharpe in here with me. From this point on, I only talk through Beth. There's no negotiating until she's here."

"Do you mean the pretty Beth who works here?" A line etched between Mrs. Williams' brows. "Why do you want her? What can she do for you? I-I don't understand."

"Understand this, lady." José spoke through gritted teeth. "Beth showed me that I have to fight for what I believe, and I want her in here with me. You got that?"

Mrs. Williams curled her shoulders inward and nodded repeatedly. "Yes. I understand. You need her here with you," she whispered and then remained silent for a moment. "Please know that I am only trying to help you by saying this. I just wonder." She paused again. "Do you think she will help you? And do you think Warden Hayward will allow it? I cannot imagine him sending a defenseless woman into a prison that is completely out of his control."

"A defenseless woman is exactly what you are, Mrs. Williams. And if I were you, I'd watch my mouth." José had reached the limits of his patience. "I've kept you safe so far, haven't I? I'll keep Beth safe too when she gets here, which she will. Besides, this could work out for you. I can trade one defenseless woman for another, and you might make it out of here in one piece. So, type what I told you, and finish it by saying that I'll only accept a response that's hand-delivered by Beth Sharpe. They have until five o'clock today to send her in, or else I kill hostages."

Mrs. Williams typed the rest of the letter with shaking hands and declared it complete. "I think I have everything down here correctly.

Why don't you read it over and let me know if you have any changes?" She turned the computer screen so José could see it.

"This is good."

"The only thing missing is a signature at the bottom. Do you want me to put your full name here?" Mrs. Williams asked.

José covered his mouth with one hand and crossed his other arm underneath his elbow to prop it up. He had to think carefully before he made this decision. He was absolutely going to declare himself the leader of the revolution, but he wanted to release that information on his own terms and timeline. He wasn't sure if this was it. Beth must have already guessed that he was leading the revolution. But what would the fallout be if the warden knew it as well?

He couldn't imagine how the truth might disadvantage him at this point or hurt his chances for success. The warden needed to know that he was dealing with a man who demanded respect. Plus, he deserved credit for the accomplishments he'd already made and for everything else that would happen in this revolution.

"Yeah. I'm the one in charge, and they should know it," he told her.

"Whatever you think is fine, I'm sure." Mrs. Williams completed the letter, printed it, and held out a pen for him. "Shall I put it in an envelope?"

"Yeah. And write 'Beth Sharpe' on the front." José activated his radio. "Mateo, send me back my worker bee. I need him to make another delivery."

CHAPTER SIX

Outside

DAY TWO
9:20 AM

Beth's exile status was short-lived. Colonel Mitchell found her in the field and escorted her back to the mobile command center less than an hour after her expulsion. She expected to find sanctuary among her superiors there, but instead she was met with hostility and three disdainful stares. Apparently, Captain Sullivan's briefing of the governor's chief of staff and Special Agent Dean hadn't been the best for Beth's reputation with the group. Captain Sullivan was no fan of hers, and now, evidently, neither were the other two.

The warden addressed Beth immediately. "The inmates announced over the radio that they're sending another message. And, of course, they will only give it to you," he said. "I want this hand-off done as quickly as possible, Ms. Sharpe. Do you understand? You will bring whatever the inmate gives you directly back to the command center."

She nodded.

"Let's get this over with," the warden declared.

Escorted by Warden Hayward and Colonel Mitchell, Beth passed the prison guards loitering outside the mobile command center, two police cars and the officers leaning against them, and the twenty yards of open space between them and the prison's perimeter fence. Waiting there for her was the same protective custody inmate she had met the day before.

"You have something for me?" Beth grasped the fence links with both hands.

The man averted his eyes and kicked awkwardly at the parched grass beneath his feet. Without looking up, he whispered, "He wants you to wave to him."

"I'm sorry?" Beth said, tilting her head.

"I'm not supposed to say anything else. He says you should already know who he is and what he's doing. I'm supposed to give you this envelope, but only after you wave to him." The inmate held the envelope in front of his chest as if he were posing for a mugshot.

Beth glanced over her shoulder at the warden, who stood a few paces behind her. Her waving to the leader of a prison riot was definitely not the video she wanted to appear on the evening news, nor was it the action she wanted to display to her colleagues who already distrusted her. This would make them hate her more than they already did, if that was even possible. Beth wasn't sure what to do. If she followed the inmate's instructions, everyone would assume that she approved of the violence and was encouraging them to continue. If she didn't do it, he would refuse to hand over the envelope, and the same horrific consequences of the day before would likely result. Another guard could be murdered—or worse.

Ultimately, Beth decided she should do as she was told. She steeled herself for the backlash and stepped back from the fence. Forcing an exaggerated smile, she waved her hand high above her head.

The prisoner returned Beth's smile and rolled the envelope to fit through the fence links. Beth rushed to grab it and quickly spun around. She had to veer to one side to avoid colliding with the warden, whose expression spoke simultaneously of outrage and confusion, and she scurried toward the command center.

The moment they stepped inside, the warden grabbed the envelope from Beth's hands and ripped it open. He unfolded the paper and read it through, shaking his head. "This is ludicrous! There's just no way. Ms. Sharpe, how can I respond to this?"

An awkward moment passed before Beth replied. "I haven't read it yet, Warden. I—I don't know what it says."

The warden stood with shoulders hunched looking at the floor.

"Let's stop for a second and regroup," Colonel Mitchell said, taking over the leadership role. "We all need to see what's on that paper, but let's follow the proper procedures here. This is evidence, and it needs to be treated that way. Andrew," he called to the information specialist, "hand me an evidence bag from the cabinet above you."

With the letter and its envelope sealed in a clear plastic bag, Colonel Mitchell continued. "Everyone take a seat. We'll project an image of this on the screen, so we can all read it without physically handling the paper and adding to the fingerprints we'll have to analyze later."

Beth sat at the conference table with the others. When each of the men finished reading, they turned to her with indignant stares.

"Now I understand your reaction to this, Warden," Colonel Mitchell said. "This is, well, this is upsetting, to say the least. Obviously we will need to make some decisions based on the contents of the letter, and I know we're all eager to take action, but a thorough analysis is the first and most important thing we need to do at this point. I promise it will be time well spent. Let's start at the top. It appears to be written on your letterhead, warden. What does this tell us?"

"It tells us that the inmates are in my office," the warden replied, "which I already suspected. It also means that they have logged into my computer. This gives them access to the surveillance camera feeds, and they can see everything going on inside the building."

"Can the doors between the cellblocks and the individual cells be opened from your office too?" Colonel Mitchell asked.

"No. That can only be done from the control room," the warden said. "But all the doors can be manually unlocked and opened as well. They have no doubt found the master set of keys I keep in my desk..." he hesitated, adding, "among other things."

"That's helpful information," Colonel Mitchell said. "Moving on, next we have the date, which is today. So, there's nothing new there."

"This is stupid!" Captain Sullivan stood up and banged his fist on the table. "We already have everything we need to know. Let's go in there and end this!"

Beth gasped, startled by Captain Sullivan's outburst. She had been lost in her own thoughts after reading the letter from José. Before this she had hoped to somehow avoid admitting to all of her mistakes, or at least mitigate them. But now, José's demand was giving her the opportunity to do more than that. She might be able to do something meaningful in this horrible situation. Maybe she could save Dan and the other hostages—and the inmates too. She might actually be able to fix this.

"No, captain," Colonel Mitchell said. "This is absolutely necessary. Analyzing this letter will help us understand the inmates' intentions and their capabilities. You're welcome to wait outside if you feel this is a waste of your time, but I, for one, would appreciate if you stayed and shared your insights as commander of the guards. You know best the inner workings of the prison, and your input is vital."

Captain Sullivan grunted and gritted his teeth, but he conceded and collapsed back into his seat, crossing his arms in front of his chest.

Beth's pulse raced, and she could not stop her lips from forming the slightest of grins. For the first time since this whole thing started, she had reason for hope. *Colonel Mitchell is taking the inmates seriously. He's trying to understand their position. He cares about them too!*

Colonel Mitchell cleared his throat and resumed his analysis. "The letter includes the names of several officials and specific law enforcement agencies. Agent Dean, it seems they have left out the FBI.

Perhaps that is purposeful? Maybe they're only directing the letter to state agencies for some reason? It's addressed to Warden Hayward."

"Or maybe they just don't know the FBI is involved," Agent Dean offered. "My initial observation is that this is a professionally-written letter. The inmate who wrote this must be fairly well educated and at least somewhat skilled with computers. I mean, I'm sure your computer password protected, warden. How did they get past that?"

"My secretary wrote this letter," the warden said in a subdued tone. "And she knows my password, of course. Look at the bottom left corner." He pointed to the screen. "You see, 'JA:cw'? The two lowercase letters indicate the person who typed the letter. 'cw' are Chrissy's initials—Christine Williams. She puts that at the bottom of every letter she types for me. The first two letters are the person who dictated it. It appears that is José Ayala, according to the signature at the bottom."

"So, it's obvious that this Williams woman is working with the inmates," Chief of Staff Fitzroy concluded.

The warden's eyes flashed, and he rose from his chair. "How dare you? Chrissy is not working with the inmates. They clearly forced her to do this. She's a hostage. There's no doubt in my mind about that." His voice nearly broke as he continued. "I'm sick to death thinking about the danger she's in and the terror she must be feeling right now. If we're going to lay blame, let's lay it where it belongs." He glared at Beth for a moment before turning his disdainful stare back to Fitzroy. "You should be ashamed of yourself for insinuating that Chrissy has any involvement in this."

Beth was stunned, but not by the implication that Mrs. Williams was colluding with the inmates, since Beth was sure that José was simply using her to help him. It was the warden's behavior itself that startled her. It was a major deviation from his usual professional demeanor and an overreaction to a fairly reasonable assumption about the facts of the situation. Fitzroy's eyes temporarily bulged, and Agent Dean turned his head away from the warden and cringed.

"You're right, Warden Hayward." Agent Dean turned back to the warden, his voice sympathetic. "We don't have enough information to draw that conclusion. We will assume Mrs. Williams is acting under duress." Fitzroy, sufficiently chastised, nodded in agreement. Their words seemed to appease the warden, and he sighed and sat back into his chair.

"Let's move on," Colonel Mitchell said. "The letter begins with the assertion that the inmates' actions constitute a revolution, rather than a riot. This is followed by what appears to be some sort of quotation. Is anyone familiar with this?"

"I am," Beth said, biting her bottom lip. "It's a Frederick Douglass quote."

Captain Sullivan lifted his hand and slapped it down on the table. "Of course it is."

"It's the speech that 'it must be a struggle' came from," Beth said, ignoring his contempt. "He was talking about the role slaves played in the West India Emancipation and how they could not have won their freedom without violence. He said they couldn't rely on others to change, so the only way to be free was for the slaves to stand up for themselves and fight."

For the second time in two days, the men seated at the conference table stared back at Beth in speechless disbelief.

"Well, I would say that is consistent with the message the inmates have given so far," Colonel Mitchell finally said. "That quote is followed by more about freedom and injustice and a commitment to winning at any cost."

"Can I interrupt here for a second?" Agent Dean asked. "I'm a little lost with this complaint that the inmates have no chance at freedom. They're in prison. Haven't they already lost their freedom? I mean, what am I missing?"

"So, you don't know about the incidents that happened this past year? Apparently, the FBI sent us a negotiator who has no clue what's going on in this state." Captain Sullivan directed this observation to everyone except Agent Dean. "If you're going to help, Agent, you need to do your homework, but I'll give you the condensed version. About nine months ago, a convicted arsonist who the parole board said was rehabilitated set an abandoned building on fire. It spread fast and killed a couple of teenage kids. One fireman died and a bunch more got hurt. It was a goddamn mess, and the news even showed the bodies of the burnt kids being carried out of the building. People started complaining about parole and early release policies for inmates because of it, and they were a hundred percent right."

Beth remembered this well. Still, she knew what was coming next, and it was even worse. She closed her eyes while Captain Sullivan continued his explanation.

"Not long after, another parolee stole a car and led police on a high speed chase that forced a school bus full of kids off a bridge and into a freezing cold river. A couple of kids drowned before rescue workers got to them, and a bunch more were paralyzed or had brain damage. The kids were all rich and white and from the suburbs, so you can imagine the public outcry. And of course, the prick who caused the accident walked away without a scratch. Everyone was pissed. The governor fired every member of the parole board and stopped all parole hearings until further notice."

"The governor was forced to take decisive action to ensure the safety of the citizens of this state," Fitzroy said, reciting the government's official statement.

"She sure did." Captain Sullivan nodded.

"Indeed," Colonel Mitchell agreed. "And with the parole board disbanded, there hasn't been a single hearing, and not one inmate has been paroled since. I assume this is the reason for the inmates' references to injustice and losing hope."

"I addressed this very issue with the governor yesterday morning," the warden said. "Captain Sullivan and I joined wardens from other prisons to explain to her that the situation is not sustainable. There is serious overcrowding in all of the state's prisons, but mine is the worst by far. Arnone was built for a maximum 1,000 inmates, and as of last week, we were at 150 percent capacity. Not to mention the building itself, which is the oldest still in operation in this state. The inmates are crammed in there and, in the middle of August on a hot day like this, the temperature in the cellblocks can reach into the nineties. Anyone in this environment would go stir crazy, but you have to remember that these aren't your average citizens. They're dangerous criminals. What did the governor expect to happen?"

A vein on Fitzroy's temples pulsed and his nostrils flared. "Warden, do not lay the blame for this riot on the governor. It's your job to effectively manage your institution. The attitudes of the inmates and the overall environment in your prison are not the fault of the governor. Let's be clear about that."

"But outright eliminating parole is ludicrous," the warden protested. "The inmates need hope that they could see the outside world again someday. That was the message I was trying to get across to her in our meeting. As you well know, Mr. Fitzroy, I was in the governor's office explaining the urgent need for change at the very moment the riot broke out. I couldn't be in two places at once!"

While the warden and the governor's chief of staff glared at each other, Colonel Mitchell squeezed his eyes shut and pinched the bridge of his nose. "Now that Agent Dean has been brought up to speed, let's deal with the inmate leader's demand," he said. "The problem, if I may state the obvious, is that he refuses to negotiate with anyone except Beth Sharpe. Not only that, but he insists she enter the prison by herself before five o'clock today."

"I—" Beth started.

"That is not going to happen," the warden declared, ignoring Beth's attempt to participate in the conversation. "There is no way I will allow a civilian woman to walk into that prison today. If she goes in there, she will never come out alive. I guarantee it."

Beth opened her mouth to speak, but this time Captain Sullivan interrupted her.

"Ya think?" Captain Sullivan retorted. "What I want to know is how this one inmate is controlling the whole prison. We heard him on the radio getting goddamn progress reports from the cellblocks. My own officers don't respond to me with as much respect as the inmates are giving him. What's his story?"

"That is an excellent question," Agent Dean said. "It will be essential to our negotiations that we find out everything we can about José Ayala. Where is he from? What crimes did he commit that sent him to prison in the first place? We need to know about his family, his friends, gang affiliation, education, everything."

"I'll put a detective on it right away," Colonel Mitchell offered. "We'll gather all the information we can about him, and I'll send my officers to his home to interview family members and neighbors."

Beth cleared her throat.

"Do you have something to add, Ms. Sharpe?" the warden asked.

"I think I can tell you what you need to know about José Ayala," she said, crossing her arms over her stomach. "I mean, I certainly know more about him than your police investigator will find out. I can tell you for sure that with José in charge of the prison and leading the riot, you need to proceed very cautiously. He is one of the smartest people I know, and he can accomplish anything he commits to. You should be afraid of what happens next if you make him your enemy."

CHAPTER SEVEN

Inside

THREE YEARS BEFORE

"Y ou had three felony convictions in four years? That's quite an accomplishment," Beth said to José during their first meeting. It was several years into his life sentence, but it was only the first month of Beth's tenure as counselor at the Arnone State Correctional Institution.

"What can I say? I got talent," was his reply.

Beth had carefully reviewed José's file before she met with him and before she chose to focus much of her energy and time on him. She learned that José was twenty-three years old when he entered prison for the last time. He had already spent time inside twice before that, but his previous sentences were punishments for minor offenses—drug possession, robbery, assault, and violating his parole conditions. They were minor offenses, that is, when compared to his last crime.

José grew up in the north end of Hartford, which at that time ranked as one of the most crime-ridden places in the country. Beth had always thought that Connecticut was a wealthy state, and it did have the highest per capita income. But she was surprised to learn that it also had the biggest disparities between rich and poor. While some sections of the state were home to the wealthiest Americans and featured gated communities and stunningly landscaped mansions, José's neighborhood was made up of public housing complexes and long-neglected apartment buildings. Gangs and violence were pervading influences.

Frederick Douglass said, "Intelligence is a great leveler here as elsewhere." But the children in José's neighborhood had no such opportunity. The achievement gap in education between white and minority students in Connecticut was profound—greater than any other state. The schools José and his friends attended were crumbling buildings with security guards and metal detectors. They bore no resemblance to the new, state-of-the-art schools in the wealthy suburbs only a few miles away.

"Tell me about your family, José," Beth said, continuing her first conversation with José and hoping to learn more about him. "Who are your parents? Do you have any brothers or sisters?"

"It's just me and my mom," he said. "My father died when I was a kid. He was black—I don't usually tell people that. And my mom's Puerto Rican. She's the one who raised me. She'd do anything for me, and I do the same for her."

Beth did not ask about José's murder conviction. She had learned everything she needed to know from his file. As a leader of the Los Solidos gang, José had found out that a member had been feeding information to the police, and José had formulated a plan to rid the gang of the informant. He had organized a dozen soldiers to carry it out, and they had cornered him in the basement of a derelict building and beaten him to the brink of death. José had stood over the barely-breathing man, commanded, "Die, Rata," and stomped on his already bloodied face, delivering the fatal blow.

All of these gruesome details had been revealed in José's murder trial, along with the fact that the informant had been an undercover police officer. Even worse for José had been the revelation that a concealed recording device worn under the officer's clothing had captured audio of the attack. When the judge had heard José's voice telling the police officer to die and the hollow sound of his boot crushing his face, his first-degree murder conviction was guaranteed, and a life sentence followed.

Mateo had also taken part in the murder and been arrested for the crime. But he had pleaded guilty to a lesser, but still serious, charge. He and José had been thrilled to find out they would serve out their time in the same prison.

Four years later, having served only a small fraction of his sentence, José and Beth were seated across from each other in Beth's office. On the surface, José was indistinguishable from the other inmates at the Arnone State Correctional Institution. At just under six feet tall and powerfully built, José looked the part. He was darker-skinned than many of his Puerto Rican friends, and a well-groomed goatee was the only hair on his head. He was a member of the Los Solidos gang, which operated on the streets and, to some degree, inside the prison as well. Beth noted the tattoo on his bicep depicting the theatrical muses Tragedy and Comedy and the words, "La Familia Solidos."

Still, it was apparent to Beth that José was different from the other inmates. First, he was smart. Not book smart, although he could have been a bright and successful student if he had channeled his energies in that direction. José was cunning and streetwise. He had an innate sense of when danger approached, and he knew how to defend himself when it arrived.

More importantly, José was a natural leader, and the other men followed him without question. Beth observed that when José played basketball in the prison yard, he always took the point guard position, calling the plays, planning the strategies, and leading the offensives. José was a leader among his peers inside the prison walls, strategizing and commanding others to do his bidding. Everyone in the Arnone prison—prisoners and staff—understood the role he played and recognized the power he held.

José was exactly the type of person Beth wanted to engage in her counseling sessions. He was smart enough to understand complex issues and strong enough to do the hard work needed to transform himself. If she could motivate him to make progress toward positive change, he had the capacity to bring the other prisoners along with him on that journey.

At the conclusion of their first meeting, Beth invited José to attend her group counseling sessions. He participated in the discussions, debating her on the finer points of the speeches and poems they read. He soaked in the new information, reflected on it, and applied his own experiences to the interpretation.

A few weeks later, Beth had evidence that her hunch about José's intelligence and influence had been correct. She led a discussion about one of her favorite poems, Robert Frost's "The Road Not Taken." The poem concluded, "Two roads diverged in a wood, and I,/ I took the one less traveled by,/ And that has made all the difference." Beth led the inmates in a line-by-line study of the piece, while José sat quietly but attentively at his usual post in the back of the room. Beth had always thought the poem was a call for courage to make the correct choice at the crossroads of life, and the group discussion focused on how making a less popular, but nobler, decision would result in a better outcome.

José added his insights to the discussion and deftly invalidated her rosy interpretation. He correctly observed that "difference" was neither inherently good nor bad, and that taking the less traveled path might actually be the wrong decision—one that results in negative consequences. In life, diverging from the norm might give rise to enormous success, but it could just as easily result in utter ruin.

José further explained his point. "A millionaire businessman might say that taking the road less traveled led to his success, but a homeless guy could say that it led to disaster. Instead of money and happiness, the homeless guy's decision to take a different path brought him pain and misfortune. What Robert Frost was trying to say in 'The Road Not Taken' was that the journey is was what matters most. The choice belongs to each of us, and so do the consequences, whether they're victory or tragedy. The outcome of each person's life is the direct result of his decisions at each fork in the road." José's analysis transcended those of literary scholars. It changed Beth's understanding of the famous poem, and she was grateful to José for enriching her experience with the poet.

During one group counseling session, when another inmate became disruptive and verbally abusive toward Beth, José stood, spoke a few forceful words, and pinned the man to the floor until the guards came to take him away. After that, if anyone dared to disrespect Beth, José would swiftly contain them. The perpetrators complied with his demands or suffered the consequences, as evidenced by the injuries they exhibited in the days following their offensive behaviors. Beth, in turn, showed deference to José, demonstrating to the other inmates that she deemed him worthy of respect. When she needed his help or he needed hers, they would simply share a look that conveyed their thoughts to the other. They built a relationship based on respect and reciprocal trust.

Their group discussions invigorated Beth, and she considered José to be an intellectual equal. He was her success story. Not only did he excel in their discussions, but he also improved his grammar and vocabulary. Encouraged by the progress they were making, Beth gradually introduced the group to more provocative essays and initiated discussions about influential historical figures, their principles, and the powerful consequences of their actions. She believed that she was inspiring José and the other inmates to choose their paths wisely and become better people. She felt conflicted about many of the choices she had made along her own life's journey, but she was certain that her overall impact on the world would be a positive one.

CHAPTER EIGHT

Inside

DAY TWO
10:05 AM

J osé left the G's to look after Mrs. Williams and monitor the surveillance video in the warden's office. Taking Krueger and Coop with him for protection, José headed to the control room where he consulted with Mateo, Fido, and Hacker.

"The cops have my demands," José said. "Five o'clock today is the deadline, so we'll see some action by then, one way or the other."

"As far as I can tell, everything's going fine," Hacker said. "The worker bees are delivering breakfast. I heard some yelling in A-Block, but that was a while ago."

"Oh, and I got orders to unlock some doors in D-Block last night," Fido added.

José jerked his head toward him. "Did you do it?"

"Yeah. That's Angel's block," Fido said, his eyes widening and the pitch of his voice rising. "I opened a couple of doors, just for a minute, and then I locked them again. He had me do the same thing this morning. Why? Did I do something wrong?"

"Why did he want the doors open? Did he give you a reason?" José pressed.

"No. He told me to do it, so I did." Fido's face paled.

José sighed and shook his head. This was not at all what he wanted to hear. "Alright. I'll deal with Angel. For now, I need to update everyone on our progress. Put me on the loudspeakers." He picked up the same microphone he had used the day before to tell his fellow prisoners about the revolution. Today, he cleared his throat and announced, "Hello, my brothers. Thank you for your patience. I gave the warden our first demand, and right now he's sweating his ass off figuring out what to do. He has until five o'clock today to deliver on it. Whether he decides to cooperate or not, we'll show him we're serious. We'll face whatever the warden throws at us, and we will win!"

José heard shouts from the cellblocks, but he wasn't sure if they were cheers or protests. He set the microphone down. "That should do for now. Hacker, unless I say otherwise, make sure all the doors stay locked. I'm gonna check in with our team leaders and see how our guys are doing. Let me know if there's any trouble."

Hacker saluted from his seat.

"Mateo, you're with us," José instructed, stepping into the corridor. "Let's go, amigos. We're doing a surprise inspection on the blocks." Hacker unlocked the door to A-Block as José, Mateo, Krueger, and Coop approached. The moment they entered, the prisoners began screaming and banging on the bars of their cells. Throwing his hands up in frustration, a chubby man with sweat dripping down his forehead rushed over to greet them.

"What the hell's going on, T.K.?" José yelled over the noise.

"You know A-Block's got the worst guys in it. I can't do nothin' to shut 'em up. They keep bitchin' about being locked up," T.K. said. "They've been throwing shit—literally shit—at me."

"Looks like you have a bunch of cell warriors here," Mateo said.

"You're absolutely right." José nodded.

"Screw you, Ayala! I want out of here!" The voice came from a prisoner who grasped the bars of his cell with one hand and pointed a threatening finger at José with the other.

No fucking way I'm letting that go. José turned to T.K. "I want you and your guys to show that guy what happens when somebody disrespects me," he said. "Bring him out here in the open, so all these dogs can see it. If his bunky tries to get in on it, give him a beat down too." José spoke into his radio. "Hacker, unlock A-12."

When the cell door opened, T.K. and two soldiers rushed in and dragged the troublemaker out. Another soldier blocked the doorway to stop the cellmate from intervening, but his role was unnecessary. The man cowered on the lower bunk and, answering an unspoken question, said, "I won't give you n-no trouble."

T.K. and his men took turns kicking the prisoner in the stomach and the face. When he curled his body, they stomped on his ribcage and his head. The prisoner rolled back and forth in a futile effort to escape the continuous onslaught of blows.

José noticed Krueger squirm as he watched the attack, and he recognized his obligation to satisfy his bodyguard's primal need for violence. "Stop!" he shouted. "Krueger, you go ahead and finish him."

T.K. and his team, panting from exertion, stopped their attack and backed away from the battered man. Krueger leered at his prey with a disturbing half smile and strode toward him, his heavy footsteps on the concrete floor reverberating throughout the hushed cellblock. The man was still conscious, which was evidence to José that he had survived many prison brawls. Yet, when Krueger stood over him with spike-covered club in hand, the hardened prisoner whimpered like an animal about to be eaten alive.

Instead of killing him with one powerful strike, Krueger first brought his weapon down on the prisoner's knee. The upper part of the man's body lurched off the floor in response to both the force and the pain. The man reached for his shattered leg, but Krueger's next blow interrupted the motion. Krueger coiled and swung the club, which landed between the prisoner's shoulder blades and sent his upper body over his legs to skid, face first, across the floor. One final blow to the back of the head shattered his skull, and blood, bone, and brain matter splattered over the cellblock floor. The victim's head no longer held its original rounded shape. Instead, his face was flattened, and the back of his head was concave. Blood spread in a growing circular pool.

Krueger turned from his kill and strutted back to his post beside José, showing no signs of exertion. José looked around the now-quiet cellblock, stifling his own desire to shudder. He had ordered the execution because it was necessary, but Krueger enjoyed it. Choosing Krueger to serve as his bodyguard was either his best decision, or his worst. *Time will tell*, he thought. *At least he's on my side.*

José turned to his team leader. "That should help, T.K. If anybody else gives you trouble, threaten them with a visit from Krueger."

"Thanks. Let me know what you need today." T.K. reached out to shake José's hand. "If shit goes sideways, we'll back you up."

José, Mateo, Krueger, and Coop left A-Block and proceeded through the grated metal gate to the hallway that held the remaining cellblocks.

Inside B-Block, José's appointed team leader sat sideways on a chair, legs pressed together in a ladylike pose, watching over the prisoners in their cells. Squeeze was tall and thin, and his chalky complexion made his black, gelled-back hair all the more conspicuous. He wore one of the guard's uniform shirts, which was unbuttoned down to his stomach to reveal his smooth, tan chest. Squeeze exaggerated his feminine mannerisms, and the other prisoners labeled him a "punk." He was not the type of prisoner one would expect to hold a position of power in the prison. José trusted him, but he recognized his weaknesses and made sure to give him ample back-up in the form of six brawny soldiers, all of whom were members of the Los Solidos gang and had sworn their loyalty to José.

B-Block housed about 250 prisoners, but it was considerably quieter than T.K.'s, which had less than half that number. The prisoners locked in their cells engaged in hushed conversations while the Los Solidos soldiers patrolled the top and bottom tiers.

José scanned the cellblock. The guards, overtaken by his men the day before, were now dressed in the light blue outfits of general population prisoners and locked in the cells left vacant by Squeeze and the soldiers. Worker bees, with their yellow jumpsuits and stooped shoulders, delivered food and carried away trash and dirty plastic trays.

"Good work, Squeeze." José nodded his approval. "This place is running exactly how we planned. You need anything?"

"Not a thing, love," Squeeze answered, leaning back and draping his leg over the side of the chair. "You do what you need to. I'm just fine here."

José and his crew moved on to C-Block, which was running as efficiently as the previous one. When José turned to leave, however, a man on the upper level called to him. "Hey, Ayala. I got a question for you. How come the rats and bitches get outta their cells, and we still locked up? It ain't fair."

José stopped, and everyone turned toward the voice. Krueger grabbed his weapon and widened his stance.

"Yeah. What's up with that? I want out too!" Other prisoners shouted their agreement, and the worker bees hunched their shoulders and dropped their heads lower. The prisoner continued. "These are the dirtiest dogs in here—snitches and punks and shit. What kinda riot is this if we don't get a chance to beat 'em down?"

José's first instinct was to crush this dissent with a decisive and violent punishment, as he had done in A-Block. But he hesitated. This protest was different. It wasn't disrespectful exactly. It was a valid complaint, and it deserved an answer.

"Hold on a minute, Krueger," José said, raising his hand to halt his bodyguard's forthcoming attack. "The man has a point." He positioned himself opposite the two-story wall of cells and addressed the entire cellblock. "First of all, this is not a riot. I told you that already. It's a revolution, and I want us to get real changes out of it. We get parole back, or else they don't get their prison back!"

He paused to scan the faces staring back at him from behind the bars of their cells. None of them spoke out, so he continued, "The worker bees are serving you, aren't they? They're bringing you food and supplies and hauling away your garbage. Believe me, I know what pieces of shit they are, but right now they serve a purpose. When we get what we want, you'll have your chance at them. I promise. For now, I need you to be patient."

José turned and marched out of the cellblock, denying the men a chance to argue further. He sighed and lifted his radio. "Hacker, open D-Block next."

"Be careful, boss," Fido's voice announced. "It's getting kinda messy in there."

José had reviewed the surveillance video before leaving for his cellblock inspection, and D-Block hadn't looked like a problem. There were more guys walking around than there should have been and there was some trash scattered on the floor, but that was it. *What could have happened in the last hour?* he thought. Still, he took Fido's warning seriously, and he pointed to Krueger. "Be ready for anything."

He peeked through the window in the door to D-Block and saw that the prisoners had tossed out the contents of their cells, leaving toilet paper, bedding, and food everywhere. It was a mess, as Fido had warned, but he was going in regardless. Once inside, José was stunned by the spectacle. A guard, stripped naked except for his socks and underwear, lay motionless on a table in the center of the block. His eyes were shut, and his hands and feet were tied to the table legs at the four corners. A man's agonizing screams emanated from a cell on the second tier, and three prisoners—José did not identify them as part of his team—surrounded a worker bee and were shoving him back and forth between them. It was utter chaos, and he didn't know where to begin to regain control.

José took a few steps into the block, held his fists close to his sides, and shouted. "Angel! Angel!" He continued until the team leader appeared and greeted him with a wide smile.

"Mi amigo," Angel said, extending his hand to shake José's. "What brings you to our little slice of heaven?"

"What the hell are you doing?" José demanded. He was beyond mad, and there was no way he was going to shake Angel's hand. He'd much rather rip it off his arm. "This isn't what we talked about. You're supposed to keep the block quiet. What if I need you? You won't even be able to hear the radio. Shut everybody up. Now!"

Angel blew a whistle, and much of the noise stopped. "No hay problema," he said. "I got it under control."

"It doesn't look that way to me. What about those three?" José said, his bicep quivering, as he pointed toward the circle of men terrorizing the worker bee.

"Just mis amigos havin' a little fun."

"That's not part of the plan, Angel. This is serious!"

Angel signaled for them to stop, and the men ended their sadistic game with one final shove that knocked the worker bee out of the circle and onto the floor. Angel spoke to Krueger next. "How you doin' man? You seeing any action in the other blocks?"

José craned his neck to watch Krueger's reaction. He hadn't realized these two were friends. Krueger's gaze was aimed straight ahead, and he gave no response. Maybe that was wishful thinking on Angel's part. But maybe not. José spied a hint of a grin flash on Krueger face as he made the slightest nod.

José felt his facing heating up, and he turned back to Angel. "And what's up with that guard on the table? You know I need the guards as hostages. He's worth nothing to me if he's dead."

"He ain't dead," Angel said. "Like I said, we're just havin' fun. That guard dropped me once, and he's been a dirty hack for a lot of years. He's getting what's due him. You can't expect us to just sit here like we're in church. You said it yourself. This is our chance to do something real."

The cellblock, which had been bedlam minutes before, was now silent. The prisoners in their cells were straining to listen to his conversation with Angel, and the worker bees huddled together in the corner. This was a delicate situation. José's own hand-picked team leader was the one responsible for fueling the dysfunction, and he could not fix this by simply killing one troublemaker, as he had done in A-Block.

Angel was a member of the Latin Kings, which was the enemy of José's Los Solidos gang both inside and outside the prison walls. While Beth had helped them set aside their differences so they could work together toward a higher goal, that trust did not extend to the other members of their respective groups. José had allowed Angel to choose his own soldiers for D-Block, and the prisoners he chose were, like him, Latin Kings. The problem, as José now realized, was that those prisoners were loyal to Angel and his gang. They had no allegiance to José. If he tried to remove Angel from his leadership position or punish him for his behavior, the Latin Kings soldiers would support Angel, which could result in a battle between the two groups. Still, José had to get D-Block under some semblance of control.

"Angel, this isn't what I meant, and you know it. Some pretty serious shit is coming our way today, and I need you to be ready to back me up. You know the plan!" José was on the verge of losing his temper, but he could not allow himself to let go. He took a deep breath and changed the subject. "Hacker and Fido told me you wanted cell doors opened last night. What was that for?"

"Well, I had to get that guard out." He pointed toward the naked man tied to the table. "And I did a little reorganizing. That's all. I moved some guys around. You know, to make 'em more comfortable."

While Angel spoke, screaming resumed from the second tier of the cellblock. José scanned the line of cells, easily identifying the source because it was the only one without two prisoners staring back at him. *What the hell else is going on here?* He looked to Angel for an explanation.

"I didn't say I was making everybody more comfortable. Some are, sure as shit, sore about their new cellmates. And that sounds like one of 'em." Angel chuckled.

José promised himself that he would bring more bodyguards with him the next time he visited D-Block, but for the moment he would work with what he had. "Coop, find out what's going on up there. Krueger and Mateo, stay here."

"I'll tell you what's goin' on. I put one of the guards in with a couple of booty bandits. They ain't killing him, but he is getting screwed," Angel said, eliciting laughter from his supporters standing behind him.

"This guard's getting banged pretty good up here," Coop shouted down to them. He winced as he glanced back into the cell. The screaming continued.

"Get him out of there," José ordered and activated his radio. "Hacker, open D-46."

"Aww. You're a real hard ass," Angel said. "Can't say the same for that guard though." He laughed and was joined again by his soldiers. "But seriously, José, I don't appreciate you coming in here and questioning me. I'm in charge of D-Block, right?"

"But seriously, Angel," José mocked. He was trying not to let his voice betray his rage, but he feared he was losing that battle. "You need to get this place under control."

"You threatening me?" Angel stood his ground. His soldiers moved in closer behind him, and Krueger and Mateo did the same for José. They were two rival gangs squaring off, and José had a critical decision to make. Did he resolve this conflict with a fight or yield and maintain his teetering alliance with Angel?

They glared at each other for a long, tense moment until José made his decision. He stepped back and purposely toned down the hostility in his voice. "Never, Angel. We're amigos, right?"

"Sure. Amigos," Angel agreed, echoing José's shift in attitude. The two men lifted their chins to acknowledge their mutual alliance, and the fight was over before it began.

Coop made his way down the stairs with the rescued guard. The man could barely stand on shaking legs, and his face was ashen, except for a trickle of blood dripping vampire-like from the corner of his mouth. Chunks of vomit, the edges dried and flaking off, stuck to the front of his shirt beside his nametag that read, "Palmer." His pants were unfastened and drooped as he staggered down the last few steps.

"That's fucking gross what I just saw up there," Coop said when he reached José, still propping up the guard with a firm grasp under his arm. "Since when do we serve guys up like that? I don't care if he is a guard. Seriously. It's disgusting."

As usual, Coop was sensitive to the suffering of others. José could do nothing to undo the abuse, but he could stop it from continuing. He had to keep moving forward.

"Put him in the first cell," José commanded. "I assume, Angel, that's the cell you had Fido open for you last night. I want both guards in there, and don't move them again." José gestured toward Angel's soldiers. "You three, untie the one on the table and put him in there too." The soldiers did not move a muscle until Angel nodded his approval, a fact that did not go unnoticed by José. He assumed that everyone else, including the prisoners watching silently from their cells, had noticed this too. His power in D-Block just got weaker.

Coop helped the first guard into the cell, and Angel's soldiers tossed the other one in after him. José radioed Hacker and Fido to lock that door, and he forced himself to shake Angel's hand before leaving the cellblock under Angel's supervision once again.

"Hey Krueger, come back and visit me later," Angel called out before the cellblock door slammed shut.

José spun around to check, but his bodyguards were still with him. Krueger's expression was as serious as ever, and he said nothing.

"Ugh. That was not good," Mateo said when they regrouped in the corridor.

"I know. I know. But it's too late to change anything now," José said. He had to trust that Angel would fall in line. "I just hope the last four blocks are in better shape than this one."

Worker bees shuffled along the central corridor, carrying supplies and pushing carts piled high with food trays. José nodded his acknowledgement to two soldiers as they passed. He found that Cellblocks E, F, and G were in decent shape. Although he witnessed his soldiers taunting the worker bees, both verbally and physically, he would allow it, so long as they were all doing their jobs.

José's last visit was to H-Block, which was farthest from the control room and protected by an additional gated door. On the second day of his revolution, the protective custody unit was quiet and nearly empty. Only a few head cases remained locked in their cells because they lacked the mental capacity to follow orders. The rest of the worker bees were preparing food in the kitchen, delivering supplies to the cellblocks, and cleaning. Straightening from his slouched seat and yawning, José's team leader in H-Block gave a positive report.

With his inspections complete, José concluded that the facility was running well enough. The prisoners were being taken care of, hostages were secure, and—with the exception of Angel and his crew in D-Block—his supporters remained faithful. José left Mateo in the control room to coordinate the activities of the worker bees and took Krueger and Coop with him to the warden's office. While José hoped for peaceful and diplomatic negotiations, he expected the opposite, and they needed to be prepared.

CHAPTER NINE

Outside

DAY TWO
11:48 AM

"**Y**ou certainly know a lot about José Ayala," Colonel Mitchell concluded after Beth completed her summary of José's background.

"Yeah. Too much," Captain Sullivan said. "Are you screwing this guy or what? You talk like you're in love with him or something—like he's your best friend."

"He's not my best friend, Captain. And I'll ignore your other comment, which is completely inappropriate." This wasn't the first time this insinuation had been used to explain Beth's skill in relating to other people. It didn't even make her angry anymore. She recognized it as a convenient way for those in power to minimize a woman's success. In her experience, it was never the correct explanation. And it was certainly not true in this case. "I know him well because he's been part of my discussion group for three years. I do respect him, though, and so should you. You'd be surprised to find out just how smart and disciplined he is."

"I am surprised," the warden said. "Very surprised. Ms. Sharpe, your job is to provide counseling to the inmates and help them learn to control their antisocial behaviors. I assumed you were teaching them to accept their punishments and conform to the rules of this institution. You were supposed to make them less violent. Based on what I've seen in the last twenty-four hours, I'd say you've failed in that assignment. And I am perplexed, to say the least, how you thought lessons about slavery and activist speeches about fighting for freedom would help the inmates learn to control themselves. It seems to have done the opposite. Don't you agree?"

"I was trying to help them." Beth sighed. The warden was right in a way. "Honestly, I wanted them to feel empowered, but I certainly didn't want them to take this kind of drastic action. Believe me, this is not what I intended."

"I'm sure you didn't mean for this to happen," Colonel Mitchell said. Captain Sullivan snorted and shook his head, but the colonel continued anyway. "I notice that you said 'them.' You did not intend for 'them' to do this. Do you know of other inmates who may be involved? We heard the leader talking to a Mateo over the radio again this morning. You said you know an inmate named Mateo Ray, so we looked him up. Nothing stood out in his file. Do you know something about him that could be helpful?"

Beth nodded. "Mateo Ray is José's closest friend, and they knew each other before they came to Arnone. Just a few days ago, they were finally able to room together in A-Block. Apparently, Mateo's previous cellmate was injured in some kind of fight."

"You make it sound like they're college students in a dorm. They're not rooming together," Captain Sullivan said, making quotation signs in the air with his fingers. "Wake up, Ms. Sharpe! The fact is they're cellmates now because another inmate got his head bashed in during rec time in the yard. I know the incident you're talking about, and the victim's been in the infirmary ever since. I bet, if I look into it more, it was Mateo or your boyfriend José who put him there."

"Do we have emergency contacts for these inmates?" Colonel Mitchell asked.

Why would he need emergency contacts? Beth thought. *I hope they're not preparing for notifications in case they're killed...*

"Give me a second," Andrew replied without turning away from the computer screen. "Yes. Maria Ray is the contact for Mateo. José Ayala's emergency contact is a Lydia Henry. Address in Hartford."

"Excellent. Print those out for me, will you?" Colonel Mitchell said. "I'll have a detective visit each of these individuals and interview them. We need to know who these women are and if they'd be willing to come here to help talk these guys down."

Oh, that's why he wanted to know their emergency contacts. They're hoping to use José's and Mateo's family members to persuade them to negotiate—or surrender. Beth didn't know how she felt about that exactly. It seemed underhanded and potentially cruel, but this was a life-threatening situation. Maybe some strategic deception was exactly what was needed.

"Lydia Henry is José's mother," Beth offered. "She still lives in the same housing complex in Hartford where José grew up. She used to visit José pretty regularly, but she hasn't for the last several months. José is quite devoted to her, though. If you can convince her to help, she might be effective in communicating with him. I'm not sure who Mateo's contact is, but my guess is it's his mother too."

"Is there something you'd like to add, warden? You look like you're confused," Colonel Mitchell said. Beth also noticed distress in the warden's expression.

"No. No." The warden waved off the observation. "I was just thinking. But it's nothing. Forget it. Just move on."

"At least we're making some progress," Chief of Staff Fitzroy said. "I need to update the governor about the demands and where we stand. Excuse me."

Fitzroy went to the small interview room at the rear of the mobile command center and shut the door behind him. Seconds later, he reemerged. "The governor's requesting a conference call. I filled her in on the contents of the letter, and she has some questions for all of you, as well as instructions." He plugged his cell phone into the spaceship-shaped sound system on the conference table. "You're on speaker phone, Governor Webb. Colonel Mitchell is here from the state police, as is Warden Hayward, Agent Dean from the FBI, and, of course, Beth Sharpe. Go ahead."

"Good morning," the governor began. "I know you're working on a plan, and I want to assure you that you have my full support and whatever resources you need. But you must understand my priorities. First, I want the body of the officer who was killed removed from the front sidewalk of the prison. The media's plastering pictures of him—gruesome pictures—everywhere. I even saw it on the morning news, for God's sake. I don't care what you need to negotiate, but get that body out of there. My second priority is to end this riot as quickly as possible. This is a public relations nightmare for all of us and for me especially. I'll be running a reelection campaign next year, and the last thing I need is for the handling of this incident to be used against me."

Those are her priorities? Hiding the evidence and protecting her image? Beth had to protest. "Governor—"

"Believe me, governor," the warden spoke over her. "We're doing everything we can to end this promptly and with as little bloodshed as possible."

"I'm glad to hear it, but that brings me to my third priority, and let me be clear about this, I want you to do whatever it takes to end this *inside the prison*," she said, emphasizing the last three words of her directive. "If you need to use force, then by all means do it. But make absolutely certain the bodies fall inside the building and not out. I don't want to see any more carnage on the news." She paused for an uncomfortably long time. "Did everyone hear me?"

Beth looked at the faces of her superiors seated at the conference table. They were as dumbfounded as she was by the obscene frankness of the governor's instructions. Only Fitzroy nodded in agreement.

"Understood, Governor," Colonel Mitchell managed in reply.

"Good. Now, before I let you get back to work, I have a few questions," the governor continued. "I'm holding a press conference soon, and there are some details I don't understand. Like, why haven't we cut electricity to the building yet? That would make the inmates less comfortable and more likely to cooperate. It seems like a logical first step."

"Cutting power isn't an option," the warden explained. "If the ventilation system goes down, there won't be enough air circulation to the cellblocks. Both the inmates and the correctional officers locked inside would get sick. That's why we installed generators two years ago. Even if we did cut power to the building, the emergency generators would kick in right away. They can keep the ventilation and surveillance systems going for forty-eight hours. I certainly hope this is over before that."

"Understood. There's another piece I don't understand, and I'm sure the media's going to grill me on it. I know a guard was shot in the head and thrown out by two inmates, but where exactly did the gun come from? It was my understanding that there are no firearms allowed inside our prisons. So, how did a gun get into the hands of an inmate in a prison riot?"

"This is Captain Sullivan, ma'am, commander of the guards. You're correct that our officers inside the prison do not carry guns because it's just too easy for inmates to get ahold of them. That said, guns do sometimes find their way in. It's never happened in all the years I've been here, but it's possible a gun was smuggled in by a visitor, and somehow we missed it. It's also possible that it was made by the inmates themselves. Again, it hasn't happened here at Arnone, but homemade guns have been found in other prisons. They can be made out of metal or even paper. I heard about one made from pieces of bunk beds with some duct tape, a clothespin, and match heads for the charge. You must understand, governor, the inmates have absolutely nothing to do all day, so they can have plenty of time to make weapons."

"I don't think that's what happened," the warden cut in. "Unfortunately, and I am loath to admit it, but the gun used might be mine. I keep a firearm hidden in my office in case of an emergency.

No one knew it was there—not my staff or any of the inmates. I can't imagine how they found it, honestly." The warden's tone was grave and he lowered his head. He did not look up to meet the others' stares. "You see, I feel it's my responsibility as warden to be the last line of defense in case a gang of inmates breaks into the administrative wing. And the only way I can defend myself and my civilian employees is with a firearm. That's my reasoning for keeping the gun in my office. That said, apparently the inmates found it, and I will accept any consequences that result from my decision."

"You certainly will," the governor said.

Captain Sullivan shook his head. "Ron, how could you? A gun in your office? Really? You know it's a violation of the rules, and, beyond that, it's just reckless. It's not like you."

Beth felt so much sympathy for the warden right now. She understood his instinct to protect himself and his employees. At the same time, she felt a perverse sense of relief that she had someone else to share the guilt. She was not the only one who had to answer for their mistakes today.

"I have a follow up question, warden," Colonel Mitchell said. "How much ammunition do you have? I mean, surely, you don't have a stockpile in there, do you? The inmates have already used one bullet, so how many more do we need to worry about?"

"It's a Glock 22," he began hesitantly. The other men seated at the conference table nodded in recognition. Even Beth was familiar with it, since most police officers carried that type of gun. It was a reliable weapon, to be sure, but it was only a handgun that held a maximum of fifteen bullets. Her relief was short-lived.

"But I also have three more magazines taped to the underside of my desk, with fifteen bullets each," the warden confessed.

"Are you kidding me?" Captain Sullivan banged both fists on the table. "Three extra clips? So, the inmates have sixty bullets they can use to shoot my men. That's just great!"

"Actually, it's fifty-eight bullets. They already used two to kill the guard yesterday," the governor said. Even through the speaker phone, she exuded intelligence and authority. "I must say I'm shocked, warden, and disappointed. But obviously, there's nothing we can do about it now. The gun is simply one of the factors to consider as we move forward. What about their demand that Beth Sharpe go into the prison to serve as the sole contact for negotiations? Can we do that?"

Maybe we can, Beth thought. *I can.*

"I will explain this again, as I did earlier to your chief of staff," the warden said, lifting his chin from his chest. "There is no way that I will allow a young civilian woman to enter the prison under these conditions. You have no idea the horrible things the inmates will do to her once she steps foot inside. Whatever abuses you can imagine, governor, the reality will be so much worse. I'll go in there myself before I allow her to enter the prison."

"But they don't want you, warden," the governor protested. "They want Beth Sharpe."

"We need to keep everything on the table if we're going to be effective in negotiations," Agent Dean said.

"Ms. Sharpe's life is not on the table." The warden took a deep breath and held it in, pushed his shoulders back, and made eye contact with each of his colleagues. "She is an innocent young woman, and I will not send her in to be slaughtered. End of discussion. We'll have to find another way."

"I agree with you, warden," Fitzroy said. "The last thing the governor needs is for the media to get pictures of a young woman's dead body and put those all over the news."

Captain Sullivan and Beth remained mute. Beth was busy with her own internal deliberations. If she did go inside the prison, what could she accomplish? Her biggest fear at this moment was that her actions—or inaction—would make matters worse.

The conversation was interrupted by the sound of static from the portable radio tuned to the frequency the inmates had been using to communicate with each other.

"Five hours and counting." It was José's voice. "You have until five o'clock to send Beth Sharpe in to me, or else, I kill hostages."

"What was that?" the governor asked. "I couldn't quite hear it."

"That was José Ayala speaking over the radio," Colonel Mitchell explained. "He was reminding us of his deadline. With all due respect, governor, if you don't have any further questions or priorities to tell us about, you should let us get back to work. We need to develop a plan and decide on the next steps."

"Alright. Keep me posted, Fitzroy. And, gentlemen, end this thing. Fast." A monotone buzz from the speaker pronounced the end of their conversation.

"We should try to establish a dialogue with the hostage takers," Agent Dean suggested. "This is my specialty. If no one has an objection, I will serve as our representative voice in negotiations." Beth read in the expressions of the others that they were glad to concede the role. Agent Dean took control of the radio. "This is Special Agent Dean of the FBI," he began. "I am here to listen to your grievances and help negotiate a peaceful solution to this riot." He waited a full minute for a response before he continued. "I read your letter to the warden, and I sympathize with your situation. Please talk to me. Give us more information on what you seek to achieve." Again, he received only silence as a response. "Mr. Ayala—José —please answer me. I've spoken to the governor already, and she is willing to consider your demands. All you need to do is communicate with me. We can work together to come up with a solution that is agreeable to all parties."

Still silence.

Over the next hour, as Agent Dean continued trying to engage José, the mobile command center became increasingly crowded. The commissioner of corrections joined the growing number of high ranking officials who added their opinions to the discussion of the government's response to the riot. Others shuffled about, delivering documents from the state police and the corrections department's records division. Two additional information specialists joined Andrew to operate the computers and communications equipment. Beth was allowed to remain in the command center, but she wasn't sure if that was merely an oversight. She didn't want to bring attention to herself, so she sat silently and nearly motionless at the conference table.

At exactly one in the afternoon, the bustle of activity was halted by a voice emanating from the radio. "Four hours and counting until I kill hostages," was all it said.

The small crowd in the command center hovered over the table as Agent Dean tried again to elicit a response. "Thank you for the update. I appreciate that you are watching the clock, and I assure you that we are doing the same. Please talk to me. I understand that you have parameters about how you will negotiate, but if we can just talk, maybe we can make progress together. Look, even if we can't negotiate formally, let me know if you need supplies or food. I'm sure there's something I can do for you now."

"Why don't we have her talk to him?" Captain Sullivan pointed at Beth. "We all know she has influence with this guy." He looked defiantly into Warden Hayward's eyes. "Surely, you can't object to that, Ron. There's no way this innocent woman could get hurt by talking into a radio."

"That's an excellent idea," Agent Dean agreed. "I'm not getting anywhere, and since Ms. Sharpe already has a relationship with the inmate leader, maybe she can get him to talk. What do you think, Ms. Sharpe? I'll tell you exactly what to say. Plus, the great benefit of using a two-way radio for negotiating is that they can only hear you if you're holding down the talk button. So, if you get stumped, you can simply let go of the button, and I'll guide you on how to respond. Think you can handle that?"

Beth thought so.

"Oh, she can handle it." Captain Sullivan answered for her. "We only have four hours until the deadline, and I won't allow another one of my men to be hurt."

Beth paid close attention to Agent Dean's instructions, despite his condescending methods. She knew José, but Agent Dean was the expert negotiator. This was his specialty. She jotted down the talking points he listed, reluctantly including some unsolicited contributions from Fitzroy. With their preparations complete and approval from the warden, Agent Dean offered a reassuring smile and said, "Remember, speak in a calm voice and try to act as normal as possible."

Beth nodded and picked up the radio. "José? Hi. This is Beth. The FBI asked me to talk to you. They want me to reach an agreement with you, so no one else gets hurt. The police say they won't let me go into the prison to help you. They say it's too dangerous. But they want you to let them remove the correctional officer's body from the ground near the entrance. His family is suffering because they keep seeing it on the news, and they deserve to have his body back to bury him."

Fitzroy flashed an unsettling smile and gave her two thumbs up. Beth let go of the talk button and shook off a chill. When she regained her composure, she continued. "I know you think this is the only way to get justice, but there are other options. I thought you understood that. 'It must be a struggle' for sure, José, but this isn't what I meant. Your freedom has been taken, but what you're doing now is stealing that away from other people instead." Beth softened her voice. "José, I don't want you to kill anyone else. Please respond. Let me know you're listening."

Time passed with no reply, and the bustle of activity resumed in the command center.

Beth genuinely wanted to communicate with José and for the prison riot to end without further violence. But siding with the government like this and arguing against José made her feel disloyal. Worse, since her pleas had failed to elicit a response, her public betrayal of him had accomplished nothing.

"Thank you for trying, Ms. Sharpe," the warden said. "I can see that difficult was for you."

Beth placed the radio speaker-side down on the conference table, closed her eyes, and slumped into her chair. Captain Sullivan, still seated beside her, shouted, "Shut up! I think I hear something. Everybody shut up!" Beth heard it too. A muffled static sound coming from the radio meant that someone on the other end was activating the talk button. Captain Sullivan picked up the radio and turned the volume dial to its loudest setting.

"Beth, I'm okay." It was José! "Don't worry. I know they made you say those things. You're the one who inspired us to start this revolution. That's why we need your help in here. This isn't a request, Beth. You know me well enough to know I mean what I say. If you're not in this prison with me by five o'clock today, I will kill guards. And you can tell the warden that they won't die as quick as the first one. Beth, if you don't want anybody else to get hurt, you need to make sure everyone understands. If they don't get it and I have to kill hostages, then that's their fault. I won't take the blame for that. This is the last time you'll hear my voice until you're inside with me. See you soon."

"Well, that's not the response I was hoping for." Agent Dean said aloud what everyone else was thinking. "Not at all."

It wasn't the response Beth had been hoping for either. "I know José," she said, "and he means what he says. More people will die if we don't give him what he's asking for. I have friends in there. We all do. And we don't want to see them hurt. In hindsight, I understand how José misinterpreted the ideas we discussed and thought that fighting for justice meant he needed to do this. I accept whatever responsibility I have in creating this situation, and I want to help put an end to it. But that means I need to go inside."

Chapter Ten

Inside

TWO YEARS BEFORE

Beth's office in the administrative wing of the prison served as the meeting place for her group counseling sessions. Two windows, one in the door that led to the central corridor and the other in the door to the lobby, allowed guards to monitor the activities inside. Beth positioned her desk at the far side of the room, so she was visible from both doors. She set up fourteen chairs for the inmates, arranged in jagged rows.

Beth met with several groups of inmates on a regular basis. The warden referred to all of these activities as "group therapy," but Beth made finer distinctions. Most were, indeed, group counseling sessions, where ten or twelve inmates talked about their problems that ranged from substance abuse to anger management and more serious mental health issues. In these groups, Beth simply listened and asked questions to encourage dialogue.

She used motivational interviewing techniques that she believed were more effective than conventional therapy approaches. She listened to the inmates' stories and showed empathy and understanding of their beliefs. She avoided arguing with them about discrepancies in their reasoning and remained constantly optimistic about their efforts to change. For some of the men, the sessions were simply an opportunity to escape from the monotony of prison life. Others sincerely wanted to improve themselves, but they had serious psychological obstacles to overcome.

José's group was different. Beth called it a "discussion group," and it met twice each week. It included José, Mateo, T.K., Angel, Coop, Squeeze, Hacker, Fido, and several others who were smart and interested in exploring literature, history, and philosophy. José and Mateo were members of the Los Solidos gang, but the other inmates represented a variety of ethnicities and gang affiliations. Anyone familiar with the intense animosity that existed between different factions in a prison would have predicted that this diverse group, put together in the same room, would surely erupt into mayhem. At first, that was precisely the outcome, but Beth worked hard to cultivate relationships between them.

During one discussion group meeting, Beth introduced the topic of violence between different factions in the same population. "Groups distinguish themselves from each other based on what I would argue are arbitrary, or random, differences," she explained, "like religion or skin color or where people happen to live. Often, people use subtle differences to justify terrible violence against one another. Many times these differences between groups are invisible to an outsider who wouldn't see any reason to divide them into separate categories at all. I'll give you some examples to clarify my point, and I want you to feel free to chime in at any time."

The men rolled their eyes, almost in unison, but Beth continued anyway. "The Hutus and Tutsis are two groups that live in Rwanda, which is in the central part of Africa. They look very similar overall. They all speak the same language and have lived in the same place for many generations. These people might have been able to build their economy and improve their country's standing in the world if they had worked together. But instead they did the opposite. They divided themselves into two enemy groups, based on some pretty flimsy genetic evidence and cultural stereotypes, and they fought battles over power and turf. It resulted in genocide when the Hutus killed a million Tutsis—seventy percent of the population. Neighbors killed neighbors in the most horrific ways, and they did this despite the fact that even the fighters themselves couldn't tell which group each person belonged to."

"And why should I care about them?" T.K. asked.

"You don't have to care about the Hutus and Tutsis. I'm just trying to show you how ridiculous it is for two groups that are essentially the same to go around killing each other. Here's another example. The Sunni and Shia share the same religion of Islam, but the two groups are split because of some ideological differences that you and I would consider pretty minor. Here's a picture of a Sunni man," Beth said, holding up a photograph, "and here is a Shia man." She walked around the room to show the photos to the inmates who stared back at her with vacant expressions. "Does anyone have an observation about them? Hacker?"

"They look about the same to me." Hacker shrugged.

Beth rotated the photos to examine them herself. "They look similar to me too." She walked back to her desk and picked up another sheet of paper. "Here's the city in Iraq where the Sunni man lives, and here's the city where the Shia man lives." She pointed to a dot on the map. Beth feared she might be making this lesson too theatrical, but the men seemed content to follow her reasoning. "To us, they are exactly the same. In fact, there's really very little about these two men that make them different from each other. Yet this Sunni man pulled Shia women and children out of buses and shot them. And this Shia man kidnapped Sunnis, simply because they were Sunnis, tortured them, and dumped their bodies in the street."

"So? Let them kill each other, if they're stupid enough to do that. There's less of 'em for us to worry about," Angel said.

"That is exactly how most people feel about the fighting between these groups," Beth said. "It's stupid for them to go to war against each other, instead of working together to improve life for everyone in their communities. So we should just let them kill each other off? It's pretty convenient, actually, for the privileged majority. That way, the rest of us—and society in general—doesn't have to deal with them."

Beth picked up two photographs she had positioned face-down on her desk. "I have another example for you," she said and held up a picture of Mateo. "This man is a member of the Los Solidos gang, and this man," she paused before revealing a photograph of Angel, "is a member of a rival group called the Latin Kings. The two look pretty similar to each other, wouldn't you say?"

Angel jumped up. "Are you crazy? How dare you compare me to that piece of shit?"

Mateo vaulted out of his seat as well.

José rose and glared at them both. "Go on," he told Beth.

"So Angel and Mateo live in the same city and speak the same language. They face the same challenges and barriers to success, like poor school systems, drug proliferation, and multigenerational poverty caused, in part, by mass incarceration. Most outsiders couldn't tell them apart, but still these two men are mortal enemies simply because they identify as members of different social groups."

"Take a seat, Mateo. You too, Angel," José commanded. Both men complied, but José remained standing.

"Don't you see?" Beth said. "The Los Solidos and the Latin Kings are the same as the Hutus and Tutsis. They're the same as the Sunnis and the Shia. Their differences are so small that they're really insignificant, or else they're completely imaginary. These groups—you call them gangs—are killing each other in wars over turf and stupid arguments over ego and respect. I'm trying to make you see that you're wasting your energy fighting each other when you should be teaming up to stand against your true enemies."

Beth held her breath. José certainly looked angry. Or was it simply resolve that she saw in his clenched jaw? She had intended to make the inmates feel a little uncomfortable. It was necessary to lead them to a revelation about themselves. But had she taken it too far and offended them? Should she make a break for the door and try to hail the guards? No matter what she did, if the inmates intended to hurt her, they could do it in seconds before a guard arrived to stop them. The ball was in José's court, as the sports metaphor goes, so the only thing Beth could do was hope that his intentions were benign.

"I understand what you're getting at," José said.

"Right," Beth continued, and she surprised herself by maintaining her composure. "So, to take it one step further, obviously T.K. and Mateo don't look all that much alike. T.K.'s skin is darker than Mateo's, and he has different tattoos and wears different colors."

"And don't forget about the hundred pounds T.K. has on him," Fido said, snickering.

"But, my point is this," she said. "These are superficial differences, and you're both more alike than you are different. You are members of different gangs—T.K. is a 20 Luv and Mateo is with the Los Solidos—but your backgrounds are similar, and you face the same discrimination and adversity. It's obvious to me that you should be standing together on the same side."

"So, if we team up with people who are like us, we'll be stronger. I get it," José said. "But, if my enemies aren't the Kings or some other gang, then who are they? Who are we supposed to be standing up against if it's not each other?"

"That's the critical question, José," Beth said, pleased with her ability to steer the conversation toward her desired conclusion. "The answer is obvious, or at least it is to me. There is no specific group of people who are your enemies, but you do have to fight. You have to stand against the system that is responsible for the disadvantages you faced when you were growing up and the obstacles you continue to struggle against. This is what's holding you down. In the big picture, it's the society in general that keeps the men in your neighborhood from being successful in life. It targets poor people for punishment, taking black and brown men away from their families and out of their communities. It causes you to believe that you're less important and your life is less valuable than everyone else's. Your enemies are the laws, the system of justice, and the values of the society itself that deny you justice by taking away any opportunity you have to succeed."

"Huh," was his reply. He sat down and crossed his arms in front of his chest.

Beth was responsible for organizing the discussion group made up of some of the smartest and toughest men in the prison. If she could prove that they were more alike than different and convince them to stop fighting each other, it would be a significant accomplishment. If she succeeded, it would demonstrate that gang-on-gang and race-on-race violence was pointless and unnecessary. Beth sought to prove that inmates, if treated well and given effective behavioral supports, were not inevitably fractious or violent, and she was confident that her efforts in the Arnone State Correctional Institution would change the world.

CHAPTER ELEVEN

Outside

The warden had flatly rejected Beth's proposal to go into the prison, and three hours before the five o'clock deadline, there had been no further contact between the inmates and the negotiators outside. Warden Hayward and the others in the mobile command center continued their planning and intelligence gathering efforts.

A knock drew Beth's attention, and she exchanged a quizzical glance with Agent Dean, who was the only other person in the command center not busy formulating the plan of attack. Those authorized to enter the command center let themselves in and out, so there was no need to request permission for entry. The two left their seats and headed to the entrance. The knocking continued. Agent Dean shrugged his shoulders and pushed open the door. A rush of humid air hit Beth, and she found herself face to face with a scowling correctional officer.

"I wanna talk to the warden," the man said. "Now."

Beth scanned the guard from head to toe. He had cast aside his uniform shirt and belt, leaving only a white tank top, black dress pants, and boots. Despite this state of undress, he was sweating profusely and his face flushed red, testament both to the temperature outside and to his apparent state of irritation.

"One moment please. I'll get him for you," Agent Dean said. The guard grunted as Agent Dean carefully shut the door and turned back to the busy room. "Ah, Warden, there's an officer outside asking to speak with you. He isn't very happy." The knocking renewed. "Or very patient, for that matter," he added. "I recommend you come speak with him right away."

Warden Hayward, Captain Sullivan, and Commissioner Holmes marched single file out of the command center. Beth and Agent Dean followed closely behind. They were immediately confronted by not only the guard who had requested the meeting but by dozens of his colleagues.

Scanning the crowd, Beth realized that the needs of this group had been ignored. So far, the people in charge had concerned themselves only with the plight of the hostages inside the prison. They had given little thought to the suffering of the prison employees and their families outside. José's hourly countdown was taking place on prison-issue radios via the frequency normally used by the guards, and many of the officers gathered outside had tuned their own portable radios to the same frequency. They had surely heard his threats. They must be worried about their loved ones, just like Beth was about Dan. They knew exactly the stakes and the timeline, and, although they were physically safe outside the prison fence, they were frustrated by their powerlessness to help.

"Good afternoon," the warden began. Captain Sullivan and the commissioner flanked him on both sides. "Someone asked to speak with me?"

"Yeah. Me," the ill-tempered guard said and held up his hand to identify himself. "We wanna know what you're gonna do. There's not a lot of time left before the inmates start killing again."

"We're planning our next steps," the warden responded. "We've gathered intelligence on the instigators of the riot, and we're developing a strategy. I assure you that the safety of the correctional officers and civilian hostages is our highest priority."

"Bullshit," the guard said. He didn't raise his voice. He simply stated it as fact. "You called their bluff before, and they shot one of our guys. If safety's so important, then how come he's dead and the riot's still going on? This needs to stop before somebody else gets shot in the head."

The others behind him grumbled their agreement.

"I understand your frustration, but I'm asking for your patience while we figure out the best course of action that ensures a positive outcome for everyone," the warden said.

"You don't understand shit," another guard said, stepping in front of the first. "We're out here staring at our buddy's corpse over there, and you're doing nothing. Nothing to pick him up off the goddamn ground and nothing to stop the next guy from ending up right next to him. We don't have time for patience. Do something. Now!"

A growing mob of guards was gathering behind their spokesmen. Beth backed up until she was leaning against the outer wall of the command center. Agent Dean did the same.

Captain Sullivan stepped forward. "Officers," he began, "you know that I'm your biggest supporter. I proved that in our contract negotiations this year, and I prove it every day when I serve right beside you on the front lines to keep the peace in the prison. I swear to you that I still support you and our coworkers who are suffering now."

"A raid is the only thing that will work," the guard insisted. "Let us go in and end this. We know the layout of the building, and we know the inmates. We're the best ones to take those cocksuckers out. Let us help!" His colleagues shouted their agreement.

Oh please no, Beth thought. There was plenty of precedent to prove that having correctional officers participate in a prison raid was a really bad idea. The guards were not trained to be SWAT officers. More than that, they had too much at stake to act dispassionately toward the rioting inmates.

Commissioner Holmes moved to stand shoulder to shoulder with Captain Sullivan. "Stand down, men," he said. "You all need to understand straight away that you won't be storming the castle today—or any day for that matter. If, and I emphasize the word 'if,' we decide to retake the prison by force, we will utilize a specially trained tactical team from the state police. I respect that you have a vested interest in what happens here today, but I advise you all to calm yourselves and let us handle the situation. You need to let the people in charge do their jobs without interruption. Otherwise, we will be forced to clear you from the area."

Captain Sullivan grabbed the commissioner's arm and squeezed it hard. "You're an asshole. Stop talking. Now."

Beth felt the tension building, and the commissioner was feeding the crowd's unrest. For once, she was glad for Captain Sullivan's bluntness. He needed to stop the insults before things got out of hand.

"Go ahead and try to clear us out," the spokesman goaded. "See what happens."

"Ignore him, men," Captain Sullivan said, pushing the commissioner behind him. "Listen to me. Trust me. I will go back into the command center now, and I will demand that we use whatever means necessary to end this riot." He paused for a moment, and none of the guards voiced an objection. "I will provide you with updates on our plans, and I will let you know what we decide before we do it. You deserve that."

The guard nodded his acknowledgement. "I'll hold you to that, captain."

Captain Sullivan turned to usher Beth and the others into the command center. When the door closed behind them, Commissioner Holmes spoke first. "Well done, captain. I'm impressed with how you handled those men. It was pretty tense out there."

"Fuck you, commissioner," Captain Sullivan said. "With all due respect, of course. Where do you get off talking to them like that? Those are the toughest guys you'll ever meet, and they deal with dangerous convicts every day. They deserve respect. If I ever hear you speak to my officers like that again, I'll let them show you just how competent they are." Captain Sullivan scowled, his pointed finger inches away from the commissioner's face.

"It's a mess out there," the warden said, ending the confrontation between his boss and his employee. "We need to act fast, or else we're going to have a riot outside the prison to rival the one going on inside. It looks like some kind of slum out there. We need port-o-potties and a dumpster brought in. We're also going to need water and food for the guards and the families of the hostages. This is a high priority, people."

"The governor's office will take care of it," Fitzroy declared.

"Captain Sullivan, I assume your men are dissatisfied with our response so far," Colonel Mitchell said.

"That's the understatement of the day," the captain replied. "They're pissed, and you know they're right. We need to do something before the five o'clock deadline. The inmates will have no problem killing another hostage. Why don't we just send Ms. Sharpe in?" The warden shook his head, but Captain Sullivan continued to make his case. "That would be the most logical thing to do. We could send her in with a hidden microphone on her, which would give us intel on what's going on inside, like where the leaders are and where they're keeping the hostages. It would help our tactical team know where to concentrate their efforts when they raid. It might help us avoid casualties."

"It's not going to happen, captain," the warden said. "We'll think of something else." The cell phone on the warden's belt rang, and he flipped it open. He grimaced and answered it, excusing himself and shuffling toward the rear of the command center.

"Then the way I see it, our only option is to send in the troops and end this thing with bullets and brawn," Captain Sullivan declared.

"Unfortunately, I agree," Commissioner Holmes said. "What say all of you?" Colonel Mitchell and Agent Dean nodded their agreement. Beth said nothing, assuming that her opinion was not welcome. The warden returned to find that the decision had been made.

"Alright, then," the commissioner said. "Assemble the SWAT team."

"I thought you might say that." Colonel Mitchell grinned slightly. "They're on the way."

CHAPTER TWELVE

Inside

"They're getting ready," Mateo announced as he entered the warden's office. "A bunch of SWAT vans and ambulances are showing up now, but it looks like we still have some time. I'll have my guys at the front door use the binoculars to watch and let us know when the pigs make their move."

"Good work," José said. "Make sure all communication is face to face from now on. We know they're listening to the radios, and we can't risk them finding out our plan. We have about two hours till the deadline. Go to the control room and tell them to get the lists of fighters ready. I'll be there soon to help."

Mateo left to set the plan in motion, and José remained in his headquarters with Krueger, Coop, and Mrs. Williams. The G's remained at their posts outside the office door.

"José," Mrs. Williams said in her gentlest voice. "Will you please let me go before the police raid? I'm afraid you won't be able to protect me while you're fighting. How could you? There's a good chance that I'll be hurt or killed. You can just let me walk out of here before it happens. Will you? Please?"

"Don't worry. You won't get hurt," José reassured her. "Did you think I wasn't prepared for this? Of course I have a plan, and it's a good one too. There's no way the cops will get to me or you. And after their raid fails and they realize they can't fight me and win, then they'll have to take me seriously. And they'll have to send Beth in. That's where you'll come into play, Mrs. Williams, and you're going to be a big help. When the raid is over, I'll trade you for her. So, to answer your question, no. I won't let you go before the raid. You stay with me."

"We have to get to the control room now," Coop said, his hand twitching against his thigh.

"We have plenty of time," José said. "First, I want to make sure this room's protected. The cops will definitely come in here to look for Mrs. Williams, so I need some of our best fighters to welcome them. You go pick some now, and tell the guys in the chapel to make sure the hostages are tied up and gagged, so they don't give away their position." José lifted the handgun from atop the warden's desk and, after examining it for a moment, tucked it into the elastic waistband of his pants. He put the extra clips in his pockets and told Mrs. Williams to prepare to leave.

Coop returned with four prisoners, one of whom had black eyes and a red, contorted nose—evidence of the discipline José had dispensed to him the day before when he joked about killing another guard. Each of Coop's recruits carried a weapon if some sort.

"You four defend this room," José ordered. "You decide if you're gonna hide and surprise them, or if you'll just stand your ground. But either way, I need you to hit them hard and fast and take out as many as you can. You're our first line of defense. Got it?"

The soldiers nodded, and José left the warden's office and made his way through the lobby toward the central corridor. The door to the chapel was closed and locked, as were the offices and the visiting area. Only the door leading to the central corridor was left open, a guard's boot shoved underneath to hold it in place.

"This door stays wide open," José said, pulling it to test its stability and jamming the boot firmly underneath. He stopped for a moment to admire the weapons piled next to the door before proceeding. There were a variety of knives, some made from sharpened toothbrushes and others razor blades inserted into the teeth of plastic combs. Some of the shanks were merely sharp pieces of shattered plastic lunch trays with handles wrapped in cloth and string. The arsenal also included simpler weapons, like blocks of wood, a piece of faucet, metal from bedframes, and electronics wires.

The group turned right into the central corridor, passing the infirmary, commissary, and library on the way. Each of these areas had been cleared out by José's crew immediately following the prison takeover. The group met up with Mateo outside the control room.

"Status update," José demanded.

"A and B are clear, but I haven't gotten past that yet," Mateo said. T.K. gave us seven cell numbers. Sounds like a lot for the smallest block, but he has some of the craziest ones, so it kinda makes sense. If all of them get killed, it's no big loss. We have Squeeze's list too, and I handed them over to Hacker already."

"And what about the worker bees? And D-Block—have you checked on Angel?"

"Not yet. I'm moving as fast as I can," Mateo said.

"I know you are," José replied. "We still have time. I'll help you check the blocks, but first I need to drop off my number one hostage." He gestured for Fido to open the control room door.

"How's it going, boss?" Fido said. He smiled at Mrs. Williams.

"I'm sure you know the warden's secretary, Mrs. Williams," José said. "She's gonna stay here with us during the raid."

"A pleasure, as always," Fido said, taking Mrs. Williams' hand in his and kissing it." She shuddered.

José pushed a chair toward the back of the room, and pointed to it. "Sit here," he told Mrs. Williams. "Hacker, how are things?"

"Going fine," he said without looking up. "I'm trying to memorize the numbers, so I can type them in fast."

José left Mrs. Williams in the control room and headed to the cellblocks. Big G and Baby G led the way, and Krueger and Coop followed closely behind. They shared the corridor with a slow parade of worker bees making their way to their cells in H-Block.

Mateo was in C-Block, so José would be the one to check in with Angel in D. *As it should be,* he thought. This was his burden as leader of the revolution, not Mateo's. To his relief, D-Block was much quieter than it had been during his last visit. Some of the soldiers scowled at him, but Angel greeted him warmly.

"Do you have your list of fighters ready?" José asked.

"Right here, amigo," Angel said, handing him a piece of paper.

José glanced at the list, estimating it included a half dozen cell numbers. *So far, so good.* "You remember the plan right? It shouldn't be too long before the police attack."

"We're ready. We got this," Angel replied.

Angel was cooperating for now. If the plan was successful and they all survived the day, José suspected that Angel's loyalty would not last. But he would deal with that obstacle when and if it became a problem. For now, he needed to focus all of his attention on the upcoming battle.

José left D-Block under Angel's supervision and coordinated with Mateo to confirm that the other team leaders were ready. They inspected H-Block together and found the worker bees safely locked in their cells. On their return trip to the control room, he noted the hushed atmosphere that permeated the prison.

For the third time since he took over the prison, José addressed his fellow prisoners using the microphone in the control room. "I told you today would be an important one in our revolution," he began. "I told you that I would be calling on you to fight. The warden refuses to negotiate, and we won't let him disrespect us. Instead of talking, he's decided to attack, and he's sending in a bunch of cops to do it. The warden is using violence against us, so we will show him violence in return. Some of you have been chosen to fight today because you're the meanest and the maddest. When the time comes, I'll let you out of your cribs and give you the weapons you need. You take your rage out against the cops because they deserve it. Beat those pigs down! We'll teach the warden that we're not his property anymore. Get ready, my brothers. Your chance to fight for freedom is here."

José knew he was putting his soldiers at risk, but he was equally certain that this was the only way to get justice.

CHAPTER THIRTEEN

Outside

DAY TWO
4:01 PM

Beth had listened in on the discussions about to finalize the strategy for the police raid. The plan was to attack with enough force and speed that the inmates would be unable to resist. They would enter through the main doors, rescue Mrs. Williams from the warden's office, assuming she was still there, storm the central corridor and control room, secure the cellblocks, and capture or incapacitate any inmates who fought back. The officers would fire their weapons only in defense of life and to subdue the inmates, rather than kill them.

When the inmates were handcuffed, the officers were supposed to send them out through the front doors, where police and correctional officers would search them and round them up. Because of Fitzroy's repeated reminders to keep any violence within the prison walls, the SWAT commander instructed the officers to secure the inmates inside the prison before sending them out and, of course, to keep casualties to a minimum. Agent Dean had advised them that the hostages would be held together, probably in the visiting area, so identifying their location and safeguarding it was an urgent priority.

The SWAT team was ready, and for the first time since the prison riot started, the mobile command center was nearly deserted. Only Andrew and the other information specialists remained at their computer workstations. Everyone else, including Beth, was outside watching.

The police raid to retake the Arnone prison would not be a surprise. Armored trucks and vans, with "SWAT" painted in huge block letters on every flat surface, were parked in the field. Ambulances joined the news vans that were already lined up along the road, their signage attesting to mutual aid agreements from surrounding communities. The medical personnel were preparing themselves in case the raid resulted in casualties. The media had their cameras focused on the prison, preparing for the same outcome as the ambulance crews and hoping to record footage of the action. Dozens of officers, dressed in full tactical gear, stood in front of the SWAT vehicles, no doubt visible from the windows inside the prison.

Beth felt unwelcome to stand beside the warden and Captain Sullivan, and she thought it was wise to stay away from the crowd of correctional officers. She had a sick feeling in her stomach, and she was sure this raid would have awful results. But there was nothing she could do to stop it. She leaned against the corner of the command center to watch the events unfold in isolation.

The SWAT officers wore army-green helmets, with spit shields covering their faces. Standing in the hot sun in their long-sleeved grey and green camouflage shirts and bulletproof vests, they were probably battling heat exhaustion even before they started their mission. They held ballistic shields, and some of them wore battering rams or bar busters on their backs. Beth saw them stuffing their pockets full of zip tie handcuffs, which they would use to secure the inmates' hands. Most members of the SWAT team carried a military-style rifle and a handgun as a sidearm, but a few officers had sniper rifles with long-range scopes. These snipers would remain outside the prison while the others confronted the inmates inside. They would take a concealed position in or near the guard towers and wait for the opportunity to support their fellow officers from a distance.

State Police Lieutenant Colonel Mitchell stood with his back to the prison and faced the SWAT team. "This is the day you've trained for," he started. "We're all counting on you to deliver the hostages to safety and end this riot. I don't need to remind you that this is a maximum-security prison and that there are dangerous criminals inside. They overtook the guards, murdered one of them, and are possibly assaulting others even as I speak. They will kill more innocent people if you don't stop them. We don't know exactly how many inmates will confront you when you enter the building, but we do know they have access to only one firearm, a Glock 22. To the best of our knowledge, they have fewer than sixty rounds left. Other than this weapon, the inmates will be largely unarmed."

He paused. "That is what I know about your targets. Here is what I know about you. All twenty-six of you are highly-trained state police officers. Your equipment is state-of-the-art, and you know how to use it. I will let your commander have the last word, but let me first tell you that I am one hundred percent confident that you will succeed in your mission today."

"Thank you, colonel. We appreciate your words of encouragement." The SWAT commander stepped forward to address the group. "You have all seen the prison schematics, and you have your mission directives. I'll consider this operation a success when we rescue the civilian hostage, retake the control room, subdue the inmate antagonists, and secure the remaining hostages. When we all meet back here, uninjured and victorious, our mission will be complete. Men and women of the Connecticut State Police Special Weapons and Tactics Unit, let's show them what we've got."

At the warden's direction, the gate opened and the SWAT team filed through in pairs. Once they passed the holding area and inner fence, four snipers broke off from the rest of the group to take positions in the guard towers. The remainder of the team advanced toward the prison, breaking formation temporarily to avoid stepping on the guard's body. They crossed the threshold of the main entrance and pressed forward into the building.

The warden watched the action with one hand covering his mouth, and Colonel Mitchell stood at attention. The correctional officers had abandoned their camping chairs and craned their necks to get a better view. Beth remained in seclusion near the command center, her arms crossed in front of her chest with each of her hands grasping the opposite shoulder and her eyes fixed on the action. She was consumed with fear for the safety of the officers, the inmates, and the hostages locked inside. Would Dan survive the SWAT raid? Would José? She held her breath while the team disappeared though the prison doors.

Chapter Fourteen

Inside

DAY TWO
4:13 PM

Mateo's lookout from the lobby pounded his fist on the control room window. "The cops are lined up at the gate," he yelled, panting. "They're almost ready."

"How many?" José shouted back through the thick glass.

"Thirty or so. They're all in camo with shields and guns."

"That's it? Alright. Go back and take the bar off the door. And let me know the second they start to attack," José said. He wanted the police to enter without breaking down the main door. If his plan was successful, he would need to bar the door again after the raid was over, and if they bashed it down, he couldn't do that. *Come right in, pigs. I'm ready for you.*

The lookout turned and sprinted back to his post.

José raised the microphone and announced, "It's time. Get into position."

Hacker started typing and José watched the surveillance screens. In every cellblock, his team leaders and soldiers were lining up in front of an empty cell. Hacker opened one cell door in each block, and the men had just enough time to step inside before Hacker typed the codes again, closing the doors and sealing them in. José's team was safe, locked in and protected for the next phase of his plan.

His team leaders had picked the most dangerous prisoners in each cellblock—the hogs and head cases. Hacker had the lists in front of him. The prisoners had been stuck in their cells for two days, and they were itching to fight. When the police raid started, Hacker would open the cells doors and let them out. José was counting on them to go off the chain and tear through the building.

In the central corridor, Krueger leaned against the control room door with weapons in-hand. Coop, Big G, and Baby G situated themselves similarly against the other three walls of the control room.

The lookout returned, but this time José spotted him before he reached the control room. The prisoner was waving his hands in the air, shouting, "It's starting! They're almost here!"

"Do it now!" José commanded.

Hacker's fingers tapped quickly on the keyboard as his eyes scanned the lists laid out on the workspace in front of him. Fido fidgeted and looked nervously toward the hallway every second or so. Even José shifted his weight from foot to foot, his hand hovering near the gun he had tucked into his pants. Mrs. Williams clutched the arms of her chair, held her breath, and sat completely stiff. To José, she looked like a passenger in a speeding car, preparing for a crash.

Hacker continued, and José watched the surveillance images of the SWAT team approaching the prison in military-style formation. The SWAT officers entered the building and moved past the metal detectors in the reception area. At the same time, the first prisoners released from their cells in A-Block were bursting through the cell-block door and entering the central corridor.

More prisoners flooded into the corridor, running wildly and pausing sporadically to throw punches at each other. Several stopped to stare into the control room. Mrs. Williams leaned from one side to the other in her chair, and it nearly toppled over. The bodyguards stationed against the outside walls of the control room pushed the newly freed prisoners to hustle along. Krueger did this without saying a word, swinging his razor blade whip at any loitering men to force them to move forward and cackling when he made contact and heard them cry out in pain. Coop and the other bodyguards urged the prisoners to move down the corridor by shoving them and reminding them of the weapons waiting for them by the lobby door.

José smiled and nodded as he watched the surveillance feed and saw four SWAT officers leave the lobby to enter the visiting area. They would find nothing there, but this served to divide the attacking force and reduce the number of officers moving forward together. Predictably, a few officers separated from the larger group to search the warden's office. José's men inside the office must have barricaded the door because the officers were using a battering ram to break it down. "Four cops against four of my toughest soldiers?" José said aloud to himself. "Those pigs don't stand a chance."

The SWAT officers tried the handles of each of the office and chapel doors. Finding them locked, a pair of officers remained to break into them, and the rest advanced toward the open door at the far end of the lobby in pursuit of their mission to reach the control room.

So far, José had correctly predicted their maneuvers, and his strategy was working perfectly.

At the same time, the newly released prisoners reached the end of the central corridor and the open door leading to the lobby. They found the pile of weapons waiting for them and helped themselves.

The SWAT officers must have heard the commotion, but they had only a fraction of a second to register the threat before the swarm of prisoners was upon them. Of the initial SWAT team force, four officers were snipers who remained outside the prison, four were searching the visitor's area, and four were battling José's soldiers in the warden's office. That left only fourteen officers to stand against the onslaught of rampaging prisoners.

The first wave charged into the lobby and bounded at the officers. The ones who came after them pushed and crawled over one another as they funneled through the doorway. In the confined area of the prison lobby, the considerably larger force of aggressive prisoners overwhelmed the SWAT team. The prisoners tossed aside the officers' ballistic shields, knocked the assault rifles out of their hands, and ripped off their helmets. They stabbed and clubbed and kicked the officers relentlessly, and every one of the forty or so prisoners struggled for a chance to land a blow.

This was a fight that the SWAT team had no chance of winning.

The officers who broke into the warden's office never reemerged, but the four who separated from the rest to search the visiting area rushed into the lobby. At the sight of the wild prisoners butchering their colleagues, they started shooting. They released multiple bursts of automatic gunfire from their assault rifles and bolted for the door. Several prisoners grabbed guns from lifeless SWAT members and fired back at the fleeing officers, hitting the slowest one in the back before he reached the door. The prisoners tackled him and finished him off with their crude knives and clubs.

The other three officers made it out of the building with prisoners in close pursuit. The snipers in the guard towers promptly leveled the prisoners with gunshots to the chest and head. More prisoners raced out of the prison, running frantically toward the gate, and the snipers shot them as well.

Still watching the surveillance video from the safety of the control room, José felt the reverberations of the gunshots and heard screams echo through the central corridor. "Holy shit!" Fido said. Mrs. Williams watched silently as both prisoners and police collapsed.

José closed his eyes for a moment and lowered his head. He felt his arms drop to his sides as the tension left his body. He sighed and looked up at the screens again. "Well, I'm calling this a win. The cops are either dead, or running away. And so are the hogs and head cases. That makes our next job a whole lot easier. Right, Mateo?"

Mateo shook his head and exhaled through nearly closed lips. "Yeah. Right. You want me to round up some guys and go take care of the rest?"

"Not yet. Let's give it a few minutes and make sure they don't send in more."

CHAPTER FIFTEEN

Outside

DAY TWO
4:22 PM

The SWAT officers ran for their lives toward the gate. An inmate wearing the prison's standard light blue jumpsuit followed. As he lifted his weapon to fire at the fleeing officers, two gunshots rang out from the guard towers and he crumpled into a heap on the ground. Another prisoner sprinted across the yard, firing a rifle randomly and spraying bullets into the air. Still another armed prisoner followed directly behind him. The state police snipers killed them all.

Five more men emerged from the prison and dashed toward the gate. Beth squatted near the outer fence and squinted through the chain links to capture every detail of the scene as it unfolded in front of her. She sensed that these five inmates were somehow different from the first group. Their movements were more panic-stricken than the others, less hostile, and she perceived more fearfulness than aggression in their mannerisms as they scurried away from the building. They appeared to be carrying rifles in their hands, just like the others.

But maybe not. She rushed to pull herself up and stood with her body pressed against the fence. She focused on these last few inmates. They each held something in their hands, but what they carried looked like sticks or pipes—definitely not assault rifles. This latter group of fleeing inmates had no firearms and, instead of chasing after the police officers, they seemed to be trying to escape the violence inside.

Beth tapped hard on Colonel Mitchell's arm, and he jerked his head toward her. She saw panic in his eyes. "Stop the snipers!" she yelled. "They're running away, not attacking."

"What?" Colonel Mitchell assumed the same position as Beth, hands clasping the fence and eyes squinting. He shouted up at the snipers in the guard towers. "No! Don't shoot! They're unarmed. Stand down! Don't shoot!" Twenty feet above, they did not hear his warning. Nor did they detect any difference between the threat levels they posed. Colonel Mitchell ripped the radio from his belt and commanded them not to shoot, but the snipers had already opened fire on the fleeing inmates.

The SWAT officers reached the fence and shoved each other to push through the gate into the relative safety of the holding area. Captain Sullivan met them and held open the outer gate to let them through. All three collapsed to the ground.

Captain Sullivan stood over them. "Are you okay? Are you hurt?" He helped one of the officers remove her helmet and face shield. Beth was close enough to read her nametag "E. Lisewski." Another officer, lying in a spread eagle position on the ground, ripped off his own helmet and threw it aside. The warden called for medical personnel to attend to them.

The third officer removed his helmet and managed to push himself to a kneeling position. He looked around at his colleagues and then back toward the prison. "Where's Steven? He was right behind me. Did you see him come out? He isn't here? There were four of us left. How did he not make it!" He sat back on his feet and turned his face toward the sky.

"What do you mean, 'there were four of you left'? Where's the rest of the SWAT team?" Colonel Mitchell's tone was heartbroken.

"They're dead," Officer Lisewski said as Captain Sullivan helped her to her feet. She took a deep breath. "It was a fucking zombie apocalypse in there, colonel. That's the only way I can describe it. They're all dead."

This time, it was Colonel Mitchell who sunk to the ground. He dropped to one knee, chin to chest. "My God. Oh, my God," he whispered.

Beth stood silently, but the other spectators gathering around did not remain quiet.

"What's going on?" "Where are the other officers?" "What's happening in there?" "What are you gonna do next?" It seemed like hundreds of voices were demanding a response.

Agent Dean was the first person with any authority to recover from the shock. "None of you looks seriously hurt," he said to the SWAT officers. "Let's get you in the command center and debriefed right away."

Commissioner Holmes snapped into action. "Get up, colonel. For Christ's sake, get up!" he urged through clenched teeth. "Who is your second-in-command here?"

"That's me, sir. Major Shaw," a man dressed in the same uniform as Colonel Mitchell answered. "What can I do, sir?"

"Take charge of this scene," Commissioner Holmes instructed. "We have no idea what's going on, so make sure nobody goes near the prison. Tell the officers in the towers to remain at their posts and keep a close eye out for any movement inside or out. Report any developments immediately to the command center. And get these civilians away from me. What a mess!"

Commissioner Holmes waved off the medics and ushered Colonel Mitchell, Officer Lisewski, and the other two SWAT officers into the mobile command center. The warden and the rest trailed behind. Beth waited by the door, not sure if she should follow them inside.

Captain Sullivan pushed her roughly aside and slammed the door behind him as he ascended the stairs.

Beth leaned against the outside wall of command center, closed her eyes, and banged the back of her head softly against it. She was afraid of making things worse—of compounding the mistakes she had already made. She had been counting on the men in charge to know what they were doing. But she was beginning to realize that they had no idea.

Beth had known that the police raid was doomed. Colonel Mitchell and the others had made the assumption that this incident was similar to previous prison riots and that the SWAT team would face a bunch of rioting inmates who were only looking out for their own best interests.

The authorities had been wrong—dead wrong. And now, Beth thought that her input might actually be helpful. Her resolve finally overpowering her insecurity, she opened the command center door and went inside.

"Out! I want everyone out of here!" Commissioner Holmes was shouting. Beth entered the command center against the tide of support personnel who were being expelled. She remained by the door, hoping no one would notice her.

"Andrew stays," Agent Dean said, referring to the information specialist who had staffed the command center since this whole thing started. He turned to the commissioner. "We might need his help."

"Fine," Commissioner Holmes conceded. "Officers, take a seat. Tell me what exactly happened."

Officer Lisewski opened her mouth to speak, but her colleague interrupted. "Shit! It's on TV already," he said, pointing to one of the screens. A version of the same video played on each of them, though they were tuned to different channels. "That's the three of us running out of the prison ... Those inmates were right on our tails. Well, our snipers are badass anyway."

"Just wait," Colonel Mitchell warned.

Beth knew what revelation was coming next. After the first wave of inmates were shot, another group emerged from the prison. By this time, the television cameras had zoomed in close enough to see that their expressions were terror-stricken, rather than fierce, and that they did not have assault rifles in their hands. The sniper's bullet struck one inmate in the chest, and the same happened to the others. Stationary photos followed.

"What?" Chief of Staff Fitzroy shouted, squinting at the screens. "They were unarmed? I thought I saw guns in their hands. But no. Our state police shot unarmed people? And the media caught video of all of it!"

"But, our guys didn't know they were unarmed," one of the male SWAT officers protested. "How could they know? The first ones came after us with bullets flying. Our snipers just assumed the last ones were doing the same thing, and I'm glad they did, since they were protecting my ass. You can't blame them for that!"

"Is that true?" Fitzroy asked. "Are these shootings legitimate? Or will we be criticized for this?"

"The snipers have scopes on their rifles," Colonel Mitchell explained. "And they're supposed to identify each target individually before they fire on it. They should have determined the precise threat posed by each of the targets and confirmed that they were deadly threats before they fired. Technically, the snipers should not have killed them. But I understand why they did. It was a highly-charged moment, and they felt responsible to keep their fellow officers safe. They simply missed a critical observation, and I will defend them vehemently." He paused. "But, yes, to answer your question, Mr. Fitzroy, we're going to take some serious flak for this."

"This is an absolute disaster," Fitzroy said, leaning forward to rest his head in his hands.

The room went quiet. Then the speaker in the center of the conference table awakened with a loud ring. Beth gasped and then snapped her mouth shut again. She wasn't doing a very good job of keeping her presence secret. Still, no one seemed to notice her.

"That would be the governor calling," Fitzroy announced into the table, his face hidden by his hands. "And, I assure you, this will not be a pleasant conversation."

"We're not having any kind of conversation with the governor right now," Commissioner Holmes declared. "We're going to find out everything these officers know and come up with some kind of response. Then, we'll talk with the governor." The phone rang again, and the commissioner reached across the conference table and started hitting random buttons on the speaker system. "Come over here and shut this thing up," he yelled, "or I'm going to rip the cord out!"

Andrew rose from his workstation, walked over, and pressed a button on the speaker that instantly stopped the noise. "There. I put it on mute," he said. "Let me know when you want it turned back on. Banging it like that's gonna break it."

Commissioner Holmes glared, but he would need Andrew's help to turn the phone system back on later. "You," he said, pointing at Officer Lisewski. "Tell me exactly what happened."

"Well," she started, "the front door was unlocked when we went in, so we didn't have to use the battering ram. The plan was for the four of us," she motioned to her remaining teammates, "well, the three of us plus Steven, to break off from the rest and search the visiting area. It was the first door on the right. The commander told us that's where the hostages would be, so we were supposed to secure them and take any inmates we found into custody. But we didn't find anyone. It was totally empty."

"You said the hostages would be in there," Colonel Mitchell said, turning toward Agent Dean.

"I said, 'I thought' the hostages would be there. That was based on how quickly the inmates killed the guard earlier. I figured they would have the hostages close by, and the visiting area is perfectly situated. That was my best prediction, based on the information I had and on similar incidents in the past."

"We acted on your supposedly expert advice and followed your recommendation," Colonel Mitchell said. "If I thought the hostages would be somewhere else, I might have done things differently."

"What about the other officers? Where were they?" Commissioner Holmes asked.

"We had a lot to search. There's a couple of rooms in the visiting area and half walls that people could be hiding behind, so it took us a while to clear it. We couldn't see the other officers at that point, but they were supposed to be searching the warden's office and the lobby, and then they would push forward to the control room." She paused. "But I don't think that happened."

"So, you determined the visiting area was empty. What happened next?" The commissioner pressed her to continue.

"We heard gun shots, which wasn't totally unexpected," Officer Lisewski said. "But then we heard screaming, and it sounded like there was a fight going on. So, the four of us ran into the lobby, and ... I can't even tell you what we found. It looked like there were a hundred inmates, and they were all over our guys—hitting them with bats and stabbing them. There was blood everywhere—literally everywhere. I think we were stunned for a second, but then the inmates saw us, and they started coming at us. We were obviously afraid for our lives, so all four of us started shooting. I have no idea how many times. We took a bunch of them out, but they were still coming, so we turned and ran out of there as fast as we could. And you just saw the rest on TV."

"Did any of the other officers get out?" Colonel Mitchell pleaded. "How do you know for certain they're all dead? Surely it's possible that maybe even one of them survived after you fled the building."

"I'm sorry, Colonel, but I don't think so. If you'd seen it in there ..." The officer shook her head.

Beth had remained completely silent and was still standing just inside the command center door. At the sight of this officer breaking down, Beth reached up to her face for only a moment to wipe away a tear.

"Get the governor on the phone," Commissioner Holmes said. "We need to decide what to do, and whatever it is, we need to do it fast."

Andrew reactivated the speaker phone system, which rang immediately. He glanced over his shoulder at the commissioner before pressing the button to accept the call. The governor's voice immediately filled the room. "What took you so long to answer? You think I don't know you're in there? I watched you all walk in there on freaking live TV. Apparently I need to remind you that I'm the one who purchased that command vehicle for the state police, and I should be able to reach you in it whenever I need to. You answer my calls immediately from here on out, or I will fire each and every one of you! Now, what the hell is going on over there? Fitzroy, talk to me!"

"We have a serious situation here," Fitzroy said.

"It's a disaster!" the governor interrupted. "From what I gather from the news, all but three of the officers that went into the prison are either dead or captured. The ones who came running out look like a bunch of cowards, and our snipers are shooting at anything that moves. The correctional officer's body, which I told you to remove as my top priority, is still lying there. And now, there are more bodies next to it. We are no closer to ending this riot, and you have not retrieved even one of the hostages. Did I fail to mention any other appalling facts about the current situation?"

"No, you haven't missed anything," Fitzroy answered, although Beth guessed that he understood quite well the rhetorical nature of the governor's question. "We're no closer to ending this riot than we were this morning, and now nineteen state police officers are presumed dead. Actually, governor, now that I think of it, you did forget to mention that, on top of everything else, the five o'clock deadline set by the inmate leader is approaching. We can expect more dead bodies if we don't meet his demands."

"We should assemble another SWAT raid, but this time we'll use the National Guard and go in with twenty times more officers," Colonel Mitchell offered. "I can set that in motion right away."

"Correct me if I'm wrong," the governor said, "but there's no way you can muster a stronger raid in this short a time. The inmate leader has, thus far, been unwilling to negotiate, and he's made it clear that he will kill hostages if we don't meet his demand. If another SWAT raid is your only strategy, it seems to me that we have no other option but to give the leader what he wants. Cooperating in the short term at least gives us time to assemble a larger attack force."

"Governor Webb, may I remind you that what he wants is for us to send a civilian—a young woman—into the prison alone," Warden Hayward said. "It will most certainly lead to another death, and I don't want that blood on my hands. I won't allow it."

"Your opinion on this matter, warden, is not the least bit important to me," the governor replied. "I am the commander in chief for this state, and I will not allow another guard to be killed and tossed out of that prison. If your precious civilian is killed by the inmates, as you predict, at least it will be behind the walls and not in front of the television cameras. Plus, from what I understand, she's at least partially responsible for inciting this riot in the first place, so we can and should use her to buy us some time."

Beth's heart thudded.

"Send her in!"

CHAPTER SIXTEEN

Inside

The follow-up raid José had anticipated never arrived. Hacker and Fido began unlocking doors to release the soldiers from their temporary safe havens in the cellblocks, and José and Mateo ventured out of the control room. Two prisoners, bloody and crazed, appeared through the open lobby door with weapons raised. José's expression scarcely registered concern as they raced toward him, and Krueger and Coop swiftly eliminated the threats with a few powerful blows. Leaving these two dead on the floor, José and his crew proceeded to the end of the central corridor where a few weapons remained unused in the stockpile near the door. They stepped over them and over the body of a dead prisoner to cross the threshold into the lobby.

Mateo headed straight to the main door to secure it, but José paused for a moment to take in the scene. He guessed this was what a battlefield looked like in the aftermath of a massacre. Police officers' bodies lay on the vinyl floor in contorted poses and framed in still-spreading pools of blood. Dead and dying prisoners lay beside and intermingled with them. Some moaned, and a few called out for help. José and his crew methodically made their way through the tangle of bodies, kicking and prodding them to confirm which ones were dead and which were alive. José had no need for the wounded, and Krueger enthusiastically bludgeoned them.

This was the final phase of José's plan to withstand the SWAT attack. He had to eliminate any threat posed by the men he had just used to defend his territory. Releasing forty of the prison's most volatile prisoners and giving them weapons was a huge risk, since those same men could easily turn against him after they had served their purpose. If many of the head cases and hogs survived the raid, they could wreak havoc, starting fires, attacking the worker bees, diverting José's men from their duties, and disrupting the smooth operation of the prison. Worse than that, they might weaken José's authority and threaten his control.

Mateo tiptoed through the lobby, pointing at the bodies with one hand and counting on his fingers with the other. Four soldiers emerged from the warden's office, smiling and patting each other on the back.

"Oh," one yelped and jumped backward, holding a hand to his chest. "I didn't know you were here already, José. You scared me. Looks like we won this fight though, huh?"

"We sure did," José agreed. "How's it look in there? I hope you didn't make too much of a mess. I want to use that office again."

"Yeah." The prisoner winced. He exchanged a furtive glance with his fellow soldiers. "You're gonna need some clean up in there for sure."

José sighed and shook his head. "Then you better get started," he barked and turned away from them. "Status report," he said to Mateo, who was still assessing the scene.

"All the cops are dead. I count fourteen here." Mateo gestured with both hands to encompass the lobby. "Plus, one more by the entrance. So, that's fifteen. And four more in the warden's office. On the control room screen, I saw another three running out across the

112

yard. Not counting the snipers, that should be all of them, so I don't think we need to worry about stragglers causing problems."

"What about the guys we let out?" José asked. "Are they all accounted for?"

"Yeah. Well, that's a little more complicated," Mateo said. "Hacker opened twenty-three cells. Assuming each of them had two guys in it and that every one of them made it out of the blocks and into the lobby, that should give us forty-six or so. I count thirty-four here. Plus, the two who came at us near the control room makes thirty-six. The cops took out five or six more who ran outside. If my numbers are right, forty-one or -two of the ones we released are dead now. That leaves three, maybe four unaccounted for."

"Not bad." José nodded. "I expected there'd be more, but the cops shot a bunch when they came back from the visiting area. Still, a couple of head cases running loose somewhere could create a hassle for us. Have some of our guys search the place."

Krueger stepped forward, blood spattered on his arms, neck, and head and holding a rifle in each hand. "They're all dead," he said, placing the weapons at José's feet.

That was fast, José thought. *It's a good thing Krueger's voluntarily giving me the guns. He's plenty dangerous without them. Besides, he probably wouldn't use one anyway—he likes to be close to his kills.*

José's men stripped the bodies of their gear, making piles of handcuffs, helmets, goggles, shields, and bulletproof vests covered in blood. They collected the dead SWAT officers' assault rifles and handguns. José instructed them to stockpile the weapons in the warden's office and the control room. They put the rest of the gear in Beth's office.

"For you," José said, offering a handgun to his second-in-command. This was a significant gesture of trust on José's part. He was no longer the only person inside the prison with a firearm. Now Mateo had the same level of power as he did.

"Appreciate it," Mateo said, tucking the gun into his waist band and covering it with his shirt.

By this time, Hacker and Fido had freed the team leaders in each cellblock and opened the cells in H-Block to release the worker bees again. They began arriving in the lobby, each one in turn registering an expression of disbelief at the carnage. After the initial shock, they set to work cleaning up the mess. They piled the bodies of the police officers and the prisoners in the visiting area and began mopping the lobby floor.

José settled back into his headquarters. He had risked so much already, but his incredible gamble had paid off. He was committed to the ideal of justice, and he knew for a fact that more struggle and sacrifice would be needed to achieve his goals. No matter what happened, he would see this through.

Chapter Seventeen

Inside

B eth's discussion group engaged in passionate, logical debates about history and politics. The inmates followed José's lead and listened attentively to Beth's lectures, and they all contributed to the group discussions.

Beth introduced them to the writings of former slave and abolitionist Frederick Douglass. At the time, she didn't think it was radical or dangerous. It was the logical next step in their intellectual journey together as a group. It just made sense to her that these men, who grew up poor and with fewer opportunities than most, would relate to Douglass. She thought they could learn from his story and writings. She wanted to instill in them the motivation to make their lives better, and she wanted them to understand that they too had the power to change the world.

Beth read aloud several of Douglass' sermons and letters, but the inmates focused on one particular piece. It was a speech asserting that freedom could only be won if the slaves themselves rose up to fight for it.

"Was this speech before or after the Civil War started?" Coop asked about the passage.

"Before, I think, but let's see." Beth rifled through her papers. "It was delivered in 1857. So yes, that's four years before the war began."

"Douglass was telling the slaves they needed to fight," José observed.

"It's true. It was a call to action. After years of advocating for peaceful opposition, in the end, Frederick Douglass welcomed the Civil War," Beth told them. "He said it was the only way to rid the country of the evil of slavery. During the war, he recruited former slaves for the Union Army, and he even served as an advisor to President Lincoln."

"Well, there's definitely no way the South would've given up slavery without war," T.K. said. "They would have gone on treating the black man like an animal they could own. What did Douglass say about people in power not giving it up unless they're forced?"

"Power concedes nothing without a demand. It never did and it never will," Beth recited.

"Yeah. I like that part." T.K. nodded.

"Me too," Beth agreed. "Now, let's take it to the next level, as we always do. How can we apply Frederick Douglass' lessons to today? Do they have any relevance now?"

"Hell, yeah," Fido said. "We're just like the slaves were back then. We're locked up because of who we are. We had no choice about where we grew up and what we had to do to survive. And now the system owns us, just like the slaves."

"Plus," T.K. said, "since we got no chance at parole now, we can't ever get free. We're slaves for life. We can't even escape like Douglass did."

"Even if we do get paroled someday," Coop added, "we still won't be free. We'll still be labeled 'criminals,' which means we can't find decent work or a safe place to live. No matter what happens, nothing can ever make up for the years I missed watching my little girl grow up."

"I'm sorry for that, Coop," Beth said. "I know your daughter would be better off with you in her life. But what can we do about the injustice in the way the system is run? What kind of action might change things?" Beth was guiding the conversation to a particular conclusion.

"Well, we obviously can't start a war," Mateo said.

"No. Of course not, but there are plenty of other things you can do. What about petitioning the governor to let her know your opinions?" Beth suggested.

"No offense, but that's pretty gay," Squeeze said in his distinctively hoarse voice. "And I should know." He paused while the other inmates chuckled. "Hell, writing love notes to politicians is the first thing everybody does when they're looking for favors, and it never works."

"Understood." Beth nodded. "Then, the next question I have is, 'What would the governor respond to?' My sense is that politicians react to public opinion, especially the priorities of people who will vote for them in the next election."

"That doesn't help us at all," Mateo said. "Prisoners can't vote, not even when we get out. That right is taken away from us when we're convicted."

"What about sending an editorial to the newspaper to get publicity for your cause?" Beth suggested.

"That would be a waste of time," Coop said. "Nobody cares about prisoners."

"We could talk to the warden. I can pull some strings with the guards and get us a meeting with him," Fido offered.

"That's an excellent idea! Anyone else?"

"Let me think on it," José said. "Douglass was right. He had a real strong message. He probably thought slavery would end after the war. But we know that's not true. It's still going strong. Our brothers are in prison for crimes that white people get away with all the time. And when we get out, we don't have any of the rights Douglass fought for. We can't vote. Hell, we can't even get a job because of our record. We need to do something."

Beth felt energized by the discussion. She thought she was making a difference in the inmates' lives by teaching them that they could advocate for themselves.

"Will you support us, Beth, if we do something to change things?" José said.

"Of course I'll support you. I will help in any way I can. I promise."

Chapter Eighteen

Outside

DAY TWO
4:49 PM

Ordered out of the command center after the SWAT debriefing, Beth leaned against the wall of the vehicle with the support personnel who had been expelled earlier. She considered the governor's order to "send her in." Would they ask her to go into the prison, as José was demanding? Would she—could she—do it? Importantly, what would happen if she refused?

Beth had the best of intentions. That much was indisputable. She had inspired the inmates to take bold actions to change their lives. Still, thinking back on the discussion group sessions, Beth was ashamed at her blindness to their intentions and her unwitting encouragement of their choices. It seemed obvious to her now that the thirteen men in her discussion group knew in advance about the plans to start a revolution. They had been planning it for months. She had stirred in José and the others enough outrage that they felt compelled to commit brutalities in order to change their predicament. More than that, she had given them the validation they needed to justify their violent behavior. But now that she had convinced them so thoroughly of the need to fight for justice, was there anything she could do to stop them?

The crowd pushed closer to Beth and her fellow outcasts, becoming increasingly restless as the five o'clock deadline approached. She glanced at her watch and then at the command center door, wishing for it to open and allow her to escape from both the heat and tension outside.

Finally, the door swung open, and Captain Sullivan emerged. Beth's relief quickly faded, however, as he shut the door behind him and stepped onto the grass.

"I promised to give you periodic updates about our plans to end the riot," he announced to the crowd. "Here's what I can tell you. The SWAT team raid was unsuccessful, as I'm sure you've figured out already. Nineteen state police officers are unaccounted for, and an unknown number of inmates were killed as well. Governor Webb assures me that she will not allow anyone else to die today. We're preparing to negotiate with the leader of the riot to find a peaceful solution."

Voices resounded from the crowd. "But it's almost five o'clock." "Are you going to give the inmates what they want?" "What about the guard's body and the officers'? When do we get them?"

"That's all I can say at this time. I need to go back to help with negotiations. I'll update you as soon as I can." Captain Sullivan motioned for the expelled support personnel to precede him into the command center. "You too, Ms. Sharpe," he grunted and let the door slam closed behind him. Beth had to reopen the door for herself, but she was grateful that her banishment was over.

Once inside, the support staff returned to their workstations. "Have a seat, Ms. Sharpe," Commissioner Holmes instructed. "We're contacting the inmates now. There are only minutes left before their deadline, and your cooperation is essential."

"José, this is Special Agent Dean of the FBI," Agent Dean was saying into the handheld radio. "We are ready to negotiate, but we would like to speak privately. Please allow us a more secure method of communication."

"He's not answering," Fitzroy breathed. "What do we do?"

"Calm down," Agent Dean assured him. "He'll respond."

"Yeah. Right. Because your expert guesses have been accurate so far." Captain Sullivan scoffed and let out an exasperated grumble.

Static from the radio confirmed Agent Dean's prediction, and José's voice filled the command center. "I told you there are no negotiations until Beth Sharpe is here with me. Haven't enough of your people died today? You're gonna force me to kill another guard, and this one is on you."

Beth's body tensed. *Kill another guard? No!*

"Please, José, let me finish. Wait," Agent Dean said. "I want to negotiate with you about how we can safely deliver Ms. Sharpe. We are willing to grant your request to send her into the prison ... for support."

This was news to Beth. No one had asked her opinion on this plan. The men seated at the conference table turned toward Beth. Even Andrew turned away from his computer screen to stare at her. Beth knew they were expecting her to show surprise, fear, or even anger. It took all of her willpower, but she sat perfectly still, her head held high and her expression resolute.

Agent Dean continued, "But we must discuss in detail exactly when and how that will happen."

"I'll give you all the details you need," José responded. "She walks in here now."

"José, you know it can't be that easy. We need to consider the specifics, and that discussion must take place on a secure line. Are you near a phone? How can we reach you?"

"The warden knows the number," José said. "Hurry up. I'm losing my patience."

Warden Hayward called out the numbers, and Andrew dialed, turning the speaker phone's volume higher. Commissioner Holmes ordered everyone in the command center to remain silent.

José answered on the first ring. "Now we're talking in private, but I'm still saying the same thing. Send Beth in here now, or else I kill hostages. It's simple as that."

"José, we will allow Ms. Sharpe to enter the prison," Agent Dean explained, "but you need to give us something in return. That's how negotiation works. We give you something you want, and you give us something we want." Agent Dean nodded. Beth thought he seemed pleased with himself for establishing what he considered productive communication with José. He continued, "First, we would like to remove the body of the guard who was killed yesterday. We also need any police officers you've captured to be released."

"You mean the pigs you sent to kill me?" José said. "They're all dead now—except for the ones who ran out the front door. And it's your fault for sending them in here in the first place. You gave me no choice but to kill them. So, releasing any live cops isn't an option. I have their bodies here though. You can have what's left of them."

A faint sigh escaped Colonel Mitchell's throat, but Agent Dean pressed on. "Yes. We want the bodies of the officers. That will go a long way to establishing a basis for negotiations. It will show that you're making a real effort to end this riot without further bloodshed."

"Okay. You get the dead cops, and I get Beth Sharpe," José agreed. "Works for me."

"Actually, José," Agent Dean said, "and I'm being completely honest with you here, that's not exactly a fair trade. We're getting the bodies of our people who you killed, and you're getting a live woman who will become another one of your hostages. You're getting the better end of the deal in that trade. Don't you agree?"

"I don't have to give you shit," José countered. And he was right. "I can just keep right on killing hostages until you realize you need to do what I say, and you'll have to give me Beth in the end anyway. I already showed you that attacking me won't get you anywhere."

Beth clenched her hand over her mouth. The situation could unravel quickly, and Agent Dean needed to tread lightly.

"You're right, José," he said. "You can keep killing hostages, and you can force us to take more aggressive action toward you. But, if that happens, we won't be able to work on your grievances. In the long run, that won't result in any kind of institutional change, and I assume that's the reason you started this riot in the first place. If we can agree on a fair deal now, you'll have a better chance of getting what you want later on."

"Continue," was the entirety of José's response.

"I think it's only fair to trade one live person for another. So, in addition to allowing us to remove the officers' bodies, which we both agree is a good will gesture on your part, we'll give you Beth Sharpe if you release the warden's secretary, Christine Williams."

"Tell me she hasn't been harmed," the warden cut in. "I know you used her to write the letter for you. Please say that she's safe."

"Ah, Warden, is that you? I thought you might want your little lady back. I'm happy to tell you she's doing just fine," José said. His next words were directed away from the phone. "Hey, say something so the warden knows you're alive."

"I'm alright," came the faint voice of Mrs. Williams. "I haven't been harmed. I want to go home."

"Thank God." Warden Hayward sighed, intertwining his fingers and pressing them to his lips.

"Then, you will trade Mrs. Williams for Ms. Sharpe? Is that what I'm hearing José?" Agent Dean said.

Beth was relieved as well. It would be awful if Mrs. Williams was hurt. She seemed like such a nice lady. Plus, José had managed to protect her through an all-out SWAT raid, which meant a lot. This tempered some of the worry Beth felt for what she might have to do.

"Yeah. I agree to that trade," José conceded, with obvious amusement in his voice. "So, send in Beth, and then I'll let Mrs. Williams out. How does five minutes sound?"

"Actually, José, we'd like to retrieve the officers' bodies before we make the trade. I think that's in everyone's best interests. My counter proposal is this. You allow our people into the prison tonight to remove the bodies of the fallen officers. First thing tomorrow morning, we make the trade—Mrs. Williams for Beth Sharpe."

"You got balls asking me to give you yours before I get mine," José replied. "Tell me this, Mr. FBI. Why should I trust you? The last time I gave you a deadline, you sent the police in to attack me. How do I know you won't use this chance to do the same thing? How do I know this isn't a trick? I think you're full of shit."

Agent Dean's response was measured. "The difference, José, is that this time you have my word. If you remember, you wouldn't negotiate with us before now. We had no other choice but to try to take the prison by force. But now that we're talking to each other and we've worked out a deal, I promise you that we will uphold our end of the bargain."

"Your word isn't enough. What else you got?" José objected. "Even if you don't come at me again tonight, what's my guarantee that you'll give me Beth in the morning?"

What about me? When do I get to say something? Beth opened her mouth to say exactly that.

But Fitzroy cleared his throat. "This is Artie Fitzroy speaking. I'm Governor Webb's chief of staff, and I have full authority to speak on her behalf. The governor gives you her personal assurance that Beth Sharpe will walk into that prison tomorrow morning. That is, if we're allowed to remove the officers' bodies from the prison and you release Mrs. Williams unharmed. We promise to follow through with the agreement."

"This is Warden Hayward. You have my word as well. That's all I can give. You'll have to settle for a gentlemen's agreement on this."

"Not good enough, Warden. If it's coming from the justice system, a gentlemen's agreement is garbage. You sacrificed your own men today instead of negotiating with me. That was stupid. Why should I trust you at all? How about this for an agreement? I'll let you have your people's bodies, but you need to take the other ones too. Our lives matter just as much as the cops'. That's what we're trying to make you understand. You take all of them, and you give them to their families. Tomorrow morning, we make the trade. In the meantime, I'll be holding a gun to Mrs. Williams's head—your gun. If I see a SWAT team coming, I'll kill her. If I think there's something shady going on, I will shoot her in the head. And it will be your fault."

"It's a deal then." Agent Dean said. "We'll contact you over the radio when we're ready to enter the prison to retrieve the bodies. The hostage trade happens tomorrow morning."

Really? Still not a word to me? Beth felt like she was about to explode.

"No," José said. "Nobody comes inside. My men will put the bodies out in front of the prison, and that's where you can get 'em. Only two people come at a time because I still don't trust you."

"Alright. I understand, José," Agent Dean agreed. "We have to get moving. There's only a few hours before sunset."

That's it! They can't keep ignoring me. "I have another condition," Beth said, her voice commanding as she straightened herself against her seat back. The men glared at her. "José, I'd like you to free someone else too. For me. Will you also release a friend of mine?"

Agent Dean grabbed the arms of his chair and twisted his body aggressively toward Beth. Sneering, he half-mouthed and half-whispered, "Shut up. You'll ruin everything."

"Is that you Beth?" José asked, the change in his voice noticeable despite the speaker system's poor sound quality. "You want me to release another hostage?"

"Yes. Please," Beth replied. "A guard. His name is Dan Cooney. He's a close friend of mine, and I would consider it a personal favor if you released him along with Mrs. Williams."

"I don't know if he's alive, but I'll try to find him. And, for you, I'll let him go. See you in the morning." A dial tone pronounced the end of the men's negotiation, but Beth saw it as the beginning of her own.

"Are you crazy?" Agent Dean spat at Beth, who had braced for a reprimand. "You could have derailed the entire negotiation. Asking him to release a second hostage is huge. The whole deal could've fallen through. Why didn't you say anything before?"

"I know José, and I believed he would do it if I asked as a personal favor," Beth explained, her frustration level increasing with each word. "And I was right. Plus, you didn't give me a chance to say anything. You didn't even ask me if I was willing to be part of a hostage trade."

"She's right," Colonel Mitchell said. He turned to Beth. "Will you go into that prison tomorrow morning? Do you accept the risk? Will you be able to do it—walk in there with no protection and no guarantee that you'll come back out alive?"

"Who the hell cares what she thinks?" Captain Sullivan interrupted. "It's her fault this riot started. She's the reason people are dead, and she's the reason we're forced to make a deal with an inmate thug. How convenient for Ms. Sharpe that she gets her boyfriend released too, while the others are still suffering inside. I say we feed her to the wolves!" His eyes pierced Beth with pure malice. She leaned away from him, an instinctive reflex to move away from a threat.

"Captain, unlike you, I care about Ms. Sharpe's welfare," the warden said before he was interrupted by the ringing of his cell phone. He pulled it from the case on his belt and looked at the number. "Sorry. I have to take this," he murmured, pushing away from the table and turning his back to the group. But his actions served only to pique their interest, and discussion about the hostage deal stopped entirely. Everyone in the command center listened to the warden's side of the phone conversation. "Nancy, stop crying. I can't understand you … It's okay. I know you've been alone for too long. I'm working on it. No. I don't know what happened to your health aide. You can stand it for a little while longer. You'll be okay. Listen, I have to go. I'm dealing with an emergency here, and I don't have time for this right now … Nancy, take one of your pills. I'll be home as soon as I can."

The warden swiveled around in his chair and met the gazes of his colleagues. Beth heard a voice say, "Ronnie! Wait! Ronnie!" as he flipped his phone closed to end the call. "Now, where was I?"

"You were telling us how much you care about Ms. Sharpe and that you're willing to let your secretary die if this one doesn't feel comfortable going into the prison tomorrow," Captain Sullivan replied.

"Enough of the sarcasm, captain. Of course I don't want anything to happen to Mrs. Williams," the warden said. "But, I can't accept that the only option is to 'feed her to the wolves,' as you so eloquently put it. There has to be another way. What about José's mother? Did we find her yet? Maybe she can talk some sense into her son. And what about the other one—Mateo?"

"We've located Mateo's mother," Colonel Mitchell answered. "She is willing to help us, but we only know about Mateo's involvement because we heard José use his name over the radio. I'm not sure how close he is to the decision-making or whether his mother will have any influence. My investigators are working on it. We haven't been able to get ahold of José's mother. We tried to get a search warrant for her apartment, but the judge won't issue one because she hasn't committed a crime. There's no evidence that she's done anything wrong or that she would even be helpful to us. We'll keep searching for her, but I don't have high hopes. I honestly can't think of another way out of this deal. Unless we're willing to see more people killed, I think Ms. Sharpe has to walk into that prison tomorrow. Now, if you'll excuse me, I need to coordinate recovery of the bodies."

The warden shook his head, and Colonel Mitchell stood to leave.

"Colonel, please wait," Beth said. She was determined to make these men listen to her. They had failed so dramatically during these past two days. They had no clue what the inmates' motivations were, and they had outright refused to heed her warnings about the consequences of their actions. Beth was becoming increasingly confident that she could do better than them. Or, at the very least, she couldn't possibly do any worse. "Let me answer the questions you asked me first. Yes. I will walk into the prison tomorrow. I understand the danger, and I accept the risks. I believe that I'll come back out again. I also accept some of the blame Captain Sullivan has assigned me, and I'll do my best to help end this without further violence."

Colonel Mitchell nodded and exited the command center.

"If we're done here, I'll update the men outside and help with the retrieval," Captain Sullivan said. He didn't wait for an answer.

The warden turned to Beth. "How are you so confident that you'll be safe?"

"I know it sounds strange to you, warden," Beth explained, "but I trust José. He's smart and a gifted leader. And I obviously understand him better than you do. I thought he would release Dan if I asked him, and it worked. Besides, he's kept your secretary alive for two whole days. I'm sure he will keep me safe too."

"I'm not nearly as confident as you," the warden said. "I just don't know what else to do at this point. It's going to be a while before we finish up here. Why don't you go home and get some rest?"

"You should do the same, Warden," Beth said, noting his drooping eyelids and pained expression. "Based on what I overheard from your phone conversation, someone needs you at home."

The warden nodded his weary agreement and motioned for Beth to exit the command center. When she descended the stairs, she glanced toward the prison and witnessed the first pair of police officers approaching it with a stretcher. She scanned their path and caught sight of the pile of bodies awaiting them. There were so many more than she had imagined. She noticed that there were far more inmates than police officers. Some of the lifeless bodies wore the yellow jumpsuits of the protective custody unit, but most wore the light blue ones of the general population. Thankfully, they were too far away for Beth to see the expressions on their individual faces. Still, the sight of it made her catch her breath, and she tripped over the command center's bottom step.

Captain Sullivan glanced over his shoulder as Beth made her clumsy exit, but he didn't acknowledge her. She heard him explaining the plan for that evening and the next day. He was imploring the spectators to leave for the night, so that the bodies of the dead police officers could be recovered and identified with the highest level of respect. It didn't seem to Beth as if the crowd would comply with his request, but she decided that it was none of her concern. She would follow the warden's instructions to go home and rest. She would need every ounce of her strength and courage to walk into the prison tomorrow.

CHAPTER NINETEEN

Outside

At home, Beth changed into comfortable shorts and a thin grey t-shirt. She turned the air conditioner in her bedroom window to high, pulled the bedspread and blankets off the bed, and splayed onto the mattress. After tossing and turning for what seemed like hours, she resigned herself to the fact that, though she was exhausted, she could not fall asleep. She lay awake as her mind sorted through all of the experiences that had led her to this moment.

So much responsibility weighed on her—Dan's life not least among it. Dan had already been a prison guard for several years before Beth met him. This was a dream job for a guy like him, who made a decent salary and benefits with only a high school diploma and more than his fair share of machismo. On the attractiveness scale, Beth thought, no one could argue that he wasn't at least an eight and a half. Intellectually, Dan was not the smartest guy around, but no one could have it all, and at this point in Beth's life she wasn't looking for "the one." To her, their relationship was about convenience, companionship, and sex. Beth thought of him as a close "friend with benefits," although "boyfriend" was the title he desperately wanted her to use.

Beth knew that Dan wanted more—a girlfriend who was sincere, caring, and wanted to live a simple, quiet life with him. But this was not how she envisioned her future. She'd told him as much, and he'd said that he was okay with it.

Still, she cared for Dan, and she was willing to risk a lot to save him. She'd already deserted one important man in her life, and she would not do that again.

Beth recalled the first time Dan had visited her apartment. She'd left him alone in the living room while she retreated to her bedroom to finish getting ready for their date. Dan had amused himself by perusing her bookshelves.

"This is quite a collection," he'd hollered, reading off the book titles. "*Understanding Serial and Mass Murder, When One Victim is Never Enough, Confronting Antisocial Personality Disorder, Overkill, Terror By Night.* You better hope you never get accused of a crime, Beth."

"What do you mean?" she'd asked, emerging from her bedroom to sidle up beside him, leaning gently into his arm.

"I can see it now. The news reports will say, 'Police found a gruesome collection of books about murder and violence. She had a virtual how-to library for being a psychopath,'" Dan had said, using hand gestures to emphasize the fictional headlines. "They'll think you're guilty for sure, just because of the books you own. Yikes!"

"Funny. You're right, I guess," Beth had said, chuckling. "That's the kind of thing I like to read about. Plus, a lot of these books were required for the classes I took in college."

"I'm just saying, if you're ever accused of a murder or something, you better hurry up and burn these books." Dan had turned toward her, his eyes had widened, and he'd nodded his head. "But, you'd be the most attractive killer I know. You look great!"

That had been their first outing together, and they had continued to date despite the disparities in their goals for their relationship.

Beth's life to this point had been shaped by her own drive to succeed, rather than by external circumstances. But the prison riot and the revelations of the past two days were forcing her to question even her most fundamental assumptions and beliefs.

She thought back to her childhood growing up in a small Vermont town, the youngest of three children. While her older brothers had followed the same path as their parents—graduating from high school, working at the local factory, and starting a family—Beth had made different choices. She had refused offers for steady relationships and instead dated unceremoniously throughout her high school years. She preferred her romantic interests to be buff and beautiful, rather than smart and ambitious. This had made it possible for Beth to keep those relationships casual, and her heart had never been broken by a boy. Beth had enrolled in community college right after high school, and she'd worked several jobs, saving every penny she could.

But while no boy ever broke Beth's heart, one man did. Throughout her childhood, Beth and her father had enjoyed spending time together. They would go to the movies, fix up old furniture, and drive around on Saturday mornings to search for bargains at yard sales. As Beth matured, she and her father had grown apart, and they had frequent, emotionally-charged arguments about their most fundamental beliefs. Beth could not accept the religion that her father believed to be absolute truth, and her father could not accept her denial of it.

"Beth," her father had reminded her, "means 'vow to God.' Your mother and I named you after Mary of Bethany, who listened to Jesus' words and cared for him. How can you ignore the call to serve him?"

"Well, if I ever hear a voice telling me to do something, Dad, I'll be sure to let you know," Beth had replied. She'd then reminded her father that their last name was Sharpe, which meant "smart," so her name actually meant that she was predestined to be intelligent and educated.

They had gone back and forth—her father emphasizing the importance of religion and Beth emphasizing her drive to accomplish more than a small-town life, no matter how rooted in religion, would allow. Their respective arguments had failed to satisfy or persuade the other.

The last argument between Beth and her father had happened when she announced that she would be leaving home to continue her education. Over Sunday dinner, she had informed the family that she had earned enough scholarships and financial aid to attend a four-year college in Massachusetts. It would be difficult, but she would be able to support herself financially while working toward a degree. She would double major in criminal justice and psychology, and she'd believed with every fiber of her being that she would change the world.

After dinner had ended and Beth's brothers and their families had left the house, her mother stayed in the kitchen while Beth and her father sat beside each other on the front porch.

"I just don't understand why you work as hard as you do, Beth," he had begun. "You're already killing yourself working sixty hours a week. If you move away, you'll have to add living expenses to that too, and then you'll have school work on top of everything. Why? Listen to me, Beth. Settle down. Start a family of your own. You want to 'make a difference' in the world. I get that. But why can't you make a difference here? Just take a step back. Refocus. Stop depending on yourself, and start trusting in God. Everything will work out fine."

Looking back, Beth could see that, at only twenty years old, she had been exhausted. She had been besieged with responsibility and had a deep-rooted fear that she might lack the commitment or the ability to achieve her goals. Maybe that was why she'd lost her temper, or maybe she had simply reached the end of her tolerance for the "trust in God" mindset. In either case, she'd shouted at her father.

"That's why you're a loser, Dad!" she'd screamed loudly enough for her mother in the kitchen and the neighbors across the street to hear. "You and Mom and your sons too. You do nothing to improve things because you have faith that your God will take care of everything. Don't you think God would want you take responsibility for what goes wrong in the world? Don't you think he wants you to do something about the terrible things that happen to people? You go to work and to church, and you think that's enough. Well, that kind of thinking is why you're stuck here in this shitty town and in this shitty life. And, I won't do it. I won't live a useless life. I'm taking control of my destiny, and, unlike you, I'm going to make something of myself."

Her father had been quiet for a moment. "I didn't realize I was such a disappointment," he'd said. "I actually thought my life was pretty good, but obviously you know better." He rose from his seat and disappeared into the house.

Beth should have gone after him and apologized right away, but she had been too proud at that moment and too self-righteous. That argument had been the final blow to their already-strained relationship. They didn't speak to each other for several weeks. Beth had worked late every night, and her father had deliberately avoided her when she was home. He worked an extra shift at the factory the day Beth's mother drove her to the bus station.

Even after Beth had graduated from college and moved to Connecticut to take a job at the prison, she and her father never spoke about the argument they'd had or about the hurtful things she'd said, and they never revived their friendship. They were both deeply hurt, and neither of them knew how to fix it. So neither of them tried.

Beth had committed herself to the ideal that she would improve the world. But what if she'd made it emptier instead? She had suppressed that idea, and put all of her energy into her work. She'd focused on the criminal justice field and, in particular, on correctional institutions and the inmates themselves, whom she'd deemed most in need of support. Her ambition was to give the worst criminal offenders the tools and motivation they needed to turn their lives around and become productive members of society.

She had taken the prison counselor position and embraced her role as therapist, teacher, and advocate for the inmates. It was a good job, a hard job. She had replaced the sadness of her loss with the day-to-day challenges of her work.

And now, three years after Beth had first stepped foot inside the Arnone prison, she found that she had, in fact, changed the world. She had succeeded in encouraging the inmates to become their own champions.

But the changes she'd brought about, rather than improving the world, had made it worse. All of her efforts and her passion for justice had so far only caused suffering and death. She'd convinced the inmates of their worth and how they deserved happiness and fair treatment. But how did she not foresee the consequences of her actions?

These thoughts flooded Beth's mind until she gave up on sleep and decided to use her restlessness for a productive purpose instead. She had resources right in her own apartment that she could use to prepare herself for the complexities of the situation she now faced. This was how she'd handled every other decision in her life—through careful research that led to a logical solution. Why should this be any different?

Beth got out of bed and headed for the collection of books she kept in the built-in shelves of her living room—the same ones Dan had commented on during their first date. They amounted to a mini-library of reference material on all aspects of the criminal justice system. She perused the titles, searching for anything about prison politics, riots, and working with offenders. Her search yielded a half dozen books, and Beth sat on the floor with her selections scattered around her.

She focused first on one that chronicled the history of prison riots in the United States. The first few chapters covered a handful of riots that took place in the 1920s, but Beth flipped through the pages until she reached the chapter on the Attica riot of 1971. She skimmed the chapter to remind herself of the details. Fights between inmates and guards had created tension in the prison, and it all came to a head one morning when the inmates in Cellblock A overtook the guards and gained access to the tunnel that connected the cellblocks to the prison yard. Sheer luck, rather than careful planning, allowed a group of one hundred rioting inmates to advance into other areas of the prison, freeing over a thousand from their cells. Many inmates hid or escaped, but others gathered in D-yard, where they stayed for four days. They held fifty guards and civilians hostage, keeping them in a circle in the center of the yard.

Several inmates emerged as spokesmen, protesting poor conditions in the prison and issuing a list of demands. Negotiations failed, and the inmates threatened the lives of hostages if they came under attack. The governor ordered that the prison be taken by force, and an army of correctional officers, state police, and sheriffs' deputies dropped tear gas on the yard and opened fire. Ten hostages and twenty-nine inmates were killed by police gunfire, and another eighty were seriously wounded. The government failed to provide prompt medical care to the injured inmates, and the correctional officers who participated in the raid brutalized them in the ensuing hours. In the end, the inmates failed to achieve any of their goals, and more than sixty of them were eventually indicted on riot-related charges. Later, the government settled a class-action lawsuit and had to pay twenty million dollars to the surviving inmates and the families of those who were killed by police. Neither party gained anything.

Beth read on, digesting the information and correlating it to the current situation. A significant portion of the book focused the 1980 riot at New Mexico State Penitentiary where the brutality of the inmates was intense. The worst atrocities were perpetrated against personal enemies, snitches, and those held in the protective custody cellblock. Victims were burned alive with torches, had their eyes gouged out, and suffered horrible mutilations. Of the twelve guards taken hostage, several were stripped, beaten, raped, and degraded.

Negotiators on the inside were simply those who had found the guards' radios, and as many as eight different inmates issued contradictory demands. A day and a half after the riot began, state police charged in, finding inmates trapped inside the then-burning building or hiding in fear, and there was ample evidence of murder and torture. Over thirty inmates died—most of them brutally killed—and hundreds were injured. The inmates gained nothing from the riot in terms of improved conditions or dispensations, and the government was left with a prison building in ruins and the repercussions of their slow, feeble response.

Reading about the horrific details of these riots left Beth feeling demoralized. She rifled through the remaining chapters that described incidents in several states that spanned recent decades. With no exceptions, they were stories of gratuitous violence, ineffective communication, and failure to achieve anything of value for those on either side of the prison walls.

Frustrated and even less hopeful than before, she pushed the books aside and searched the bookcase for something that would offer more inspiration than despair.

A stack of magazines in the lower corner of the bookcase caught her attention, and she pulled it onto the floor in front of her. Over the years, Beth had saved copies of *The Angolite* magazine, which was written by inmates at the Louisiana State Penitentiary, called "Angola." In six issues published each year, the magazine featured articles about the realities of prison life, how families were impacted by incarceration, issues with parole, and new rehabilitation programs. Beth had always been captivated by articles about the injustice of nonviolent offenders dying in prison and stories about inmates who acknowledged their crimes and committed to turning their lives around.

She flipped through the magazines and read the poetry written by the inmates of Angola. They told of sadness, hurt, and regret, but they also revealed determination, sincerity, and strength of character.

Reading these essays reminded Beth of the reasons why she chose to work in the field of corrections. Many inmates were good, intelligent men who had simply been caught up in unfortunate circumstances. They had made poor decisions and caused harm to others, but that did not mean they were evil or worthless. On the contrary, some, like those who wrote for *The Angolite,* were thoughtful, moral people with enormous potential.

Reinvigorated, Beth sat back and tried to clear her head.

Other riots had ended in disaster, but this one didn't have to. The revolution at the Arnone State Correctional Institution differed from the others in significant ways. For one, it was led by one powerful and principled leader. With José in charge, there were strict controls on the inmates, as evidenced by the status reports heard over the radio and the precise planning behind their effective response to the SWAT raid. For another, the inmates' complaints were not absurd or extreme. They were motivated to act by the inherent unfairness of justice system. They were simply asking to be heard and shown some respect.

Most importantly, the one thing the Arnone revolution had that none of the other riots did was Beth Sharpe. Not one of the riots she read about featured an advocate for the inmates who had an established and trusting relationship with them and a demonstrated commitment to improving their plight. For years, Beth had supported José and the other inmates in their struggles for justice. She alone had the ability and the power to ensure that this riot did not result in the same tragic consequences as the others.

At that moment, seated on her living room floor, Beth realized that she could be the decisive factor in determining the outcome of this revolution. She would continue to serve as counselor and advocate for the inmates. She would mediate the negotiations in an innovative way with skills that no other person possessed. She would pour all of her energy and insight into helping the inmates, hostages, families, and everyone involved. She would do her best to make sure that the prison revolution ended peacefully and that it resulted in positive and constructive change.

When Beth had walked into the prison for the first time three years before, she had been a moral, determined, and idealistic person. Since then, she had not let anything discourage her or impede the progress she was making to improve the lives of the inmates she counseled.

But for the last two days, she'd felt self-doubt taking its toll on her mind and influencing her decisions. She had lost her way. And she had cowered before the administrators, negotiators, and strangers—before her own painful memories. But she would not cower any longer. No more running, no more hiding.

When she walked into the prison the next morning, even if it was for the last time, she would do so with the same principles, dedication, and ideals that she had maintained throughout her life. She would fix this.

She had to.

CHAPTER TWENTY

Inside

Angel was causing trouble again. Only a few hours ago, he had helped to resist the police raid. But now, from what José saw on the control room's surveillance screens, his cooperation had only been temporary. D-Block was a mess.

José decided that he needed to have an in-person conversation with Angel. Remembering his earlier vow to take more reinforcements with him the next time he visited, he gathered his team. It included his usual bodyguards—Krueger, Coop, and the G's. But this time, he would also take Mateo and three more Los Solidos soldiers borrowed from Squeeze's backup force in B-Block.

The group proceeded through the gated door into the cellblock hallway. They spotted Squeeze peering through the small glass window of the B-Block door, his fingers appearing near his cheekbone to make a flickering wave. No one in the group returned the greeting.

Their arrival at D-Block went unnoticed by the men inside. This time, it was José's turn to peer through the little window in the door, and what he saw made bile rise to his throat. He moved aside to let the others take a look, and their reactions echoed his own. Coop winced and muttered, "Jesus." Mateo shook his head and turned away. Only Krueger stared expressionless while watching the sordid scene.

A limp body dangled from the railing of the cellblock's second tier. Its head was crooked, forced to one side by a large knot tied in the sheet-rope that was lodged against its neck. Whether this was the body of a general population prisoner, a worker bee, or a guard, José could not ascertain. It had been stripped naked and the facial features that he would have used to identify it were bloodied and distorted.

About fifteen men roamed the main floor of D-Block, kicking at the toilet paper, food trays, clothes, and mattresses scattered everywhere. These were not the worker bees who should have been tending to the needs of those locked in their cells, nor were they the soldiers who had enlisted to help José's cause. They were Angel's buddies, no doubt members of the Latin Kings.

Still scrutinizing the scene, José asked, "Where is Angel?"

Mateo pointed to the far corner of the cellblock.

Following the path of his finger, José saw him too. The five-point crown tattooed on Angel's back identified him as his bare ass gyrated roughly and repeatedly. Two legs protruding on either side of Angel's revealed that another man, bent over a table, was the recipient of his assault.

The bile rose more forcefully this time, and José turned away, his face set like stone. He had no choice. He had to get D-Block under control, but he knew it wouldn't be easy.

"Let's do this," he said.

José and his men filed into D-Block and grouped together. A few of Angel's dogs noticed them immediately and positioned themselves in a line facing José. Soon another dog joined them, and then another. Finally, Angel came over, flanked by several other supporters. He stepped in front of his gang, adjusting the waistband of his pants and smoothing his shirt down over them.

"What's goin' on?" Angel said, scowling at José.

A few more men joined Angel's ranks. José did a quick count. His crew of eight was outnumbered by Angel's. He scanned the faces of the dogs who stared back at him. These were good fighters, for sure. But his soldiers were better. Krueger alone could take out more than a few of Angel's guys easy. Plus, he and Mateo had guns and, if they found themselves in trouble, they would be the decisive factor in his success. He concluded that, if a fight was necessary—and that possibility was looking more and more likely by the second—he would clearly have the advantage.

José took a step toward Angel. Both gangs closed in behind their respective leaders. "That's my question for you, Angel. What the hell is going on?"

"It's none of your business, man," Angel replied. He held out his arms as if baffled by José's anger and offended by his intrusion. "D-Block is mine. You got the rest of the prison to worry about. Why don't you just leave us alone in here?"

"Because, Angel, what you do reflects on all of us. And this," José said, gesturing to include the whole room, "isn't what our revolution is about." *Plus, you're showing me disrespect,* José said to himself. *And I won't let you get away with that.*

He moved even closer until he was standing nose to nose with Angel. "Get in line," he said, poking him hard and repeatedly in the chest. "Or I will take you out."

This was a direct threat, and Angel's dogs reacted immediately. One rushed at Mateo, landing a face punch before José even realized what was happening. The confrontation quickly turned into a full-fledged brawl, and the block exploded with excitement and shouting from the prisoners watching from inside their cells.

José hit Angel squarely in the jaw, pushing him backwards, and Angel collided with one of this own men who had been rushing in the opposite direction. Angel fell to one knee.

This is it, José thought. I finish this now. He stood over Angel and pulled back his fist. He swung, putting all of his strength into the punch, but his hand was stopped mid-air by an unseen barrier. Confused, he looked up to see that it was Krueger. José's bodyguard had caught his fist before it made contact with Angel.

The other men surrounding them continued to battle, but to José, the scene was playing out in slow motion. Angel got up and shook off José's punch. He did not seem at all surprised to find that Krueger was protecting him. In fact, he was almost smirking. José tried to wriggle out of Krueger's hold, but he could not. In terms of brute strength, Krueger had him beat. José reached with his left hand for his gun, but it was positioned so he could grab it easily with his right hand, and Krueger still held onto that hand with an iron-tight grip.

Krueger snarled. "No," was all he said.

The fighting around them died down some, and the once-frenzied cellblock went quiet. José felt all eyes on him. The other prisoners must have been wondering what would happen next. He wondered too, since it no longer seemed that he was in control. Somehow, with just one word, Krueger had taken that from him.

Still, José managed to compose himself. "Enough!" he shouted. "That's enough." But everyone else had already stopped fighting. José turned to Krueger. "You can let go now. This fight is over." Much to José's relief, Krueger did as he was told.

Angel nodded to Krueger, whose face did not reveal any sign of an acknowledgement back.

José looked over one shoulder and then the other. He found that his men had dominated the fight, as he had predicted they would, and Angel's dogs were scrambling to their feet licking their wounds. He and Angel glared at each other as their respective supporters re-grouped behind them.

José could not think of any persuasive, inspiring, or even threatening words to say. He was dumbfounded by Krueger's actions. This confrontation, though technically a win for him since his men had beaten down Angel's, had not gone as well as he'd hoped.

I better cut my losses now, he thought. "Let's go," he said aloud to his crew.

José did not make eye contact with Krueger or any of the others as they left D-Block and made their way into the central corridor. Everything had gone down so fast. He hadn't even had a chance to ask whose body was hanging from the second tier railing and who Angel was raping on the table. It was no matter though. José was coming to the realization that Angel and D-Block were beyond salvation. There was nothing he could do to change that. Going forward, he would simply contain them and limit their impact on his mission.

For now, José would return to his headquarters and wait out the night. Angel's betrayal was disappointing, but Krueger's was grave. If Krueger turned on him, it would be the end of everything. Without José, there would be no more revolution. No chance for justice. And he would not allow that.

CHAPTER TWENTY-ONE

Outside

DAY THREE
12:20 AM

It was after midnight when Warden Hayward left the grounds of the Arnone State Correctional Institution. To his welcome surprise, he felt a reprieve from the oppressive stress he had been under all day. His mind was unencumbered during the short drive to his home in a bedroom community north of the prison. He focused only on the narrow section of road illuminated by his car's headlights until he reached the white picket fence that signified the edge of his yard, and he turned into the driveway. As he did every day after work, he dreaded the possibility that his wife was still awake, waiting to tell him about the trials of her day and demanding his sympathetic attention.

He entered the house through the garage, gently closing the door behind him. Only the ticking sound of the antique grandfather clock greeted him. He sighed and crept down the hall to the kitchen, where the answering machine blinked on a small table against the wall. He turned the volume lower and leaned over to listen.

"Ronald, it's your mother. I heard your name on the news and saw the awful pictures of what's happening in your prison. Are you alright? I'm worried sick. I've called your house a hundred times today, but nobody's answering the phone. Is Nancy okay? Call me. Please."

He glanced at his watch and decided that it was too late to call her back. The front page of his church's monthly newsletter, which his wife made him post on the corkboard above the phone, caught his eye. As always, it listed the contact information for the church leaders, important dates, and an inspirational phrase. This one read, "God will give you strength for every battle, wisdom for every decision, peace that surpasses understanding." Rather than inspiration, it felt like a personal insult to him. At the moment, he felt neither strong nor wise. In fact, he felt that he had been given nothing but battles to fight. He ripped the newsletter off the corkboard, sending the tack that held it flying across the room. Then he crumpled the paper and threw it in the garbage.

He opened the kitchen cabinets and perused their contents, but he found nothing appetizing. He concluded that the feeling in the pit of his stomach was exhaustion rather than hunger, and he tiptoed to the bedroom, peeking around the door before he entered. His wife was sleeping soundly, though the lamp was still illuminating the open bottle of pills and a glass of water on the bedside table. He tiptoed over and picked up the medicine bottle. Verifying that there were pills left inside, he secured the cover and returned it to the table. He leaned over to listen for his wife's breathing and shut off the lamp.

Nothing could wake his wife after she took one of her pills, so he trudged to his side of bed, sat down heavily, removed his shoes, and placed them neatly on the floor beside his night stand. He rested on top of the covers, arms by his sides, and fell asleep.

Ronald Hayward had married his high school sweetheart and planned to live a quiet, conventional life filled with church picnics and family outings. As newlyweds, they'd talked for hours about how they would be moral leaders in their community and the greatest-ever parents to their future children. Theirs had been realistic goals, but they'd been young and naïve, and they could not have predicted the challenges they would face or the losses they would suffer. Bit by bit, as many couples before and after them, they'd come to understand that the reality of life was often painful and unfair. After thirty years of marriage, they had achieved none of their original goals.

When they married, Ronald worked as a guard in one of the nearby prisons. He had already achieved more than his father, who had worked as a mechanic in other people's garages, only ever making as much money as the family needed just to get by. Ronald had wanted more for himself and his family, so he had worked tirelessly to move up the ranks in the state prison system. He was eventually appointed Warden of one of the state's largest prisons, making his professional life an unmitigated success.

His family life, on the other hand, was exactly the opposite. He and his wife had tried for years to have children, but every one of Nancy's pregnancies ended in miscarriage. They'd considered infertility treatments and adoption, but they'd been forced to put their plans on hold when Nancy had become ill. It had started ten years into their marriage, as Nancy had approached her thirtieth birthday. Days turned into weeks and months, and her health had failed to improve.

Doctors had tried various diagnoses, ranging from Lupus to depression, and a wide assortment of medications and treatments. Nothing helped, and both the warden and his wife had grown increasingly disheartened. Finally, a specialist had made a diagnosis that seemed to fit her symptoms—Chronic Fatigue Syndrome. It had been a relief to finally solve the puzzle of Nancy's illness, although her diagnosis had not brought with it an effective treatment. Her suffering had continued with headaches, joint pain, trouble concentrating, and severe exhaustion that left her unable to get out of bed.

Nancy never returned to her job at the bank, and she fell into a downward spiral of isolation and depression. Most days, it would take all of her energy to get out of bed, dress, and prepare a meal for dinner. As the years went on, even that became too much for her, and the warden had to hire outside help to care for her while he was at work.

When he was young, newly married, and just starting his career, Ronald Hayward had envisioned a much different future for himself than the reality in which he currently existed. He had imagined that, at age fifty-six, he would be celebrating his children's graduations and helping them find their way in the world. He might even have grandchildren playing in his backyard, asking him to toss around a baseball or begging him to tell another joke. He'd thought that he would be preparing to retire after thirty years as a state worker and that he would travel the world with his wife. Instead, he had no children, and his father and brother had passed away years before, leaving him the sole caretaker to his elderly mother and ailing wife.

The beeping of his alarm clock awakened him from a deep, albeit brief sleep.

"Ronnie, are you home?" his wife whimpered. She kept her eyes tightly closed when she spoke.

"Yes. I'm here," he sighed, forcing himself to rise from the bed.

"Yesterday you weren't here," she said, shifting to face him. "I had to get up and shut off the alarm clock myself." The warden saw in her glassy eyes evidence that she had taken more than the recommended dose of her medication.

"I'm sorry," he said. "I'll shut it off in case I don't make it home again tonight."

"What? Why, Ronnie?" she whined. "Why wouldn't you come home tonight? Yesterday was awful for me. Lydia didn't show up, so I was alone for the whole day."

"It was a bad day for me too, Nancy," he said, choosing a clean suit from his closet and laying it on the end of the bed. "I'll call the service and find out what's going on. If your usual aide isn't available for some reason, they should be able to send someone else."

"I do hope Lydia can come today. She's my favorite. She's so nice and helpful, and she talks to me about all kinds of things." Nancy chattered on. The warden thought it was more an effort to satisfy her longing for his attention than anything else, so he was only half listening. "I've told her my whole life story and all about you too. I can tell she's really listening because she asks me questions and tells me to describe all the little details. She's told me about her life too," Nancy continued. "She just adores her son. She always says she'll do anything for her José. He's the best thing that ever happened to her. Apparently he gets himself into trouble, though, and she's always worried about him and hoping he makes the right decisions. Just the other day, she was nervous that something might happen to him. Gosh, I hope everything's alright. It would be just terrible if—"

"Wait. Stop!" the warden interrupted, his voice louder than he intended. "Did you say José? José what?"

"Why are you yelling at me, Ronnie? You know I hate when you get angry with me." Nancy propped herself against the headboard.

Instead of apologizing the way he usually did, the warden rushed over to his wife and gripped her shoulders. "Answer me, Nancy. Think! Is her son's name José Ayala?"

"I-I don't know," Nancy said. She tried to shrug her shoulders, but she was unable to complete the movement because he continued to hold them tightly. "Yes. I-I think that's what she said. Her last name is Henry, I remember, but her son's name was something else. Ayala sounds right."

The warden knew he'd heard that name before—Lydia Henry. In the command center when they were discussing José's family connections, he hadn't been able to place the feeling of familiarity at the time. But it was clicking for him now.

"I can't believe this!" The warden let go of his wife's shoulders and ran his fingers through his own hair instead. He paced back and forth by the foot of the bed. "What did you tell her? Does she know that I work in the prison?"

Nancy sniffled. "I don't know why you're asking me all of these things. So what if I told her about you? What's the harm in that?"

"Nancy, you have no idea. Tell me everything you said to her." He continued to pace, and he began closing his fists and stretching them out again as he waited for her to reply.

Nancy took a calming breath. "We were both saying how we worry about the men in our lives," she explained. "Like, Lydia's always worried about her son because she knows that he puts himself in danger. I told her that I worry about your safety too. Every day when you leave for work, I'm worried that you won't make it home—that one of the criminals in the prison will hurt you. She told me that what helps her anxiety is knowing that her son can fight to defend himself. And I told her that I feel better knowing that you can defend yourself too, if anything bad happens."

"Oh, what have I done? How could I be so stupid? I never should have told you." He groaned. "You told her about the gun I have in my office. Didn't you? Even though you promised me you would never say it to anyone. Tell me the truth, Nancy."

"Yes. I told Lydia about your gun. I'm sorry. It just kind of came out. I only told that one person, and she's a home health aide, for goodness sake, Ronnie. She doesn't have any connection to the prison. What harm could possibly come from telling her? I don't understand why you're so upset."

The warden stopped his nervous twitching and stood at the foot of their bed, his shoulders hunched and arms dangling by his sides. "She was using you, Nancy. And you had no idea. Her son José is an inmate in my prison. He started a riot, and he's the leader of the whole thing. You told his mother about my gun, and she gave that information to him. And he used it, Nancy. He used it to kill a guard. Someone died because of what you did."

Nancy's eyes flooded with tears, and her lower lip trembled. "I'm sorry, Ronnie," she whispered. "I didn't know." She laid her head back against her pillow and sobbed.

The warden froze. Then he gasped and his eyes lit up. "Wait," he said more to himself than to his wife. "I think I know how we can use this. This could change everything." He darted into the living room and dialed the phone. "Who is this?" he barked. "Get me Captain Sullivan. No? How about Colonel Mitchell? Who is in charge of the command center right now? Fine. Put Agent Dean on." He slapped his thigh impatiently. Finally, he blurted, "I have new information, and we need to act on it fast. Call everyone in right away. Send a car to pick up Ms. Sharpe. I'm getting on the road now." He hung up the phone before Agent Dean uttered a word.

CHAPTER TWENTY-TWO

Outside

DAY THREE
7:14 AM

"**A**re you saying your wife had something to do with this?" Fitzroy raised his hands as a sign of surrender and shook his head. "This just keeps getting better and better."

Beth was stunned by the warden's disclosure. He had already admitted that the gun José had used to kill a guard was likely taken from his office. But now, he was admitting that his wife was the only other person in the world who knew it was there. Beth couldn't imagine any worse situation for the warden to be in.

"Not in the way you are implying, but yes," the warden explained. "As some of you know, my wife has some significant health issues, and she requires assistance when I'm away from home. I hire home healthcare aides through an agency to provide services for her. It came to my attention this morning that the most recent aide was, in fact, José Ayala's mother, Lydia Henry. She has worked in my home for several months, and during that time she kept her affiliation with the prison a secret. She gained my wife's confidence and convinced her to divulge things about me and the prison, including the presence of the firearm in my office. My wife is beside herself, and I'm furious at the invasion of my private life."

How awful for him, Beth thought. She was not at all surprised that José had made this complex, long-term investment of effort to ensure his success. He was more than capable of such multifaceted strategic planning. She was surprised, however, and disappointed in herself, that she had no inkling at all that this plot had been in the works.

"I'm so sorry." Agent Dean spoke when no one else did. "I understand your outrage, and I share it. Believe me. This serves to demonstrate the intense level of preparation on the part of the inmates. It's truly unprecedented, and it's no wonder we've been forced to negotiate on their terms. But I don't see how this changes anything."

"Really? It's perfectly obvious," the warden insisted. "The state police are trying to find José's mother because she might be able to convince her son to surrender. The investigators located her apartment, but, as Colonel Mitchell informed us, no one answered the door. They couldn't get a warrant because she hadn't done anything wrong. But now, don't you see? Now we know that she's committed a crime. We can get a search warrant for her apartment and an arrest warrant for her."

"You have certainly been deceived, warden," Commissioner Holmes said. "But what crime has she committed?"

"This woman's actions definitely constitute a felony," Colonel Mitchell said in support of the warden's claim. "We can charge her with aiding and abetting and inciting a riot. And I would even go so far as to say that she's an accessory to murder, since the firearm she helped her son acquire was used to kill a prison guard."

"Exactly," the warden said. "Now, get your people on this, colonel. If we move fast, we can find José's mother and avoid sending Ms. Sharpe into harm's way."

"Whoa. Hold on a minute. That's quite a stretch in logic," Commissioner Holmes contended. "How exactly does locating the inmate's mother translate into keeping Ms. Sharpe safe? Even if a judge issues the warrant right away, and even if we find something interesting in her apartment and we arrest her, that doesn't change the fact that we still need to exchange Ms. Sharpe for your secretary. If we don't want anyone else murdered," he said, pointing at Beth, "she needs to walk into that prison this morning."

"No! We'll find Lydia Henry, arrest her, and charge her with a felony. Then, we'll dangle that in front of José and see how he feels about putting his mother's life in jeopardy. We'll tell him that she will go to prison herself unless he cooperates with us." The warden began his argument with confidence, but as he continued, his tone betrayed recognition of the flaws in his reasoning. "Surely his mother can convince him to give up before anyone else gets hurt."

"Warden," Beth interrupted, "José loves his mother, but I doubt she'll have much influence over his behavior. I also don't think that you'll find Lydia Henry anytime soon. I would assume that José has made arrangements for her to hide out until this is over. If, by some miracle, you do find her and arrest her, and you try to hold that over José's head, it will only make him angry. And, honestly, you haven't seen him angry yet. So far, every one of José's actions has been calculated and deliberate. If you provoke him by threatening his family, his reaction will be severe."

The warden slumped into a chair. "I'm trying to save you."

"I appreciate that, warden. I really do," Beth said. She stood tall, squared her shoulders, and made deliberate eye contact with each of the men seated at the command center's conference table. "Let me make this clear. I don't need to be saved, and I've never asked anyone to protect me. In all the time you've known me, warden, have I ever asked you for help? Have I ever given you the impression that I wanted or needed you to intercede for me when I'm working with inmates in this institution?" The warden shook his head. "Since this revolution started," Beth continued, "I've stayed quiet as all of you have made ridiculous assumptions about the people involved in this—about everything! I've kept my mouth shut while you came up with plans and took actions that I knew would fail. I even let you speak on my behalf and promise to trade me for a hostage—all without even consulting me."

Fitzroy pointed at her and started to rise from his seat. "Sit down," Beth snapped, cutting him off before he uttered a word. *All of these men can just shut up now. It's my turn, and they will listen to what I have to say!* "Until now, I've gone along with all of this because I thought that you knew what you were doing. But obviously that's not the case. I admit that by teaching the inmates to stand up for themselves against injustice, I may have inspired them to take this drastic action. That was my mistake. But you all have made plenty more mistakes over these past few days, and they've had effects far worse than mine. You've made a mess of things because you didn't realize who you were dealing with. I'm through cowering to all of you. I am the only person here who truly understands the inmates and their motivations. I'm the only one who has a chance to end this without more people being killed."

"What exactly is your point, Ms. Sharpe?" Captain Sullivan fumed.

"My point is, captain, you've ignored my opinions and outright belittled me, but the truth is that I am your most valuable asset." Beth read in the men's expressions assent to her reasoning thus far, so she continued. "Whether you realize it or not, the best thing you can do right now is trust me. From this point on, you will listen to what I have to say because you recognize that my insights are critical. I will walk into the prison today under my terms, and I will use my considerable skill in counseling inmates to negotiate a deal. I will convince José to cooperate, but I will insist that you hear his grievances and come up with an honest plan to address the issues he brings to your attention."

The faces staring back at Beth revealed a wide range of emotional responses. Warden Hayward's was one of sadness and defeat, while Captain Sullivan's was characteristically annoyed. Colonel Mitchell beamed, which Beth perceived as a sort of fatherly pride. Most everyone else in the command center wore an expression of disbelief, but

Beth remained confident and poised. No one spoke out to disagree with her assertions or protest her demands. She had succeeded in gaining their respect.

The next few hours would reveal whether she could achieve the same respect inside the prison walls.

Chapter Twenty-Three

Inside

FOUR DAYS BEFORE

The members of Beth's discussion group were uncharacteristically quiet while she tried to initiate a discussion about their latest reading assignment.

"I thought this book would strike a chord with at least some of you. *Way of the Peaceful Warrior* is a book that changes lives. It even says so right on the cover," Beth teased, struggling to elicit their participation. "No one? Well, I certainly got something out of the book. It's a 'seize the day' sort of message that offers a path to find happiness within ourselves. I particularly liked the quote, 'There are no ordinary moments.' It's a simple idea, but if you internalize it, you realize that every day is precious and valuable."

"That's the truth," Mateo said.

"What's going on with you guys today?"

"Nothin's going on," José assured her. "I think maybe we should use the peaceful warrior message and just enjoy the moment. I'm thankful—I think we all are—that you started this group. It's really made a difference to us. You changed the way I make decisions, so thanks."

157

"You showed me that I don't always have to be a victim, and I can stand up for myself. Thank you," Squeeze said.

Hacker raised his hand. "You helped me realize what my strengths are and how I can use them. Thank you."

"You introduced me to all these guys, and now I have a lotta friends who back me up and protect me. Thank you," Fido said.

T.K. put his hand over his heart. "You gave me confidence. That's something I never had before."

Beth put the book down. She wasn't sure how to respond. "Wow. I'm touched, truly, by what you've all said." Her voice caught. "But what brought this on? Don't get me wrong. You've really been amazing to me, and I appreciate every word. But why say all of this today?"

"We just wanted you to know all that, in case we don't have another chance to tell you," Angel said.

José glared at him and turned to smile at Beth. "Well, like you said, there are no ordinary moments. And this unordinary moment belongs to you."

Beth was moved by their sentiments. *They appreciate me*, she thought. *I really am making a difference.*

CHAPTER TWENTY-FOUR

Outside

On the third day after the riot began, Beth stood near the outer gate, flanked on either side by Warden Hayward and Colonel Mitchell. They stared at the front door of prison, waiting for any sign of activity.

Mrs. Williams emerged. "Oh, thank God," the warden whispered. The door shut behind her, and it appeared that she would be the only hostage released that day. Beth breathed a disappointed sigh. She supposed this meant that Dan was dead or injured, or—she allowed herself a shred of hope—maybe he was hiding somewhere and José couldn't find him.

All eyes were fixed on Mrs. Williams as she walked away from the prison. She seemed to be focusing on the gatehouse, but something on the ground must have caught her eye. She hopped away from it, held her hands out in defense, and started running toward the gate. Hers was not the smooth sprint of an athlete but the desperate scuttle of an animal caught in the talons of a predator and somehow managed to escape. She lost one shoe by accident, and she kicked the other one off purposely to expedite her retreat.

Beth made a move toward the gate, but Colonel Mitchell stopped her. "Not yet," he said, catching her by the arm.

"But José will think we're tricking him," Beth protested. "I need to go now. He's trusting me." She felt panic rising in her chest, and she was suddenly short of breath. She couldn't let José think for even a second that she had deceived him. She needed him to believe that she was on his side, since she was going into the prison under his protection.

"I said 'not yet.'" Colonel Mitchell was still holding her arm, but his gaze alternated between Mrs. Williams and the prison door.

Mrs. Williams pushed through the inner security gate and into the holding area between the two fences. State police officers held open the outer gate to allow her through, but Warden Hayward ran past them and into the holding area to meet her. She leapt up to wrap her arms around his neck, and he held her close, closing his eyes and resting his cheek against hers. Their embrace was so obviously intimate and tender that what had once been secret was now public. Beth stared at the lovers and became acutely aware of the void in her own life. She had never experienced that strength of affection, and she found herself longing for it now.

The warden loosened his hold of Mrs. Williams when the prison door opened once again. A man in a black guard's uniform came into view, followed by an inmate in a yellow jumpsuit. The door shut behind them. Beth strained her neck and squinted her eyes in an attempt to identify them.

"It's Dan!" she shouted, a sense of relief coursing through her body. "José's giving us Dan too. And he's okay! I think the other man is the same one who delivered the letter yesterday. Yes. That's him."

Dan walked under his own power away from the prison, but his pace was slow and his movements labored. As he drew closer to the fence, Beth noticed that his white t-shirt, visible through the unbuttoned top of his uniform shirt, was stained red. A smear of the same color drew her attention to a two-inch gash on his forehead, and another line stretched from his nose to his chin. Beth was used to seeing a relaxed smile on Dan's face and his dirty blond hair combed neatly to one side. At this moment, staring straight ahead with a miserable expression and disheveled hair and uniform, he looked like a different person. The gatehouse sentries opened the inner gate, and Dan walked through, but the prisoner stayed behind. Beth did not go running into his arms, as Mrs. Williams had done with the warden. Instead, she waited for him to exit the holding area and greeted him with a gentle, if uneasy, hug.

"Hi," was all he said.

Beth pushed away from him and noticed that his eyes welled with tears. "Hi, yourself," she said, stepping back while still holding one of his hands. She scrutinized him from head to toe. "Are you alright? You're not hurt badly, are you?" Beth tried to think of something else to say, something compassionate or soothing, but she was never very good at this part of a relationship. A pair of medics arrived to attend to Dan's injuries, rescuing Beth from this awkwardness.

The yellow-suited prisoner remained standing inside the perimeter fence, and Beth presumed that his job was to escort her into the prison.

"I have to go now," she said gently, letting go of Dan's hand and stepping around him toward the gate.

"Wait. You have to go where?"

"Inside. That's the deal, Dan," she explained. "We're trading me in exchange for you and Mrs. Williams. It was just going to be her, but I asked José to let you go too."

"What? No!" Dan screamed, pushing aside the medic who was dabbing at the cut on his forehead. "No fucking way you're going in there, Beth!" He moved aggressively toward the warden, Colonel Mitchell, and the others gathered around, gesturing wildly with his arms and searching their faces for a shared sense of outrage. Finding only acquiescence in their expressions, he concluded, "You're all fucking crazy! You have no idea what it's like in there. There's no way I'm letting her go!"

Beth took advantage of Dan's outburst and scampered into holding area. The outer gate snapped shut behind her, and Dan turned to find Beth beyond his reach. He slammed his body repeatedly against the metal fence. "Open this gate! Open it now!"

Beth stepped backwards as she spoke, her palms open and arms outspread. "It's okay, Dan. I'll be fine. Everything will be alright, I promise." The inner gate opened, and Beth glanced over her shoulder at the inmate waiting for her. "I have to go now."

"Don't do this, Beth. Please," Dan begged.

"I have to, Dan, but don't worry. I'm going to fix this. It'll all be over soon."

"What are you going to do?" Dan said, gripping the fence links with both hands, his body wilting. "You're going to get yourself killed in there. You realize that, right? How can you possibly fix this?"

"From the inside out," Beth said. "It's the only way." The inner gate slammed shut behind her.

"No! Beth! Come back! No!" Dan yelled. He jumped onto the fence and scrambled to climb over it, but Captain Sullivan and Colonel Mitchell grabbed onto his legs before he cut himself on the razor wire lining the top. Some of the prison guards ran over to help pull him down and restrain him.

Beth nodded to her inmate escort, and the two started their trek toward the prison. The inmate limped along, although he stood taller and appeared healthier than he had on his first messenger mission two days before. Beth paused and looked back at the muddle of people and equipment assembled outside the perimeter fence. Ambulances lined the road, their engines running to keep the air cool inside. News vans shared space along the street curb, their crews fully engrossed in their duties, pointing their cameras at Beth and broadcasting the events to viewers across the country. The prison guards and family members gathered in the field directed their full attention to her, as did the uniformed police officers and National Guard soldiers. Where moments before there had been commotion and the hum of a multitude of voices, now the crowd was still. Their collective expression was one of incomprehension as they stood silently, watching a young woman walk willingly toward certain death. The warden had his arm wrapped around the shoulder of his mistress, and Beth saw both relief and shame in his eyes.

Beth's eyes met Dan's next, and she tilted her head sympathetically and gave him a delicate smile. She hoped to see some sign of forgiveness, or maybe even gratitude, for what she was doing. Instead, still being restrained by his coworkers, his expression was grim. Beth had known that it would be difficult for Dan to accept her decision to put herself in danger, and she had expected disbelief and even anger when he found that he was helpless to stop her. What she now sensed in Dan, however, was neither of those things. It was complete despair. He loved her. Beth realized that now. She had suspected it all along, but this intensity of emotion made it impossible to ignore. But she didn't feel the same. She didn't love him, and it wasn't fair what she was doing to him—staying in a relationship when their feelings for each other were so one-sided. None of this was fair.

She felt a pang of uncertainty that shook her determination. She steeled herself against the doubt and guilt, and she turned toward her objective.

Beth matched the inmate's pace, and they walked side-by-side along the paved path toward the prison entrance. As they approached the building, the grass on either side of them receded and the pavement widened. Something on the ground caught Beth's attention, and she paused to scrutinize it. She cringed when she identified it and immediately understood what had prompted Mrs. Williams' panicked dash to safety. On the edge of the path, half on the pavement and half on the grass, lay an amputated ear. Near it, she saw a shoe and a piece of fleshy tissue, the origin of which she could not determine.

Beth and her escort had reached the area where the bodies of the slain inmates and police officers had been piled in a heap and then retrieved as part of the hostage exchange agreement. She noticed the roundish blood stain on the sidewalk, still wet in the middle, and the other evidence of human remains surrounding it. It could not have been the first time the inmate had seen it, but he still crinkled his nose. This represented not just a pile of bodies, but actual human beings who had been caught up in this mess and died as a result. They'd left behind family and friends who now had to face life without them. Beth bore some of the responsibility for their pain, and she shared in their grief. She and her escort stepped around the blood, but they could not avoid it completely. The mark it left on Beth's soul would cause more lasting damage than the stain it left on her shoe.

When they reached the door, Beth glanced at the bronze plaque on the wall beside the door that read "Arnone State Correctional Institution. Julie Webb, Governor."

The inmate turned to Beth. "You ready for this?"

"It must be a struggle," she said.

He nodded and held the door open for Beth to walk in.

Chapter Twenty-Five

Inside

DAY THREE
9:12 AM

Beth stepped over the threshold. Inside the prison, she was concealed from the television cameras, from the police and spectators in the field, and from the snipers perched in the guard towers. Her eyes adjusted to the yellow-tinted lighting of the lobby, and she was surprised by the calm, quiet atmosphere that surrounded her. She knew that prison riots were bloody, chaotic events, and she expected to hear yelling from the cellblocks or see inmates running amok. Instead, the only activity she saw was a single protective custody inmate mopping the floor.

José emerged from around the corner and greeted her with a triumphant smile, his arms stretched wide. "You're finally here!" Coop followed, along with the G brothers and another scary-looking inmate Beth knew by reputation only.

"I'm so glad you're alright," Beth said, and it was the absolute truth. She felt enormous relief at seeing him and having confirmation that he was safe. "I was worried about you, but I don't know what to say. I had no idea you were going to do this. I hope you didn't think I meant for you to—"

"How about you don't say anything right now?" José interrupted. "You're overwhelmed. I know. It's taken longer than I wanted for you to get here, and we have a lot of work to do. But, I want to show you around a little, and then we can talk about what comes next."

"No," Krueger said in his raspy voice, stepping between José and Beth. "Gotta check for a wire first." He reached out for her with one hand and for the weapon on his belt with the other. A jolt of fear shot through Beth's body, and her survival instinct took over. She hopped backward and continued to retreat as Krueger advanced toward her.

José scrambled to put his body between Krueger and Beth. "Whoa. Whoa. Relax, Krueger. Just relax. She's on our side. Take it easy." José pushed Beth behind him and stood with both hands in front of him, palms open and facing forward. Beth tried her best to let him shield her, and she mimicked José's stance.

Mateo emerged through the open door to the central corridor and ran to José's side. "What's going on?" he asked, assuming the same posture as the two of them.

"Just a little misunderstanding. That's all," José said. Krueger grunted, puffing air through his clenched teeth. "Stand down, Krueger. Beth is our ally. There's no way she's wearing a wire. Isn't that right, Beth? Tell our friend that you're here to help."

"I'm not wearing any wire. I don't have any kind of communication device on me, not even a phone. And I don't have any weapons either," Beth said, managing to maintain her composure. She opened her black blazer to reveal the same color shirt underneath, and she ran her hands across her pockets to show that they were empty. She felt justified in her stubbornness with Colonel Mitchell that morning when she had refused to smuggle in any tracking or listening devices.

"I don't believe we've met." Beth extended her hand to Krueger, although she kept the rest of her body behind José's. "My name is Beth Sharpe. I'm the counselor here. I've known José and Mateo for several years now, and I am absolutely here to help."

Beth looked into Krueger's eyes and, where everyone else saw madness and rage, she sensed a traumatic history and lingering emotional pain. She knew about Krueger's background from the inmates' files. Timmy Brown was his real name. He had a violent criminal record, but Beth's assessment of his character was more thorough and more accurate than any file could be. She heard in his gruff voice evidence of smoking and hard alcohol consumption throughout his four decades of life. She also heard in his limited vocabulary that his formal education had ended at a young age. His demeanor spoke of quick shifts from calmness to rage and, once he turned that corner, she guessed that he had almost no control over the violent outbursts that followed. Beth noted the many scars on Krueger's body, from the disfiguring burn on his face to the many cuts, in various stages of healing, on his arms and shoulders. Beyond these wounds, which everyone could see, Beth also perceived in Krueger the hidden wounds of a childhood filled with neglect and abuse and of an adult life spent in prison. Beth had no trouble explaining the reasons for his distrust and aggressiveness toward her, but she could not ignore that he posed a real threat.

Krueger grunted and rebuffed her handshake invitation, but he settled down.

"This one's on me, Krueger. It's my bad," José said. "I should've told you about Beth. I forgot you two don't know each other. Beth is our friend, and she's gonna help us get justice. She's very valuable to me." He gestured to the entire group. "I want to make this clear to all of you. While Beth is in this prison, her safety is your number one priority. You protect her even before you protect me. Understand?"

The men nodded. Mateo spun around and smiled at Beth. "Never a dull moment, huh?"

"Never." She noticed Mateo's swollen cheek, and she pointed to her own. "Are you alright?"

"Oh, that's nothing," he replied. "It's busy in here. I'm organizing the worker bees and keeping everybody in line and what not. It's a tough job, but somebody's got to do it."

For a moment, Beth stopped thinking about the dangers surrounding her and the risks that she was taking. "It sounds like you have a lot on your plate, Mateo, but we both know you're capable of major responsibility. I assume you're talking about the protective custody inmates when you say, 'worker bees?' That's clever."

"That was my idea," José interjected, turning the conversation toward himself like an attention-hungry toddler. "Get it? They're worker bees because they wear yellow, and I'm using them to do all the work to keep this place going? They're scared shitless about what'll happen to them if we lose control of this place, and they're right. If I let the dogs out of their cells, they'll get the shit kicked out of them, so it's in their best interest to keep this place running smooth. They're the ones getting the food for everybody and doing the cleanup, as you can see." José motioned toward the man mopping the lobby floor.

The inmate who had escorted Beth into the building was leaning against the wall, seemingly worn-out from his most recent trek to the perimeter fence. "You, get to work!" José ordered, and Krueger reinforced the message by shoving the prisoner. Beth winced. She knew protective custody inmates were especially vulnerable during a prison riot. It appeared that José was protecting them from serious abuse—even if he was allowing some harsh treatment and using them as free labor. Beth's thoughts went to Frederick Douglass, and she wondered if José had considered that he was acting as the slave master in this situation.

José continued before she verbalized these ideas. "Mateo's my right hand man for sure, but I'm running the show in here. Impressive or what?"

"José Ayala, you are undeniably impressive," Beth agreed.

The phone in the warden's office started to ring. "That's probably for you." José snickered. "Ignore it for now, and I'll give you the grand tour." He pointed to the different rooms that were accessible from the prison lobby. "The warden's office is my headquarters, and the copy room in the corner is where I found his secretary. The other offices are unlocked, but they're all empty except yours. We're storing some of the weapons and equipment in there because your office has a door to the corridor too, and we can get to them from both sides if we need to."

The disappointment on Beth's face must have been obvious, and she opened her mouth to speak, but José beat her to it again. "I mean no disrespect in that, Beth. I know you're not a fan of violence."

"You're right. I hate violence," Beth said. "I'm just taken aback a little that you're using my office as an armory. I always thought of it as a sanctuary for us and a place for thoughtful discussion, even though I do see the practicality of storing the weapons there. Go on, please."

José motioned for the group to follow him to the chapel. The inmate mopping the floor kept his eyes turned downward. Beth looked into the bucket as he wrung his mop and noted that the water was dark red. This was the sole piece of evidence to corroborate the killings that had happened in that exact location only one day before.

"This is where I'm keeping most of the hostages," José said, opening the chapel door to allow Beth to peer inside. The stench of body odor and urine hit her with the same force as a punch in the face, and she jerked her head to the side, covering her nose and mouth with her hand. Still in the doorway, her eyes adjusted from the well-lit lobby to the relative darkness in the chapel, and she spotted two inmates watching over the room. They were sitting on one of the long wooden pews. Their eyes opened wide when they saw Beth's figure in the doorway, and they enacted a military-style salute to José. The rest of the chapel's pews were piled along the wall behind them. There were about twenty prison guards sitting or lying on the floor, their hands secured behind their backs and their mouths gagged. Beth noted their disheveled hair, bloodied brows, and swollen faces. Their pleading eyes stared back at her, but she could not discern whether they were warning her to escape or imploring her to save them. It didn't matter one way or the other because, at the moment, she was powerless to do either.

José signaled for her to back out of the room, and Beth eagerly complied. When the chapel door closed, the hand she had used to shield her face against the odor fell to her side, and she took a long, deep breath.

"Come on. I wanna show you how everything's running," José said, motioning for the others to follow.

"I'll keep watch from the office and radio you if I see anything happening outside," Mateo said. "Enjoy the tour, Beth."

They left the lobby, but Beth hesitated as she stepped through the propped-open door into the central corridor. She felt safe in the administrative wing of the prison, but the cellblocks were a different story as she rarely ventured down the central corridor. The cellblocks were where the inmates slept and dressed and took care of their business, and Beth felt that she owed them a modicum of privacy. They were not animals to be observed in their cages.

Beth's chest tightened, but she reassured herself that José and his crew would protect her from harm. Her panic eased, and she could not suppress a smile when she spotted Fido waving vigorously in the control room. He squished his face against the glass before he opened the locked door and ushered Beth and José inside.

"Well, look who's here," Fido said. He held an imaginary microphone in his hand and announced, "It's everyone's favorite prison counselor—the beautiful, the elegant, the talented Ms. Beth Sharpe. Welcome, my lady. We're happy you've decided to join us here today."

"Alright. That's enough," José said, pushing him into a chair.

"It's good to see you, Fido," Beth said, though not nearly as cheerfully as he. "And you too, Hacker."

Hacker nodded his greeting.

"We can see into all the blocks from here and the yards too," José began. "Plus, we can lock and unlock every single door, just by pushing a few buttons. I'm keeping the rest of the weapons in here, mostly the ones we took off the cops yesterday. Hacker and Fido are the only ones, besides Mateo and me, allowed in the control room. You guys are good here, right?"

"Right, boss," Fido replied.

"I'm taking Beth into the blocks, so open the doors for us when we get there," José instructed. "Got it?"

Again, Hacker nodded and turned his lanky body toward Beth. "You take care of yourself. You understand? I don't want anything happening to you. Be careful."

"I'll take care of Beth," José rebuked. "I'll make sure she's safe. You worry about yourself."

José stomped out, and Beth followed after waving a stealthy goodbye to Fido. At the access door for A-Block, José looked over his shoulder and nodded toward the control room. The click of the lock sounded, and Coop opened the door to allow Krueger and Big G to enter before the others. José sauntered in, and Coop signaled that it was Beth's turn to enter next. She grasped the doorframe to steady herself and held her breath until she finally mustered the courage to take the last few steps. Coop and Baby G followed. The door slammed shut behind them, and Beth found herself locked inside a maximum-security prison cellblock with a hundred convicted criminals.

T.K. greeted José with a combination handshake and one-arm hug. Beth remained frozen by the door until Coop put his hand on her back and gently pushed her forward.

"Unbelievable," T.K. exclaimed. "I can't believe you're really here, Beth."

"It's all part of the plan, T.K.," José said, nodding his head with smug satisfaction.

"No. Seriously. I'm stoked that you get to see this," T.K. said. "We put aside our gang alliances just like you told us to. Who would've thought this lifelong 20 Luv would be helping out a Los Solidos?" T.K. punched José teasingly on the arm. "And now we're working together."

Beth couldn't access any words of reply. Instead, she simply smiled and nodded, hoping that would be enough.

José, at least, seemed to accept this as a sign of approval. "I wanted you to see the cellblocks for yourself. Nobody's burning the place or messing each other up. I have a team leader in every block and soldiers to back him up. T.K.'s keeping the peace here in A-Block."

Beth scrutinized her surroundings. "I'm amazed that everyone is so calm. Aren't they upset that they're still locked up?"

"It wasn't so quiet in here yesterday," José said. "Some of these guys were giving T.K. a hard time, throwing shit out of their cells and such, but we took care of it." He glanced at a spot on the floor for half a second, but it was enough to make Beth look too.

Another smear of blood. Another person dead.

José continued. "That's why they're behaving so good. Plus, most of the head cases and fighters are dead now because of the cops' attack yesterday. The only ones left in here are the guys who get time off for good behavior." He grinned, and his shoulders twitched with a silent chuckle.

Beth took a staggered step back. José was expecting her to say something, but she was at a loss. What could she say to that? Finally, she decided the truth was best. "I'm speechless."

"Well, that's a first," José teased. "Come on. I want to show you around some more."

Beth had never heard better news. She whipped around and headed straight for the exit. Without uttering another word or even waving goodbye to T.K., she hurried through the door Coop held open for her, and the group made its way into the central corridor, heading for the other cellblocks.

CHAPTER TWENTY-SIX

Outside

DAY THREE
9:12 AM

The warden did not let go of Chrissy's hand as they walked away from the prison's perimeter fence. The released guard, Officer Dan Cooney, had twisted free from his coworkers after Beth disappeared into the prison, and they all headed toward the ambulances lined up along the road. They didn't make it far before Officer Cooney was intercepted by a crowd of prison employees and family members of the hostages.

"How ya doin' buddy?" a coworker asked.

"What's going on in there?" another demanded. "Are the other guys safe?"

"What the hell happened yesterday? How did the inmates take out the whole SWAT team?"

One woman slammed into Officer Cooney and clutched him by the shoulders. The force of the collision pushed him off balance, causing him to stumble backward. "Have you seen my husband? His name's Palmer. Tell me he's okay. Please!" Officer Cooney nearly collapsed under her weight, and the two would have ended up in a heap right there on the grass if Captain Sullivan had not intervened.

He put one arm around the officer and used his other as a shield. "Move out! Give him some room! Injured man here! Get out of the way!" Captain Sullivan made a path through the crowd, and the warden used it to guide Chrissy to the edge of the field.

He found the double doors of an ambulance open and a team of medical personnel ready. He settled her onto the stretcher inside, and she closed her eyes and rested her head against the white sheet. He stroked the silky material of her shirtsleeve and spoke gently to her. "You're alright. Everything's alright now, Chrissy. I won't let anything happen to you."

A snort and grunt from outside the ambulance brought the warden back to reality, and he looked down into the disapproving face of the governor's chief of staff. Agent Dean stood beside Fitzroy, but he averted his gaze.

"What are you staring at, Fitzroy? What do you want?" the warden asked. He just wanted to be alone with Chrissy for a minute. He set aside his professionalism and replaced the deference he would normally have given Fitzroy with contempt.

"Excuse me, Warden," Fitzroy said. "I'm sorry to interrupt your— uh—reunion here, but I must remind you that there are plenty of hostages left inside the prison. We need to find out what she knows."

"Back off, Fitzroy," the warden snapped. "Can't you see she's exhausted?"

"It's alright," Chrissy said. "I can answer whatever questions you have."

"Tell me about the leader of the riot," Agent Dean began. "Did you have much contact with him? How did he manage to defend against the SWAT raid, and what did he do with their weapons? Where are the hostages? How are they being treated?"

Chrissy related what information she had. Agent Dean prompted her with follow-up questions and concluded the interview by thanking her and asking that she contact him if she remembered any other details. Fitzroy insisted that the warden accompany them to interview the other released hostage, and the warden reluctantly agreed.

"I have to get back to work, Chrissy," he explained. "The ambulance will take you to the hospital to make sure you're alright. Call me when you're set, and I'll come get you."

"I'll be fine," she said. "I can call my husband to pick me up. Don't worry about me. You take care of things here, and I'll talk with you soon."

The warden didn't like to think about Chrissy's husband, preferring to pretend that he didn't exist. Normally that was easy to do. Though their affair had been going on for years, her husband didn't seem to have a clue. But, of course, he must be worried about her as well, and he should be the one to meet her at the hospital.

The warden pursed his lips and nodded. He set aside his desire to stay by her side and stepped out of the ambulance to return to his responsibilities.

He followed Fitzroy and Agent Dean to another ambulance where they joined Captain Sullivan and Colonel Mitchell to form a semicircle around Officer Cooney. Instead of lying on the stretcher, as he was supposed to, he was seated on the edge of the ambulance floor, his feet dangling outside of it. Captain Sullivan was leading the debriefing.

"How could you send Beth into the prison?" Officer Cooney demanded. "You realize she'll die in there. I would never have come out if I knew you were trading her for me. Why the hell would you do that?"

The warden understood the officer's concern and sympathized with his pain. "It was the only thing the inmates wanted," he explained. "The leader insisted that Ms. Sharpe go into the prison, and in return he would spare Mrs. Williams' life. It was Ms. Sharpe's request that you be released as well. We didn't even know if he would comply until we saw you walk out the door."

"Where are the hostages? How are the inmates controlling the facility?" Agent Dean asked. "Please tell us everything you know."

"When everything started—was it two days ago?" Officer Cooney began. "I was patrolling the administrative wing when the inmates attacked me. There was no warning at all. They tied me up and threw me into the chapel with a bunch of other guards. They didn't let us talk, but I knew the inmates were controlling the whole facility."

"How did you know?" Captain Sullivan asked.

"Because the other guards in the chapel with me had been assigned to the cellblocks. All of us were pretty banged up, but at least we're still alive. I'm not sure about the rest of the men. There were only about twenty of us in the chapel, and there's always at least sixty guards on duty overnight, so they're either dead or hiding or locked up somewhere else."

This was worse than the warden thought. If the hostages were all together, they have a better chance of survival. Having them spread throughout the prison would definitely complicate things and make it harder to rescue them if it came to that.

"What do you know about the SWAT raid? Did you see or hear anything?" Colonel Mitchell joined in the questioning.

"I'll tell you what I know about the SWAT raid," Officer Cooney said. "It was a fucking disaster. The inmates guarding us in the chapel stood by the door expecting the cops to come in, but they never did. I don't know why. I couldn't see. I heard plenty, though. Plenty of screaming and then shooting. Listening to it, and not being able to do anything ..." He shook his head and sighed. Captain Sullivan motioned for him to take a drink. He complied and continued, "The inmates were a hundred percent ready for the raid. That much was obvious. It was all over in a couple of minutes. The ones guarding us stepped out afterwards, and they were all excited—slapping each other on the back—when they came back in. How many officers died?"

"Nineteen." Colonel Mitchell's voice was quiet.

"Plus one of our guys was shot on the first day," Captain Sullivan added.

Officer Cooney set his water bottle down on the bumper of the ambulance and covered his face with both hands.

"What else? There must be something more you can you tell us!" Fitzroy demanded. "You and your guard buddies just sat there and did nothing while real cops were being killed right outside the door?"

Officer Cooney lowered his hands, and his face contorted. He launched out of the ambulance and reached Fitzroy in a fraction of a second. Before the others could stop him, he landed a punch squarely on Fitzroy's chin, causing him to fall backward onto the pavement. Fitzroy held his face and moaned, rolling from side to side. Captain Sullivan and Colonel Mitchell managed to grab hold of Officer Cooney, but he did not attack again. Instead, his face paled, and he leaned back against the ambulance.

"Son of a bitch," Fitzroy spat, rolling onto his hands and knees.

"Get up," the warden ordered, fighting the urge to smile. This was an appropriate consequence of Fitzroy's pompous and condescending behavior. Gathering as much composure as he could muster, he continued, "Everyone has their breaking point, Mr. Fitzroy. You were out of line just then, so just be quiet. You deserved that."

Captain Sullivan did not suppress his snicker. He addressed Officer Cooney again. "Is there anything else you can tell us?"

"That's about it, really," he said. "After the SWAT raid was over, somebody announced over the loudspeakers that they were looking for me. They wanted me brought to the lobby, and since I was in the chapel, the inmates just pushed me out the door. I didn't see any more of the prison than the chapel and the lobby, and nobody told me why I was there. They kept me tied up and sat me in the corner facing the main door. There wasn't much to see except a few protective custody inmates cleaning the floors. I sat there all night long, and no one said a word to me. And then this morning, I saw your secretary actually," Officer Cooney motioned to the warden. He had forgotten about Chrissy for a minute there, but this brought back his despair in full force. "José Ayala was leading her by the arm. He walked her to the door and said something I couldn't hear, and he let her go."

"And what happened next?" the warden pressed, motioning for Officer Cooney to increase the speed of his storytelling. He glanced down the road as the ambulance carrying Chrissy drove past them, headed for the hospital.

"Then he told me to get up. Apparently I didn't do that fast enough because Krueger—you know who I'm talking about, right?" he said to Captain Sullivan who nodded. "He's a real badass, real scary. Anyway, he cut the zip ties off me and dragged me across the lobby. Then he pushed me out the front door, along with a protective custody inmate. I had no idea if they were going to shoot me or what, so I just walked out of there and straight to the gate. You all saw that part. And then, for some insane reason, you let Beth walk in. I promise you she's going to get killed in there."

"She wanted to go in," the warden said, defending the action that he had once argued vehemently against. "She practically demanded it. She even admitted that she helped cause the riot, and she's convinced that she can talk the leader into giving up."

"I have no doubt that she wanted to go in," Officer Cooney said. "Believe me. Beth thinks she can change the world, but you and I both know she can't."

"Officer Cooney, that's the only thing the inmates wanted," Captain Sullivan added. "That was their only demand. They refused to even talk to us unless we sent her in. They'd already executed one of our men, and they would have killed more if we didn't comply. Obviously, the raid didn't work, so we had no choice."

"You always have a choice," Officer Cooney whispered. His shoulders slumped.

"We should get you to the hospital," Captain Sullivan said.

"I have just a few more questions before you go," Colonel Mitchell said. "What can you tell us about the hostages? How were you treated? Did you see any guards being assaulted?"

Officer Cooney breathed deeply and sat slightly straighter. "I told you already. I only know about the twenty guards in the chapel. The rest have to be somewhere else in the prison, or else they're already dead. I haven't seen anyone killed, but it won't be long before that happens on its own. They'll all be dead soon enough."

"What do you mean by that? How will they 'all be dead soon enough?'" Colonel Mitchell's forehead creased, and he leaned in toward the officer.

"I mean, they're going to die of thirst. The inmates haven't given us a drop of water since this whole thing started," he explained.

"What?" the warden said. *No!* "The hostages have had nothing to eat or drink in two whole days?"

Officer Cooney shook his head.

"This changes everything," Colonel Mitchell said. "The hostages could die. What is it three days without water before the body shuts down? Unless the hostages get water soon, we have no choice but to end this riot by force."

"I need to inform the governor," Fitzroy said. He held his hand against his swollen chin and scurried toward the command vehicle.

"Get yourself taken care of, Officer Cooney," Colonel Mitchell said. "We'll contact you if we need you."

CHAPTER TWENTY-SEVEN

Inside

J osé glanced over at Beth as they approached the door to B-Block. Her face was pale and she looked like she might throw up.

"Hey, you okay?" he asked.

"Yeah. Yeah. I'm okay," she said, shaking her head.

"Really?" José didn't believe her. "Because you don't look too good. Maybe we should do this later. I just thought you'd want to see for yourself how it's going and check in with our guys, but we can stop if you want."

"I do want to see everyone," Beth replied. "I want to be able to report back to the warden that everything is going fine in here and everyone's safe. But, if I'm being honest, I'm not all that comfortable in the cellblocks."

"I get it. And I want you see it too." More than anything, he wanted Beth to appreciate what he had accomplished, and he wanted to start working toward his goals with her at his side. He turned to his bodyguards. "Krueger and Coop, get the team leaders and bring them to the chow hall. We'll talk in there. This is better anyway," he concluded, directing the group to reverse direction. "You've already seen one block, so you know how those are running. My guys can get a break for a couple minutes, and you can see everyone else all at once."

José led Beth through the central corridor with the G's following behind. He stopped at the control room and leaned in to talk to Fido and Hacker. "Coop and Krueger are gonna get all the team leaders together, so you can let them in all the cellblocks." He lowered his voice to almost a whisper. He didn't want Beth to hear this part. "Except D-Block. You got that?" He continued through the central corridor, stopping again for just a moment to peek through the propped-open door to the lobby. Everything was quiet.

Hacker buzzed them through to the cafeteria, and José motioned for Beth to have a seat at one of the long dining tables. He scanned the room, spotting worker bees laboring in the kitchen and one of his soldiers seated in the far corner of the room. Their arrival had apparently interrupted his nap, and he was scrambling to an upright position. José shot him a look that he hoped conveyed his disgust at him for literally falling asleep at his post. José knew the cafeteria's back entrance could be an access point for the police, so he had made sure someone was watching it at all times and that they had a radio to alert him at the first sign of trouble.

"You feeling any better?" he said to Beth.

"Much better. Thanks," she replied.

This time he believed her. "You want something to eat? I have the worker bees in here cooking food and delivering it to the blocks. I figure, if I can keep everybody fed, that'll keep them quiet."

"I'm fine. But won't you run out of supplies sooner or later?" Beth asked.

"Naw. We have more than enough," José said. He was pleased that Beth seemed interested in his management of the prison. "What else do you want to know?

"Actually, I do have a question for you, José," Beth said. "Why did you make me wave to you? Before, when you delivered the letter to me at the fence, the protective custody inmate told me I had to wave to you before he would give it to me. You had to know that would make me look bad in front of everyone."

This wasn't the kind of question he was expecting. He hadn't really thought of it from that perspective. He had asked her to wave to him because he wanted everyone to know that she was with him on this. "I don't think it made you look bad at all. I think it did just the opposite."

Beth nodded.

"And now that you're here," José continued, "you can help me negotiate, and everyone will know that this revolution is real."

The clack of a door echoed through the open space, and Coop led a group of men in.

Squeeze promenaded past the others, his arms stretched out with palms up and fingers flared. He kept his legs pressed together as he walked, forcing his hips into an exaggerated sway.

"Darling," he said in his best Zsa Zsa Gabor-inspired Hungarian accent. "How arrr you?"

"Squeeze!" Beth smiled. "Oh my. That's quite an outfit!"

This guy's too much. José shook his head. But Beth seemed amused.

"What? This old thing?" Squeeze said, petting the collar of his stolen guard's uniform. He tugged at the unbuttoned shirt to reveal a bit more of the smooth skin of his chest. "I just wish I had my makeup kit. Some red lipstick would really complete the look, don't you think?"

"I do," Beth agreed. "But, please tell me that no one was hurt in the process of you acquiring that uniform."

Squeeze's expression turned somber, and he said in his melodramatic voice, "Not under my watch. You know me better than that. I promise you nobody's been hurt in B-Block. I can't say the same thing for the other blocks, or so I heard."

"That's enough, Squeeze," José said. "You concentrate on your business and let me worry about everything else. I wanted Beth to see you. That's all. Go back to your block." He needed Squeeze out of there before he blabbed any more.

"Just for the record," Squeeze whispered, tilting his chin to the side and fluttering his eyelashes. "The guard who gave me this uniform was fabulously happy to donate it. I exchanged his outfit for mine, and I think we can all agree that no one has looked better in a uniform than I do right now. Ta ta." He waved his goodbye and made a hip-swaying exit.

José stood back while his other team leaders, one at a time, welcomed Beth and chatted with her. After a while, he instructed them all to go back to their responsibilities in the cellblocks. When the others had gone, leaving only Beth, Coop, and the G's left, José leaned back with his elbows against the table.

Beth had a puzzled look on her face. "I notice your team leaders are all part of our discussion group," she said. She was counting on her fingers as if taking an inventory. "Where's Angel though? I feel like he's the only one missing."

José had hoped to avoid this topic, but Beth was too smart not to notice. "Angel's not missing," he explained. "He's the team leader in D-Block, but he's not exactly following orders. We had some words about it yesterday. He wasn't too happy about it, and neither was I. So, I'm just leaving him be for a while." He didn't need to tell Beth everything.

"I hope you two can work it out," Beth said.

"Oh, we will," he assured her. But then he noticed something. "Speaking of missing people, where in the hell is Krueger? Coop, he was with you, wasn't he?"

Coop shrugged his shoulders. "He was, and we got all the team leaders out of the blocks, but then he was gone. I'm not sure where he went."

José wasn't sure either, but he had a pretty good idea.

"I'm sure he's just taking care of business," José said to comfort Beth, though it was he who needed reassurance. He had a bad feeling about this.

"José?" Beth interrupted his thoughts. "Please tell me the truth. Were our discussions about justice the reason you started this riot?"

"It's a revolution. Not a riot." José corrected her. She wasn't helping him at all with this sort of question. "And yes. You brought us here, Beth. You have to know that. You're the reason we had the courage to do this and how we know this is the way to get justice. Only the ones who are oppressed have the power to change things. Right?"

Beth nodded slowly, staring into the floor. "But," she murmured.

"But what, Beth?" José said. He felt his face heating up, and he heard his voice growing coarser, even though he was trying to keep his cool. "What? How could you disagree with what we did? You're the one who taught us that the only way to get freedom is to fight for it. I didn't think you'd be surprised. You even helped me write the speech I gave right after we took over."

"Is that what that was? A speech?"

"Yeah." Of course it was a speech. He had forgotten that she hadn't known that at the time. "And it was perfect for explaining the reasons for the revolution to all the guys who don't understand what we do about slavery and freedom and justice."

"I support you, José, you know that," Beth spoke softly. "You're one hundred percent right in principle about the need to stand up for yourself and demand justice. It's the level of violence that upsets me. So many people have been killed in the past two days. I think there's nineteen police dead, plus the one guard, and something like forty inmates too. There was a huge pile of bodies outside, and I couldn't stand to watch them all being carried away. I just wish we had thought of a peaceful way to reach your goals. If we had worked together, I know we could have achieved justice without killing so many people."

José studied Beth's face. So this was why she seemed unhappy with him. It wasn't that she disagreed. She believed in the same ideals that he did, and she wanted justice just as much. It was the violence that was upsetting her. That was all. Finally, he sighed. "I get it, Beth. You're a compassionate person, and you hate to see people in pain.

That's why I didn't tell you about our plan beforehand because you would've tried to stop us. But you know deep down that violence has to be part of a revolution, and we had no other choice. So, I forgive you for questioning me because I know it's coming from a good place. We have to work together now, you and me, to make sure no one else has to die. We need to get the negotiations started."

CHAPTER TWENTY-EIGHT

Inside

DAY THREE
10:40 AM

Beth followed José into the prison's central corridor. Throughout their conversation in the cafeteria, she had struggled to convey to José how she truly felt about his efforts to achieve justice. She couldn't say that she disagreed with his motivations, but she had at least made him understand that she didn't support the violence he had used. He seemed to get that.

Big G and Baby G went first, and Coop followed closely behind as they made their way to the warden's office.

"I've been thinking," José said. "Who is that hostage you asked me to release? What's he to you?"

Beth found herself temporarily speechless. She never shared personal information with the inmates. This was the cardinal rule of working in a prison, and she held fast to that directive, keeping the details of her private life—both past and present—confidential. Normally, she would divert their curiosity about her and redirect their attention toward their own lives. She was truly interested in the inmates' personal histories and aspirations. Since most men were eager and willing to talk about themselves, she found it easy to manipulate the subject matter of their discussions back to the inmates themselves. Even when she interacted with José, Beth kept the details of her private life secret. Now, noting that the other inmates surrounding her were listening too, she realized that there was no way to deflect his question. She had no choice but to respond.

"He's a friend of mine. I–I guess you'd call him my boyfriend," she said, avoiding eye contact.

"How come you never told me you had a guard for a boyfriend? I mean, you know everything about me, but I didn't even know this one simple thing about you. It bothers me."

This question and the deeper issues tangled within it stirred the butterflies in Beth's stomach. Before this, José had overlooked the inequity of their relationship. Beth's private life was secret, while she knew everything about his. Beth noted José's anguished expression, and she wondered if he felt deceived or betrayed. Maybe it was both. Regardless, this imbalance put José in a position of vulnerability, and Beth knew he wouldn't be comfortable with that. She needed to do something to ease the tension.

"I guess it just never came up," she said, deciding that casualness was her best strategy.

"But seriously, you know about everything that's important to me. And I didn't even know you had a boyfriend," he protested.

Beth didn't know what to say. She shrugged her shoulders slightly.

"What is important to you?" José stopped walking and turned to face her. "Tell me. Who is your best friend, since you know Mateo is mine? What do you do when you leave here every day? I should know all of this."

"I would have to say that you are the person I feel closest to at this point in my life," Beth said. This was true to a point. But Beth saw this as an opportunity to restore José's confidence in her. "Even if that sounds strange. I feel like I understand who you really are. And although you don't know about the little details of my life, we understand each other. My father used to be my best friend, but I ruined that. So, that leaves you and my job, and that's pretty much all there is to know about my boring life. You see why we always talk about you and not me?"

José laughed out loud. Beth assumed this was an exaggerated reaction that accompanied a release of tension. She joined him and welcomed the restoration of their comfortable rapport.

When Beth and José reached the prison lobby, they saw Mateo and a few others surrounding a protective custody inmate. Mateo had a handful of the man's collar and was holding him at an arm's length away, while he squirmed in an effort to escape. The inmate's hands were bound behind him with one of the zip tie handcuffs carried in by the SWAT team, and there was a circle of wetness on the crotch of his yellow jumpsuit. "I'm sorry," the prisoner cried over and over again. The sound of a ringing phone emanating from the warden's office added to the chaos.

"What the hell's going on here?" José shouted.

The man continued to chant, "I'm sorry. I'm sorry."

"Shut up already!" Mateo shouted. He turned to José. "This one's a head case, and he's making me crazy too. He came running out of D-Block with some of Angel's guys chasing him—"

"Who let him out of D-Block?" José interrupted.

"I have no idea. But I saw it on the surveillance screen, so I took some soldiers and ran out to cut them off. It was all we could do to pull Angel's guys off him. I told them I would take care of it. I thought this one might give us some idea what's going on behind the scenes in D-Block. But," Mateo groaned and rolled his eyes, "I don't think he can do that."

Beth took in the bewildered look in the inmate's eyes and the distorted features of his face, and she concurred with Mateo's assessment. His incessant, "I'm sorry," served only to reinforce their conclusions.

Krueger entered the lobby. Without saying a word, he rushed over and relieved Mateo of his burden, seizing the prisoner by his hair and forcing him to a kneeling position on the floor.

Beth noticed that José frowned at Krueger. He seemed annoyed. Or maybe worried. She wasn't sure which. And she wondered what was really going on there.

"Good thinking, Mateo," José said. "But obviously this guy's missing a bolt or two. He probably annoyed the hell out of Angel. I bet that's why they went after him. He won't give us anything." José dismissed him with a wave of his hand.

Krueger raised his jagged club over the kneeling inmate's head.

"No! Wait!" Beth screamed. She couldn't let this man be slaughtered. The panic in her voice caused Krueger to freeze in place. "José, please. Krueger, please. Don't kill him." Beth's eyes darted back and forth between the two men. "He's obviously scared to death. You can't just murder him."

Krueger looked to José, and then turned his attention back to Beth.

"José, you know I support you. I do. But I can't support this," she pleaded. "Ask yourself, 'Does killing this man further your cause?' If the answer is 'no,' then murdering him would be senseless violence, and that's not what you stand for. That isn't who you are!" Beth hoped she was correct on this last point.

José remained silent. Beth held her breath. She was becoming frightened and less sure about how much influence she actually had over him.

"Alright," José finally said. "Krueger, you can stand down. Put him in with the hostages in the chapel. It'll be extra torture for the guards to listen to him babbling."

Krueger returned his weapon to its pouch on his belt, dragged the prisoner across the lobby, and tossed him face first into the chapel. He muttered something to the men inside that Beth couldn't hear and slammed the door. Beth felt enormous relief, but she recognized that the incident might have bruised José's reputation with his men. She bowed her head and mouthed, "Thank you."

"Hey, no problem," a seemingly indifferent José replied. He instructed Krueger, Coop, and the others to stand guard and held the door open for Beth. The two entered the warden's office together.

Beth noticed several dark red stains on the beige carpet, but she didn't mention them.

"Here, sit down at the desk," José said. "I'll show you how the surveillance system works." Beth complied and felt him leaning over her shoulder. He told her how to toggle between camera views and change the screen from a single camera feed to show several simultaneously. They looked in on each of the cellblocks. All of them were calm with the exception of D-Block. Beth watched with dismay as Angel and several others took turns punching a man who was tied to a chair. She and José shared a disapproving look. Beth was beginning to understand the extent of Angel's disloyalty and its potential impact on José's plans.

The ringing of the phone startled Beth, and they both spun toward it. The phone on the warden's desk was a replica 1950s rotary-style, heavy and black, with a spiral cord connecting the hand-held receiver to the base. Old-fashioned and classic but still practical, it reminded Beth of the warden himself.

"Don't answer it," José commanded. "We need to get to work typing on the computer. And by 'we,' of course, I mean 'you.'" He chuckled and pointed at her. "The next step is to tell the warden our demands. I figure the best way is to write it up in a letter, like the other one. What do you think?"

"Sounds good, but the constant ringing is driving me crazy. Maybe we should just answer and find out why they're calling," Beth suggested. *Okay. Maybe I'm being slightly manipulative here. But surely it's in José's best interest to keep the lines of communication open. Maybe the warden had some new information for them.*

"Nope," was José's verbal reply, and he accompanied it with a physical one, reaching over to yank the cord out of the phone.

José took a seat on the opposite side of the desk, and Beth turned to the computer. She located the document Mrs. Williams had created the previous day. It was saved to the desktop and titled, "Ayala Demand Letter."

"I'm ready," Beth announced. "I'll use the last letter as a template. At the top, you listed the state police and the governor and the commissioner of corrections, but you missed the FBI."

"Yeah that Agent Dean's been hounding me. We hit the big time, huh?" José said.

"You have no idea," Beth replied. "But in all seriousness, there are so many agencies involved now that you really can't list them all. How about just addressing it to the warden? They're all going to read it anyway."

"Done," José said. "Let's start by saying that we're ready to negotiate, and this can go quick or it can take a long time. It all depends on them. Got that? These demands are for the sake of justice, not for anyone's personal gain."

"That's excellent." Speaking as she typed, she continued, "The inmates of Arnone State Correctional Institution demand a written response to the following problems of injustice within this facility specifically and in the criminal justice system as a whole."

"The 'prisoners' of Arnone State, not 'inmates.' Inmates are pussies." José corrected her. "The first thing is that parole is restored for everyone. You can't take away hope, or else there's no chance for redemption. We shouldn't all have to suffer because some parolees killed people when they got out." Holding up two fingers, he continued, "Second, everyone who should've been up for parole gets a hearing in thirty days. It's only fair. Third,"

"Wait, wait. Let me catch up," Beth interrupted. "Okay. Third?"

"Third is the overcrowding. Because of no parole, there's too many people crammed into this place."

"So, you want a new ruling that correctional institutions in this state can't house more inmates—uh—prisoners than they were designed to hold," Beth said. "Go on."

"Next, we need more education while we're inside. We should get the skills we'll need when we get out. And more counselors like you to teach us about hope and change."

"Anything else?" Beth asked. "I think the first two demands are your main issues, but the overcrowding and education are really important too."

"Yeah. There's more. Some guards in here are dirty," José said. "They bring in drugs to make money, or else they let other people smuggle it in, and they set up beat downs on prisoners they don't like. They do so much illegal shit that they should take our place in here when we get out on parole."

"I know there are some problems, but not all the guards are bad," Beth protested. She knew that Dan truly cared about the welfare of the men he watched over. Most of the guards did their best to treat the prisoners fairly and keep them safe. But, she had to admit that these traits did not apply to all of the guards at Arnone. Some were apathetic, and others were downright cruel. She could think of a few who matched José's negative portrayal.

"No," José explained. "There's really only a couple of them, but they do a lot of evil shit. It's the same with cops on the outside that murder people on the streets. Not that many of them actually do it, but the rest cover up for the bad ones, which makes them all accomplices even if they're not totally guilty. Plus, the flow of drugs has to stop. Mateo told me that a lot of guys are going through withdrawals now because they haven't had a fix in a couple of days. Some of the guards are too. The truth is that drugs keep us down just as much as the system does. If a guy's still hooked when he gets out, there's no chance in hell that he's gonna make it. He'll commit more crimes and end up right back in here."

"So, what are you asking for?"

"My fifth demand is that the guards get treated the same as us. Full body searches every time they come inside, for starters. Justice means that all people are treated fair. I mean, that's what we've been talking about in our discussion group, right? That's why we're doing this in the first place."

I am the reason they're doing this. Beth had to keep reminding herself. She knew it was true, but it was still difficult to accept.

"I understand," Beth nodded. "We never really discussed how illegal drugs were an obstacle to justice, but you're absolutely right."

"Yeah. This is about more than them stopping parole. That was just the last straw. The injustice we deal with on the inside is an extension of what we face on the outside. The law punishes us worse than rich people, and the government treats us like we're worthless. It has to stop."

Beth didn't agree with the methods José was using to address these injustices, but she could not argue with his assertions. After all, she was the one had who introduced him to these ideals. She believed them too.

"Good. The last thing is immunity—no punishment at all—for anything that happens during the revolution. Those are my demands," José said. "Now what?"

"Here's my suggestion," Beth said, again typing as she spoke. "The next paragraph should say, 'In order to bring a peaceful end to this revolution, we require a response to each of these six demands that specifies solutions, action steps, and a timeline for completion.'"

"But, how the hell am I supposed to make them do what they say?" José asked.

It was an excellent point. The warden could agree to anything simply to end the siege and retake control of the prison. Once it was over and the warden was in charge again, the inmates would have no power to enforce his promises.

"Well, for reinstatement of parole and new hearings for everyone, that would require a legislative action, or at the very least an executive order from the governor," Beth said, scanning the half-finished letter on the computer screen. "The same is probably true for the third demand about overcrowding. For the education and drug issues, numbers four and five, I think new policies might be enough. You could require that the warden sign them and the commissioner of corrections and the governor too."

"Yeah. Sounds good to me," José agreed. "Put that in there."

"Done," Beth said, stopping to flex her fingers and stretch her arms before typing again. "When the demands are met, we will begin discussion to peacefully end the revolution, release the hostages, and return control of the prison to Warden Hayward."

José picked up where she left off. "All of it had to be done in twenty-four hours after this letter reaches you. If my demands are not met, one hostage will be killed every hour."

Beth's eyes widened. This was not at all what she wanted to come next. "I'm not typing that, José. They already know you're serious, and they know what you're capable of. The threat of force is implied. You don't have to spell it out."

"But I do," José said. "You know as well as I do that you need a deadline and real penalties to make people do anything. If everyone knows what I'm capable of, then they'll meet my demands no matter what I threaten to do. If they take me seriously, like you say, then I'll never have to follow through on the threats anyway."

Beth could not formulate a coherent response quickly enough.

José continued. "Violence is necessary. Sometimes it's the only way to stop injustice. It's like when Frederick Douglass finally stood up and fought against his slave master. He worked hard and tried to follow orders, but the white man still whipped him. It wasn't fair. Once he showed that he would fight back, that was the end of his beatings. The only thing that worked for him was violence. You remember the essay I'm talking about, right? It's in that book in your office. I'll go get it, so you can see." José sprung out of his chair and headed for the door. "The consequence has to be in the letter, Beth. Please, just put it in there," he said and disappeared into the lobby.

The door thumped closed behind him, leaving Beth alone in the warden's office. She looked around the room, at the screen on the wall, at the door to the lobby, and then at the computer monitor. She felt compelled to use this time, alone and unsupervised, to do something useful. Maybe she should send an email? No. Shutting off the internet connection was the first thing the warden had done after the revolution started, but he had left the phone line to this office active. She reached for the phone but remembered that José had disconnected the cord. There wasn't enough time to plug it in, use it, unplug it, and get back to her seat before José returned. Besides, what would she tell them anyway? She knew the identities of the secondary leaders of the riot, but she was in no hurry to tell the warden and the others, particularly Captain Sullivan, that the members of her discussion group were the ones running the prison under José's leadership. She knew that many of the hostages were in the chapel, but that would only be helpful if the police were planning another raid. The last thing she wanted was to encourage that. Plus, by now Dan would have shared any information he had about the hostages and the inner workings of the prison since the takeover, so any information she had about that was irrelevant anyway.

José could return at any moment, and she was running out of time. An idea emerged. She looked over her shoulder at the window. "I know," she breathed and pushed herself up from her chair. She did have critical knowledge—one piece of information that would be useful to the police outside. She parted the curtains covering the window, allowing them to envelop her. The brightness of the midday sun caused her to squint, but she forced herself to face directly toward the light. The one vital piece of information she had was the fact that she was safe. If Beth could make them understand that she did not need their help, it might buy them all more time. She hoped to use that precious time to negotiate a peaceful resolution. She mouthed the words, "I'm okay," and formed a thumbs-up sign with both hands. She instantly felt ridiculous for using that gesture under these most dire circumstances, but it was the best idea she could come up with. She stepped away from the window, allowing the curtains to fall back into place, and hurried back to the desk. She was standing, both hands on the back of her chair, when José returned to the room.

"Everything good in here?" he asked.

"Fine. Just stretching my legs," she said. Her voice and demeanor were calm, and she surprised herself with the ease of her deception. In truth, she felt at peace with her decision. Conveying evidence of her wellbeing was the ideal course of action, since it was neither a betrayal of José nor a hindrance to the objectives of the police outside.

José glanced at the phone on the corner of the desk and at the detached cord still lying on the floor. Beth thought she saw an inkling of suspicion in his expression, but it lasted only a split-second. He reclaimed his seat across from her, propped one ankle on the opposite thigh, rested a leather-bound book on the lectern it created, and opened to a bookmarked page.

"Here's the quote I was talking about. It's from *My Bondage and My Freedom* when Douglass finally stood up for himself," José said, reading. "'The lesson taught at this point by human experience is simply this...Men may not get all they pay for in this world, but they must certainly pay for all they get. If we ever get free from the oppressions and wrongs heaped upon us, we must pay for their removal. We must do this by labor, by suffering, by sacrifice, and if needs be, by our lives and the lives of others.'"

But this situation is different from the one Frederick Douglass faced, Beth thought.

José must have interpreted her hesitation as doubt. "Here's another one," he said turning to a different page. "This is from after the Civil War when black men still weren't truly free. 'The American people have this to learn: that where justice is denied, where poverty is enforced, where ignorance prevails, and where any one class is made to feel that society is an organized conspiracy to oppress, rob, and degrade them, neither person nor property is safe.'"

This time, Beth nodded. She didn't need to hear any more quotes. José was right in a way, but his methods were wrong. And she didn't want anyone else to be hurt.

"See? Violence is necessary, Beth. Even Frederick Douglass, who said for years that peaceful resistance was the best path, finally admitted there was no other way to get justice. That's where we are now with the prison system."

"Why don't we put that in the letter then?" Beth offered. "You could say that you don't want any more bloodshed and you don't want any more violence. You only want justice. That quote will help solidify your argument."

"Perfect," he said. "They get twenty-four hours before I start killing hostages."

Chapter Twenty-Nine

Inside

With the letter of demand printed, signed, and ready to be delivered, José moved on to another project.

"I need another speech for tonight, just like the last one you helped me write." José grinned. He hoped Beth had forgiven him for deceiving her about this. "This one's for the guys still in lock down. They've been in their cribs going on three days now, and they're getting nasty," José said, fanning his face and crinkling his nose. "I need something, you know, inspirational, to convince them to hang in there a little longer."

"I'm sure we can come up with something," Beth said.

Over the next hour, José worked with Beth to draft a speech that he considered compelling. Beth printed it, and he read it aloud as a practice run. A knock at the door announced the arrival of lunch, and a worker bee carried in a brown plastic tray. José motioned toward the oval conference table, and the worker bee put it down with trembling hands. Pressing his palms together under his chin, he bowed and left the room. José and Beth moved to the larger table to eat, and he discovered after his first bite that he was famished. He devoured the meal and relaxed back in his chair.

"You know, I think you should consider opening up communication again with the police," Beth suggested. "They have no idea what's going on, and the last thing any of us wants is another SWAT raid. If we let them know that we're making progress, maybe that will hold them off for a while."

"If you think so, then let's do it," José said. As usual, Beth was right. Another police raid was the last thing he needed. He bent over to pick up the cord and plugged it into the phone. It rang immediately, and just as quickly José felt his anger swell. He had agreed that this was a good idea, but he hated to have another conversation with that asshole FBI agent. José was insulted by his demeaning tone. It was disrespectful. He wouldn't listen to any of his bullshit. He would tell them one thing—and it was something they'd want to hear. "That was quick." He growled and picked up the receiver.

"Beth will be out by five o'clock today," José barked. "I'm keeping her safe. Don't try to attack me again because I will see you coming, and I promise I will kill anyone who tries." He slammed the receiver onto its base, picked up the heavy phone, and hurled it to the floor.

"Did you hear that?" Beth asked. José was angry and exasperated, and he shook his head. He hadn't heard a thing.

"I heard the word, 'water.' At least I think that's what it was. 'Water. Water.' But, what does that mean?" Beth asked. "Are they going to shut off the water, do you think?"

"I have no idea what that asshole's talking about," José said. He honestly didn't. Maybe the cops were threatening to shut off the water. What did he care? Their own people would suffer if they did that. He would make sure of it.

José ripped the cord out of the wall again. With the present battle won, he rejoined Beth at the conference table.

"Tell me more about what it's like out there," José said. "Is the warden freaking out or what?"

"I would say so," Beth said. "All the decision-makers are in the mobile command center planning their strategies. I'm not sure if you can see, but a bunch of guards are camped out on the other side of the perimeter fence. Family members of the hostages are there too."

"I bet they're all sweating their asses off," José said. *Like we've been doing in here for years. It's their turn now.*

"Yes, they are," Beth conceded. "Just about every law enforcement agency you can think of is represented—and the media too. The police are keeping them off the field, but the news vans are lining the street out in front, and others are parked farther away, higher up a hill, so they have a bird's-eye view."

"They must've lost their shit when the raid went bad and only a couple of cops made it out alive," José said. "We could see them coming from a mile away, so I had plenty of time to get ready. What did they expect to happen? Honestly, I thought they would've sent in more cops. If I knew there would be so few, I would've saved some of the best hogs for later. As it was, we had way more fighters than cops, and I had plenty of weapons for them to use."

"You definitely surprised them," Beth said. "They expected little resistance, and in the end only three of the officers made it out alive. The snipers in the guard towers shot unarmed inmates as they were trying to escape, and the media's ripping the police to shreds over it."

Good, he thought. *The more people who know about the injustice, the better.*

"I'm going to ask you something, Beth, and I need you to tell me the truth." José's said, his tone serious. "Are they planning another attack? If so, you need to tell me."

"Not as far as I know. As of this morning, there was nothing planned. That said," she continued, "they could very well be assembling a new SWAT team right now. I just have no way of knowing that since I've been in here with you all day."

"Fair enough." That made sense to José. But Beth might have other information that could help him. "They know that I'm the leader, but what else do they have on us?"

"They know about Mateo, but I believe that's because they heard his name over the radio. I'm not sure about anyone else. Of course, Dan might have given them some other names, and you know what information Mrs. Williams has. In the end, the hostages will surely tell them who's responsible."

"You're right. I was hoping that the rest of the group might still be secret when this is over, but I guess not. I'll have to make sure there's immunity for us," José said, hesitating before he spoke again. "What do they know about how the revolution started? I mean, how I was able take control of the whole prison so easy. Did the warden have any ideas about that?"

"Nothing in particular. They attributed your success to careful planning, strong leadership, and flawless execution of a plan," she said. "The only thing the police found puzzling was the gun used to kill the guard on the first day. They were unsure where that came from."

"Oh, that was smuggled in months ago," José answered, looking Beth straight in the eye. "That piece has been in place for a while." This was a lie, but it was a necessary one. The less the cops knew about the gun, the less likely it was that they would find out about his mother's involvement.

There was a knock at the door, but Mateo let himself in before José acknowledged it. If looks could kill, the one José gave him would surely have accomplished that.

"Sorry to bother you," Mateo said, "but I need you out here. Now."

José and Mateo rushed out of the room. Beth followed.

A small crowd waited for them in the lobby. Krueger and Coop each held an arm of a squealing prisoner. A rip in his blue shirt reached from the neckline to his stomach, and Kruger's manhandling had pulled the material down, exposing his shoulder and much of his chest. T.K. and Fido were there too, as were the G's. They were all speaking at once.

"What's going on?" Beth yelled, surprising everyone.

"There's some shit going down in the blocks that we need to deal with," Mateo said. A threatening glare from José told him shut up, and snap his mouth shut.

"Mateo, take this mess into the chow hall. I'll be right there," José said. He didn't want Beth to see any more turmoil. He needed her to report back to the cops that he still had firm control over the prison.

"You know what, Beth? I think it's time for you to leave. Our work is done for today anyway, and you have to deliver the letter with my demands. The warden will be thrilled I'm letting you out early. Tell him it was for good behavior." He winked.

"And I'll tell them you're serious about your cause and that you want to resolve this peacefully."

José retrieved the letter from the warden's office and walked her to the prison's main door. "Please come back in the morning. Promise me," he said, handing her the envelope and holding the door open. The next day, Beth would have more information about what the cops were planning outside and if they made any breakthroughs. Plus, he needed her here to support him and help him stay on track.

"I promise," Beth said. "Stay safe."

Beth left, and José replaced the metal bar on the door. He had a new set of challenges to deal with.

CHAPTER THIRTY

Outside

DAY THREE
4:05 PM

Beth felt more wounded by José's lies than guilty about her own. She had not divulged to him that the authorities knew about his mother's surreptitious relationship with the warden and his wife. She knew the police were looking for José's mother in the hopes that they could use her as leverage against him. As of that morning, they had not located her, but it was possible they had found her during the course of the day. This was the first instance she'd encountered where helping José might hinder the police response and, as much as she hated to deceive him, Beth had kept this part secret.

But José had lied to her about the gun, and she saw no good reason for him to do that. What disturbed her most was that his expressions and body language had revealed nothing. Not even a hint of dishonesty. When she saw José next, she would need to protect her own false version of the story and feign ignorance about his mother's involvement in the plot, while at the same time acting like José had not told her a blatant lie. It was overwhelming, and she wondered if it was even possible for her to juggle these conflicting accounts.

Worse than lying and being deceived in return, Beth had left the prison and abandoned José just when things were getting difficult. But what could she do to help him deal with the other inmates who were causing trouble? Nothing. The best thing she could do at this point was advocate for him with the authorities on the outside. Still, her heart wrenched.

Beth reached the prison's perimeter fence, and a state police officer escorted her to the mobile command center.

"Welcome back, Ms. Sharpe." Warden Hayward greeted her.

Colonel Mitchell shook her hand heartily, but before he could speak, Captain Sullivan rose from his seat. "Well, you made it out of there alive. You don't look any worse for the wear either."

Beth did not acknowledge them. She simply handed the envelope to the warden who tore it open, scanned the text, nodded, and gave it to the information specialist. "Ms. Sharpe, have a seat."

"I'd like to express my relief that you've returned safely," Colonel Mitchell said. "You are, in fact, unharmed?" Beth nodded, and Colonel Mitchell continued. "Good. Obviously, we have a lot of questions for you, Ms. Sharpe, starting with where you were all day. What parts of the prison did you see? What can you tell us about the welfare of the hostages and where they're being kept? We need every bit of intelligence you've gathered, no matter how insignificant it might seem."

Beth described her tour of the cellblocks and the control room, and she told them the names and roles of the collaborating inmates. She didn't mention the relationship between herself and the inmates or the fact that all of the leaders were members of her discussion group. Surely that information would come out later, and she could think of no compelling reason to offer it now.

"And what about the condition of the hostages?" the warden asked.

"I didn't see many of them. Only the ones in the chapel," Beth recalled. "But none of the hostages were being abused, if that's what you mean. I did see some of the inmates being pushed around, but nothing too serious."

"Are they being cared for? The hostages, I mean." the warden continued. "Officer Cooney was weak and dehydrated when he was released this morning. He hadn't been given food or water since the riot started. We tried calling my office and the control room all day, and Ayala answered at one point, but he started yelling and hung up on me. I don't think he heard me."

"Oh," Beth said, shaking her head. "I thought I heard the word, 'water,' but I had no idea what it meant. I thought you were threatening to turn off the water to the building."

"What? You heard him?" Captain Sullivan roared. "Why didn't you listen? Or insist on calling us back? Our men are literally dying in there, and you did nothing?"

"José destroyed the phone after that call and he refused to make contact again," Beth said. "I–I don't know if the hostages are being fed. Honestly, I can't imagine that they've gone this long without water. I'm sure José is taking care of them." But even as she spoke she remembered the ease of José's deception and his casual dismissal of the unstable protective custody inmate's life. She couldn't forget about his pride at having killed all of the SWAT officers, but she pushed the thought away.

"The truth is, Ms. Sharpe," Colonel Mitchell said, his tone grave, "the hostages will die without water. We don't have much time left and even fewer options. I will not allow—I'm sure all of us agree on this—we will not allow the hostages to die of thirst. That is not an acceptable outcome."

The others in the command center nodded their agreement, but Beth was still trying to process the information. She could not imagine that José's plan was to starve the guards to death. Perhaps he didn't realize what was happening. Perhaps the inmates he trusted to watch over the hostages were neglecting their responsibilities.

But what if he did know? Images of blood smeared on the floor of A-Block and the stain on the carpet of the warden's office flashed in Beth's mind. What if his intention was to make the guards suffer?

And, if that was part of his plan, was there anything she could do to change his mind?

"We cannot allow the hostages to die." Colonel Mitchell's words shook her out of her ruminations. "We have no choice but to retake the prison by force. Tonight."

"No." Beth found her voice unsteady. "Please don't. So many people will die. You know that as well as I do."

"I have three hundred officers ready to go, between the National Guard and our state police, and we won't make the same mistake as last time. There'll be no warning this time," Colonel Mitchell said. The growing conviction in his voice bordered on excitement. "We'll keep the troops hidden, and we'll attack from several angles." He rolled the prison schematics onto the table. "Obviously, the main doors are one entry point, but this time we'll also use the loading dock that leads to the cafeteria. We'll send the majority of our officers in through that door. It will give us easy access to the central corridor, the control room, and the cellblocks without going through the administrative wing. And it has the added benefit of keeping most of the hostages out of harm's way. See?" he said, tracing his finger along the proposed path. "Ms. Sharpe, I could use your help here. Were you in the cafeteria today? Did you see the door that leads to the loading dock? I'm asking specifically about whether and how that entrance is guarded."

Beth had seen the cafeteria door, and she knew the loading dock entrance was, in fact, a point of weakness. Colonel Mitchell's plan might result in a successful retaking of prison. But a raid would also inevitably result in massive loss of life. Faced with a choice between certain loss of life and potential resolution without further deaths, there wasn't really a choice at all. Beth made her decision.

"I did see the cafeteria, but I don't think it's a viable option as an entry point. The door is blocked. There's no way to get through it," she said, adding this to the list of deceptions she needed to keep track of. "Plus, there's an inmate guarding it, and they're watching constantly from the control room, so they will see you coming."

Colonel Mitchell went on, undeterred. "We're working to shut off the surveillance cameras. It turns out the security put in place to keep that feed from being hacked is so strong that we haven't been able to access it. But we found an expert who can shut down the system completely. That's happening even as we speak, so by the time we attack, the surveillance cameras will be off. Plus, we can get through the door, even if it is barricaded. We can ram it or even blow it up, if necessary. It's not ideal, but we can make it work."

Fitzroy raised his hand and lifted himself a few inches from his seat. "Obviously, the governor would prefer to resolve this without the use of explosives and without any more dead bodies being thrown from the building."

"There will be plenty of dead bodies if you do this." Beth found her voice again, and she was using it to convey her determination. "You all know that's true. Dead police, dead inmates, dead hostages. Please just give it one more day."

"The hostages are suffering, Ms. Sharpe," Colonel Mitchell said, interrupting Captain Sullivan who had already started making the same argument. "This is the perfect time to retake the facility, but we need to act quickly. If we launch our raid tonight, we'll catch them by surprise, and it'll all be over before the sun comes up. Look, we know where the hostages are being kept now, so that's a point in our favor. And the inmates have already used their toughest fighters to fend off our first incursion, so their numbers are down."

"There are still fifteen hundred inmates in there," the warden said.

"Yes. But certainly some of those men are important to Ayala. The inmates he used to fight the SWAT team were expendable to him. He didn't lose anyone he considered valuable. A surprise night raid will put the key players in harm's way. The best case scenario is that we take out the leader and his closest supporters, and the whole leadership structure falls apart."

"No! Don't do that," Beth pleaded. She paused to compose herself. She couldn't let them kill José and Mateo and the rest. They were only doing what they thought was right. "I can fix this. I can. I'll make sure José feeds the hostages. He already has the protective custody inmates delivering meals to the cellblocks. I'll tell him to do the same for the hostages. I promised him I would go back into the prison tomorrow morning. When I do, I'll make sure the hostages are taken care of right away. No one else has to die. Just give me another chance."

"Let me interject here," Agent Dean said. "I see the benefits of taking decisive action to end this—" Beth inhaled loudly, but the FBI negotiator held up his hand to silence her. "Let me finish. I would be all for it if I thought we could successfully end the riot tonight, but I have some strong reservations about that. First, I don't have confidence in the assertion that a night raid would be a surprise. Second, the colonel pointed out that many inmates were killed during first SWAT raid and contends that another raid would meet weaker resistance. I say the opposite is true. The inmates may be fewer in number, but now they have firearms and other gear taken from the SWAT team, which makes them much more dangerous than before. So, while a stealthier and more forceful raid tonight might be successful, it would come at a very high price. The number of police, hostages, and inmates killed and injured could reach the triple digits. I don't think we're willing to pay that price. I certainly am not. Not unless we've exhausted all other options. We haven't even discussed whether we can meet the inmates' demands. I think we have an obligation to at least try to end this peacefully."

"I agree wholeheartedly," Fitzroy said. "Deaths in the triple digits would be a public relations nightmare." The others nodded reluctantly.

"Plus, we're making progress on some other strategies," Agent Dean said. "Colonel Mitchell's investigators are providing regular updates, and I think we can expect significant developments on that front." Beth wasn't sure she if agreed with Agent Dean's assumptions, but he was on her side now, so she chose not to interrupt.

"We have one more day before the hostages are in real trouble health-wise, and it's possible they have already been fed since Officer Cooney left this morning. Is everyone in agreement that, for the time being, we postpone the use of force in favor of negotiation? The governor's office is on board, and I see the commissioner is nodding his assent. What about you, warden?"

"As much as I want this to be over, we have to make every effort to avoid further loss of life," he said.

"I thought I would come down on the colonel's side," Captain Sullivan admitted, "but the losses on our side would be extremely heavy now that the inmates are armed. Believe me, I'd like to kill as many of those cocksuckers as possible, but another SWAT raid would end up killing my men in the process. Their best chance for survival is if we negotiate and get the inmates to surrender." When Colonel Mitchell began to object, he pressed on. "That said, we need some assurance that the hostages aren't going to die because we delayed taking action. We need proof that they're given food and water. If that doesn't happen first thing tomorrow morning, I say we retake the prison by force, no matter what the cost."

"Obviously, I disagree," Colonel Mitchell protested. "If we wait until tomorrow, we lose our tactical advantage."

"Your opposition is noted, colonel, but we will renew our negotiation efforts," Fitzroy asserted.

The warden spoke next. "We will continue to reach out to the inmate leader by phone and radio. But if that fails, Ms. Sharpe will insist on proper treatment for the hostages first thing tomorrow morning."

"Yes. I will," Beth said. She felt so much relief at that moment that she would have agreed to almost anything.

"You," the warden motioned to Andrew who had already scanned the paper and was paying close attention to the present conversation, "put the letter on the screen, so everyone can see what the inmates want."

Colonel Mitchell sat down hard, his face set. Beth's side had won, and she would have another chance to find a peaceful resolution.

The group discussed the specific demands outlined in José's letter. Warden Hayward seemed surprised by José's accusations about dirty guards and their flagrant mistreatment of the inmates. Captain

Sullivan predictably refuted the claims. Beth thought there was agreement among the group that the complete elimination of parole was unfair, and there was consensus about the need for more drug treatment and counseling services for inmates. Every one of the men rejected the idea that the inmates should receive immunity for the crimes they committed during the riot. Fitzroy made several phone calls to the governor, securing her acquiescence on some of the requests and outright denial to others.

"Let's go over each of these points again," Agent Dean said, seemingly the only one still enthusiastic about the exercise. "Ms. Sharpe, would you please review your explanation and the significance of this Frederick Douglass quote?"

"I've heard enough about Frederick Douglass," Captain Sullivan said. "Haven't all of you?"

"I have already explained it twice." Beth sighed. "And we've been at this for hours. I really don't have anything else to add."

"We still have more work to do," the warden said. "But Ms. Sharpe has to go back into the prison tomorrow morning. I think she should go home and get some rest." Nods all around approved his proposal.

The warden ordered Beth to return the next morning, and she headed straight out the door. She marched past the makeshift camp lit up by generator-powered lights and arrived at the staff parking lot. "You've got to be kidding me," she said, scanning the vehicles. A police officer had picked her up that morning and driven her to the prison, so her car was still parked miles away outside her apartment. She seriously considered walking home, but her exhaustion overruled her pride. She turned on her heels and trudged back to the command center.

Silent glares greeted her. Only Agent Dean spoke. "Did you forget something?"

"Um," she stammered, her embarrassment crushing. "I need a ride home."

The commissioner snickered, and Captain Sullivan guffawed at full volume. The others maintained their composure, but barely.

Colonel Mitchell was the only one of the group who appeared un-amused by Beth's humiliation. He rose and, directing his comments to everyone except Beth, said simply, "I'll have one of my officers drive her."

CHAPTER THIRTY-ONE

Inside

DAY THREE
11:21 PM

José found that the prison's central corridor, which had been quiet and empty only hours before, had turned to bedlam. Worker bees were running in circles outside the control room, dodging blows from the unruly prisoners who were chasing them. José recognized the pursuers as Latin Kings, associates of Angel from D-Block.

Krueger stepped in front of José. He stood only a few inches away, his broad chest blocking José's view of the chaos. Recognizing Krueger's bloodlust, José looked straight up to meet his eyes.

"I want you to kill every single person in this hallway," José said quietly. Krueger, Coop, and the G's set to work. Mateo remained by José's side. Fido, who had peeked his head out of the control room, pulled it back in and slammed the door shut. Krueger and Coop, with brutal skill and speed, killed two of the worker bees. Their flattened skulls and crumpled bodies fell to the floor. The G's were less efficient, and Big G struggled to strangle a worker bee with his hands, while Baby G wrestled the writhing man's legs to keep him pinned to the floor.

Angel's supporters turned and ran away. Krueger caught up with one before he made it through the propped-open access gate between the central corridor and the cellblock hallway. Krueger dropped his club to the floor, wrapped one massive arm around the prisoner's head, and used the other to clasp his torso. With one violent contraction, he broke the man's neck. Another dashed away with Coop following closely behind. They both disappeared through the gate.

José and Mateo walked past the G's still atop the now-motionless worker bee and signaled for Fido to open the control room door.

"What the hell's going on?" José started. "Why are there dogs in the hallways when they're supposed to be locked up? That's your job, Hacker, to keep the blocks locked down and let me know if anything goes wrong. Who the hell told you to open D-Block?" *This wasn't supposed to happen.*

Hacker shook his head and pointed at Fido, placing the blame squarely on his partner. José glowered at Fido, demanding further explanation.

Fido twitched nervously. "Angel made me do it," Fido insisted. "He called and told me to unlock some cells for him. As a personal favor. Then, he said to open the door to D-Block, so I did that, and some worker bees came running out with two guys chasing them."

"I told you not to do it," Hacker scolded.

Fido glanced to one side, winced, and turned back to José. José looked over his own shoulder to follow path of Fido's eyes and saw Krueger glaring at him from outside the control room. Maybe Krueger had somehow intimidated Fido into doing what Angel told him to.

José was angry, but he recognized Fido's shortcomings and understood his actions. Like an obedient pet, Fido followed his master's commands. But the only power stronger than respect was fear. And, from what José could tell, Fido had good reason to be afraid.

Coop burst through the gated access door and leaned over with hands on his knees. "I lost him," he said in between gasps. "He's hiding in H-Block. I need some help before he finds his way back into D."

Krueger shifted, determined not to miss out on an opportunity to hunt and kill. At a jog, he and Coop set out to find the traitor.

José grabbed Fido by his shirt. "Do not open any more doors," he said. "And, no matter what, don't let anyone into the control room or give anyone weapons. Promise me, Fido. Hacker, you too."

Fido nodded vigorously. "Trust me," Hacker said, adjusting his glasses. "I won't let anyone in this room."

Suddenly, the video screens in the control room went dark, and José took in a sharp breath. "The warden finally decided to shut off the surveillance cameras. Took him long enough! It's no big deal. We know we've got this place under control."

His statement was almost true. At last check, the prison's perimeter and cellblocks were calm with the notable exception of D-Block.

José dreaded his next move, but he knew he had no choice. He wasn't sure exactly what kind of relationship Angel had with Krueger, but it appeared they were working together somehow. He guessed that Angel had allowed Krueger to brutalize his enemies and the worker bees in D-Block, and that was the only reason for their alliance. But at the moment Krueger was busy chasing down a rogue prisoner with Coop. This was the perfect time for José to do something about it.

He grabbed some SWAT gear and weapons from the control room floor, and he instructed the G's to do the same. Then he, Mateo, Big G, and Baby G headed for D-Block.

This time, his arrival did not go unnoticed. It appeared that Angel had a lookout waiting at the door because as soon as José peeked through the tiny window, a man rushed away calling Angel's name. José instructed his guys to leave the extra gear in the hallway, and he radioed Hacker to unlock the cellblock door.

José wasn't playing any games. Once inside, he immediately drew his gun and shot the first one of Angel's dogs he saw. He shot another square in the chest, and the cellblock erupted into earsplitting chaos. The prisoners scrambled to take cover, hiding behind poles and the little furniture there was on the cellblock floor. He saw one dog trying to conceal himself under a mattress. José kind of wanted to shoot him too, but he figured he'd already made his point.

"Angel!" José yelled, scanning the cellblock. But Angel didn't show himself. *Fucking coward,* José thought. "I know you're in here, Angel. So you listen to this. The door to D-Block will not open again—not until this revolution is over. You're on your own now, Angel. I hope all your dogs appreciate what you've done. There will be no more supplies. No more food. You can all sit in here and rot for all I care. You go to hell, Angel!"

José spun toward the door and motioned for Mateo and the G's to leave before him. Just as he crossed the threshold, he heard Angel's voice. "I'll meet you there," it said.

Angel had the last word, and José tried not to let it bother him. He gritted his teeth and slammed the door shut behind him.

José had Baby G jam some of the SWAT gear under the cellblock door. He shoved a longer piece of wood between the door handle and the floor. This way, even if Fido unlocked the door to D-Block remotely, Angel wouldn't be able to get out. Coop and Krueger rejoined the group. José looked for a sign that Krueger was upset at the sight of the barricaded door, but he saw nothing of the sort in Krueger's fixed expression.

Satisfied that he had the Angel problem under control, José and his crew returned to the central corridor. There, they found worker bees laboring to clean up the mess and dragging the bodies of the slain prisoners to the visitor's area. His confidence was partially restored by this example of efficiency in the organization that he had put in place.

In the control room, José once again addressed the entire prison via the intercom system. Reading from the speech he and Beth had written earlier that day, he started, "Attention, my fellow revolutionaries, I am pleased to report that our demands have been delivered into the hands of the warden. They include the restoration of parole and a fair hearing with the parole board for all of us within thirty days."

José expected to hear applause in response to this news, but instead there was an almost continuous hum of booing and general chatter. He wondered if anyone was listening.

Despite the inattention, he continued. "We demand that overcrowding is stopped and that we get more education and counselors. There will be justice in this prison, with guards punished for their crimes and illegal drugs eliminated. Finally, there will be absolute immunity for anything that happens during this revolution. No punishment for me or for any of you."

The shouting from the cellblocks continued. José understood that the prisoners were angry at still being locked in their cells, but they seemed uninterested in the principles of the revolution and the potential for change inherent in his list of demands.

"The world cannot honor a helpless man, although it can pity him. We are not helpless, and we will not be pitied. I know it's been hard for you, but you need to be patient a little longer. In the end, we will be victorious."

José acknowledged that few had listened to his carefully crafted speech. Even the team leaders in the cellblocks would have had trouble hearing him over the thunderous protests. Only his closest, most loyal supporters listened well enough to understand. But maybe they were the ones who needed to hear it most.

Chapter Thirty-Two

Outside

DAY THREE
11:31 PM

Beth's police escort dropped her off in her building's parking lot. She opened the building's dimpled metal door and went up the stairs to her apartment. When she reached the top, she froze, hand poised on the door knob. She heard scuffing noises inside, and Beth found herself wishing that she'd asked the officer to walk her all the way to her door. Someone was in her apartment. *Why? Had they expected me to stay away all night? And if not, what were they planning to do to me when I came home? What the hell am I supposed to do now?*

Beth cocked her head, putting her ear as close as possible to the door without actually touching it. She closed her eyes and focused her remaining senses on identifying the threat. The ever-present odor of cooking oil from the restaurant downstairs overpowered her sense of smell, but her hearing detected one footstep and then another. There was at least one person inside, but the pace of the movements seemed dawdling, and she questioned the legitimacy of her fear. Perhaps the intruder was not there to hurt her, but was simply searching the apartment. For what?

A loud clattering sound startled Beth, and she let out an involuntary shriek. Her presence was no longer secret. A quick succession of footsteps brought the intruder closer, but Beth's body was still deliberating the fight or flight decision. She was paralyzed by fear when the door flew open.

There, standing in the doorway with light from the kitchen illuminating him from behind, was an angelic-looking Dan Cooney. Overcome with relief, she acted with uncharacteristic enthusiasm and jumped into his arms. She looked over his shoulder and noticed the open takeout containers on the table. The sound that had startled her must have been Dan dropping two of her plastic dishes, and the food smell emanated from inside her apartment, rather than simply residue wafting from the restaurant below. She had not seen Dan's car in the parking lot outside, but maybe he had been dropped off, or she simply hadn't noticed it in the darkness. He must have used the spare key she kept hidden atop her door frame to get in. Either way, Beth's fears were eased. This intruder she didn't mind.

"I'm so glad you're alright." Dan was the first to speak. "I got you Chinese again. Sorry. You know I'm not much of a cook."

"No, it's great. Thank you!" she said. "I'm famished."

Beth retrieved the plates from the floor, and the two sat across from each other at her tiny kitchen table. Leaning back in his chair, Dan broke the progressively awkward silence.

"I can't believe you made it out of there alive, Beth," he began, touching the bandage on his forehead. "I don't understand why you walked into that prison in the first place, though. That was an insane thing to do."

"I know," Beth said. She was so sick of being lectured about all the things she was doing wrong. "But I really don't need any criticism from you about this. I went in because I had to, and it saved your life and who knows how many more. I helped the inmates write up their demands and stopped any further violence for the time being." *So there*, Beth said to herself. Dan's silence confirmed his tacit agreement to let the matter go.

"How are you?" Beth asked, pointing to the injuries on his face.

"I'm fine. Just some bumps and bruises and a couple of stitches on my head. I had an IV for a while, but I'm doing much better now." Dan shrugged his shoulders.

"How did you know I was coming home? Or did you get all this food for yourself?" she teased.

"I came straight here from the hospital to wait for you. I had the TV news on all day, so I watched you walk out of the prison around three o'clock. Like I said, I couldn't believe it, but I was so tired that I fell asleep waiting for you. Your couch is pretty comfortable." Beth grinned and nodded. "When I woke up, you still weren't here, so I ordered food before they closed downstairs. What took you so long?"

Beth sighed and twisted her top lip. "After a couple hours of de-briefing, I was just about done, and then everyone else felt the same after another four. They finally called it and sent me home. I have to go back in the morning."

"Oh. Your phone was ringing like crazy," Dan said. "I went in your room to put it on silent. I hope that's okay. I'd guess you have more than a few messages."

Beth rose and made a sullen trek to her bedroom, where she had left her phone plugged in when she rushed out that morning. She scrolled through the list of missed calls. Some were numbers she recognized—her mother and her brothers. Others were unfamiliar, and there were dozens of them.

Beth listened to the first message. "Beth, it's mom. I've been watching the news and praying that you're okay. We're all so worried about you. Please, Beth, call me back. And please, please be safe."

Hearing the sadness in her mother's voice triggered in Beth long-festering feelings of guilt to be the cause of so much pain. It re-minded her of everything that had happened, and it brought back the anguish of the tragedy she had caused for her family. Beth hunched over and allowed herself a single inaudible sob. She placed the phone face-down on her dresser and took a deep breath to regain control of her emotions. Beth sensed that she wasn't alone and turned to find Dan leaning against the door frame.

"A lot of people care about you, Beth," he said. "And I'm at the top of that list."

This was the most vulnerable Beth had allowed herself to be with Dan, and she was troubled by the emotion it provoked within her.

She suppressed that sensation and replaced it with a more familiar one. She tilted her head and gazed up at Dan. He closed the space between them in two long strides, wrapping both arms tightly around her and kissing her forcefully on the lips. Beth reciprocated the enthusiasm of both the kiss and the embrace, and, eager to proceed, she pushed him away. Dan's body obeyed her corporal command, but his lips were last to comply.

Shuffling together and fumbling to remove their clothes, they found their way to Beth's bed. The two entwined in a practiced, almost graceful, erotic routine. This is what they did best as a couple. They had little in common in terms of ideals or interests, and though they spent time together, they did not satisfy each other intellectually or emotionally. Sex was the one aspect of their relationship where they were perfectly matched. In the bedroom, if nowhere else, she and Dan were utterly compatible.

Dan was an enthusiastic and skillful lover—the best combination. Beth reveled in it, and they moved together in rhythmic synchronicity. Her body melded with Dan's, and the nagging worries and guilt that had besieged her over the past few days disappeared. The intense physical sensations served to subjugate Beth's other emotions. This was exactly what she needed.

Even on her best day, Beth was a selfish lover. That night, she was singularly focused on prolonging her own pleasurable reprieve from reality, and she pushed the limits of Dan's endurance. At any moment, she could choose to surrender herself and achieve the satisfaction they both craved. But instead, she chose to remain there in that torturous moment, which was at the same time both magnificent and excruciating. Dan persevered despite Beth's unrelenting stimulation. Desperate and unable to hold back any longer, he begged, "Now, Beth. Please."

Dan's pleas pushed Beth over the edge, and she finally allowed herself to succumb, savoring the pulses that traveled the whole of her body. Beth rested atop him until their gasping breaths slowed and their bodies unraveled. Her mind clear and her body contented, she slept.

In the morning, Beth rose early, showered, and dressed. A knock on her door confirmed that Colonel Mitchell had followed through on his promise to have an officer drive her back to the prison. Dan stirred at the sound, but Beth pretended not to notice. She folded a blazer over her arm, shoved her phone in her pocket, and left her apartment.

She followed the officer, this time a chunky grey-haired man with curved shoulders, down the stairs. Before she reached the bottom step, she jolted to a stop. "Wait. Just a second. I'll be right back," she blurted. Fortunately for Beth, this officer was less sprightly than she, and she bounded back up the stairs before he even registered her remark. Beth turned the door handle and discovered that she had locked herself out of the apartment. She usually had a key hidden atop the door frame, but she remembered that Dan had used it to get in. Apparently he hadn't put it back yet. She sighed and knocked on her own apartment door, hoping the sound would wake Dan before the police officer made her leave.

Dan appeared quicker than she'd expected. Dressed only in his boxer shorts, he beamed through sleepy eyes and ran his hands through his tousled hair. "Did you forget something?"

"Yep!" She started past him, but Dan had already bent his face toward hers. She realized, to her horror, that he was leaning in to kiss her. Beth tried clumsily to recover, turning sideways to give Dan a quick kiss on the cheek. She rushed to her bedroom in pursuit of her original objective and reemerged seconds later, tucking a small object into the pocket of her pants.

Dan stood in her path. His stance was neither aggressive nor confrontational, but as she approached him, he grabbed her by the arms and pulled her toward him. He kissed her hard on the lips, and then he stared at her as if it was the last time he would be able to do so. His expression spoke volumes, but "be careful" were his only words.

She descended the stairs a second time and found the state police officer in the parking lot, holding open the car door. He motioned for her to hurry, and she caught sight of Bearded Bob at the repair shop next door. He was leaning against the same minivan he had been working on the last time she had seen him. How many days ago was it? Three or four? But this time, instead of waving and calling out a friendly greeting, he glared at her with his arms crossed and shook his head with blatant disgust. Bearded Bob must have heard about the riot and the role that Beth played in it. She surmised that he—and likely everyone else in town—had already tried her in the court of public opinion and found her guilty.

This was yet another reason—as if she needed more—to find a peaceful end to the inmates' revolution.

CHAPTER THIRTY-THREE

Outside

F our days after the prison revolution began, Beth found the makeshift camp outside the prison's perimeter fence still inhabited. Prison employees, gathered as a show of support for their colleagues and to monitor the government's progress in ending the riot, had erected pop-up canopies and set up folding chairs and tables. The guards' black uniform shirts hung from the canopy rods and on the backs of chairs. She stepped over plastic water bottles and other trash on her way to the mobile command center.

She welcomed the sight of the now-familiar faces that turned toward her when she stepped inside. Unfortunately, those faces did not reflect reciprocal pleasure at the occasion of her return. The inhospitable greeting was accompanied by the equally offensive aroma given off by the half dozen unshowered men who had spent a sleepless night in command center.

The governor's voice emanated from the speaker on the conference table. "And don't even get me started on the fifth demand. The media's going to have a field day with this!" she ranted. "Why the hell would inmates demand that the guards be punished for dealing drugs? Are you telling me that my state employees—well compensated employees, I might add—are bringing drugs into the prison? Of course I want that to stop, but I can't really respond to this without admitting the whole system is corrupt."

"Excuse me, governor," Captain Sullivan interrupted, "but just because the inmates say so doesn't mean it's true."

Beth couldn't believe they were still at it. Had they been up all night arguing about the inmates' demands?

"Who is that? Who is that speaking?" the governor fumed, her rage palpable even though she was miles away. Captain Sullivan did not immediately answer, giving Fitzroy the opportunity to mediate.

"That was Captain Sullivan, governor," he offered. "He's commander of the guards."

"Well, Captain Sullivan, I'm inclined to believe it, since there's no reason for the inmates to include it in their demands otherwise. If I find out this is true—that your guards are dealing drugs in the prison and mistreating inmates—I will hold you personally responsible. You will find yourself without a job or a pension."

It was a powerful threat, and Beth thought that Captain Sullivan had good reason to be afraid.

"Please, governor," Warden Hayward said, rising from his chair. "I am the warden, so I am ultimately responsible."

"You're damn right you are!" she shouted. "Believe me, when this is all over, there will be plenty of heads rolling. And you, warden, will be the first one on the chopping block."

Apparently no one could think of an appropriate response to this statement. Beth certainly couldn't. The group waited mutely for the governor to continue.

"This is a no-win situation for me. You have to realize that. Under no circumstances will I give in to the demands of a bunch of rioting inmates. The legislature refuses to reinstate parole until they can come up with a better way of making the decisions. That is taking some time, obviously, since they can't seem to do anything quickly. Plus, I fired the entire parole board, so I would need to appoint all new members before any hearings could be held. The best I can do on that is promise to make it a priority. And, as for the final demand in this letter, I will not grant immunity to the leaders of this riot who are responsible for the deaths of nineteen state police officers and at least one correctional officer. Fixing this mess is in your hands, gentlemen. You need to come up with a solution, and you need to do it fast. If your investigators come through and you get the leader to surrender, then that is obviously the outcome I want. If not, and you have nothing more to offer, you will end this riot by force. But, in case I wasn't clear last time, I do not want to watch people being gunned down on television. However you retake the prison, make sure the bodies fall inside the building."

Only Colonel Mitchell managed a reply. "We should wait until dark, then. Our officers have night vision capabilities, so we will shut off all of the outside lights and enter the prison under cover of darkness. It is perfectly reasonable for us to do that, and it won't look like we're trying to hide anything from the media. We can finish it and have everything cleaned up by morning."

"Good. That's the plan," the governor said. "Tell the counselor girl to string the inmate leader along until we get our forces organized for the final strike tonight."

Beth had stayed quiet, not moving beyond the entryway of the command center. But now she was angry. The governor knew full-well what her name was, and she refused to be called, "that counselor girl."

"My name is Beth Sharpe," she snarled. "And I heard you, governor. I understand that you're making no effort to address the inmates' concerns. While I admit that their methods are poorly chosen, their actions have given you the opportunity to improve prison policies and bring more fairness to the system. What I heard you say is that you would rather see both inmates and police officers die than make an effort to change things for the better. Am I right in understanding that you will not negotiate at all? You are even unwilling to investigate corruption among your own guards?"

"I cannot give in to their demands and maintain my authority," the governor replied. "I will not be seen negotiating with inmates who are killing police and guards and holding people hostage to get their way. And I will not negotiate with you either. Like it or not, I call the shots here. Do you understand that, Ms. Sharpe?"

"I do, governor," Beth replied. "But I think you have an obligation to respond. They have legitimate grievances."

Beth had allowed herself a speck of optimism that she would make progress toward ending the violence and achieving the inmate's goals. But now she realized that she wasn't even close to making that happen.

"I'm sure some of their complaints are legitimate, and I will address the issue of mistreatment after this is over. I will do my best to get the legislature to move on the reinstatement of parole and address the other demands about treatment and learning opportunities, as well. I am willing to put this all in writing." The governor paused. "But you need to do your part too, Ms. Sharpe. You need to tell your friend José Ayala to give the hostages water immediately. You must tell him that we are working on his list of demands and that he needs to maintain order inside the prison and make sure no one else dies. If he does this, we will have a written response to his demands by the end of the day. You will act in accordance with my instructions, or I will expel you from the command center, and you will never step foot on the prison grounds again. Your inmate friends will be on their own. What is your decision, Ms. Sharpe?"

Astonished eyes turned away from the speaker to Beth.

"I will do as you say, governor." *What choice do I have?* "But, I will hold you to your word, and you must make every effort to respect the inmates' pursuit of justice and limit the loss of life."

"Indeed," the governor said, though it fell short of a promise. "This arrangement gives you until the end of the day to stop the riot. If the inmates do not surrender, we *will* retake the prison by force tonight. That's a promise I'll keep. Mr. Fitzroy, I need to speak with you privately. Call me immediately." A dial tone signaled the end of the conversation.

Fitzroy rose and, with his cell phone to his ear, walked toward the command center's back room. With his elbow on the table and his head leaning against his fist, the warden used his idle hand to motion toward the chair Fitzroy had vacated. "Sit."

Beth's conviction was shaken. She had truly believed that José's actions would result in positive change, but the governor was belittling him and undermining his efforts.

The others echoed her hopelessness with bowed heads and dejected expressions. Agent Dean, the person least connected to the situation, spoke. "Look, Beth, we still have a chance for a peaceful resolution. Colonel Mitchell and the state police are working on their plan to force José to cooperate. Don't give up. There's still something you can do to help the inmates achieve at least some of their goals." Beth lifted her chin from her chest.

"Remember," Agent Dean continued, addressing the entire group. "As of now, the governor is acting on the assumption that the hostages are in immediate, life threatening danger. She thinks they are on the brink of death from dehydration and will not survive through the night. If Beth can make José feed the hostages, and she can vouch for their continued wellbeing, the governor might be convinced to continue negotiations into tomorrow. Now, to be sure, they won't get everything they're asking for, but maybe they'll achieve something, considering what's been sacrificed." He turned back to Beth. "You can still make a difference today."

It was only a hint of hope, but it was enough to lift Beth out of complete despair. If they needed her to convince José to agree to that one condition, she would do it.

"The first and most important thing you need to do," Agent Dean explained, "is get José to give the hostages food and water. Get that message to us right away. When we know they're safe, I promise to contact the governor and try to push off the SWAT raid."

"I'll do my best," Beth agreed. "But how do I get you that message. I told you how José slammed the office phone and pulled the cord from the wall."

"That's not a game changer," Agent Dean said. "We can have the phone company reactivate the other lines, so try the one in Captain Sullivan's office. Or, you can use one of the guard's radios to get us a message."

"Sign language through the window won't cut it this time," Captain Sullivan mocked. "We need to know for sure that my men aren't dying of thirst."

"Yes. Even if you have to come back out of the prison to let us know, understand that we need that piece of information before we can make any progress with the governor to avoid a violent end to this situation," Agent Dean told her.

"I understand," Beth said. "I'll reach out as soon as I can, in whatever way I can."

"If you feel unsafe at any time," the warden said, placing his hand on Beth's shoulder. "I want you to get out of there. Just get out."

"I'll be fine," Beth assured him.

Chapter Thirty-Four

Inside

DAY FOUR
9:59 AM

"**B**eth's on her way," Mateo announced, knocking on the glass of the control room. Her arrival was later than José had expected, but he was thankful for the extra time. He needed it to sort out the details of the previous night's events in D-Block and reinforce his authority with the other cellblocks. He nodded toward Mateo and issued directives to Fido and Hacker before joining his second-in-command in the central corridor. Flanked by his bodyguards as always, he crossed the threshold to the lobby just as Beth entered from the other side.

"We meet again," José said, greeting her with a smile. "You have good news for me?"

Beth returned his smile, but José sensed some hesitation. "I have good news and bad news, actually. Let's sit and talk about it."

"Just tell me, Beth." He had no time for games.

"Uh ... okay," Beth began. "The good news is that the governor is giving serious consideration to your demands, which is really great. The bad news is that it's going to take a while for her to put all of it into place. She has to meet with the legislature, and they have to vote.

It might not be possible to have everything finalized today, but she is putting everything in writing and promising to address most of your demands. But that takes time."

José pursed his lips but did not speak. *It would take time? That's bullshit.*

Beth kept talking. She was going on about the hostages and water and telling him to give in to the warden on this one thing. But he couldn't focus on her words. Anger was sweeping over him.

"Well, screw them," José scoffed. "I'm not doing anything those pigs say. I gave them a whole night to work on my demands, and they couldn't come up with a response to even one of them? I'm not giving them shit."

"I need to contact the warden to let him know about the hostages," Beth said. "I promised I would do that right away."

"But you just got here," José protested. "You haven't even seen anything yet. What could you possibly tell him?" He was losing his patience with everyone, even Beth. "Come with me. I have some business in the blocks."

He led the group out of the lobby and into the central corridor, passing by the control room. When they arrived at the entrance to A-Block, José saw the same panic in Beth's eyes as the day before. Remembering her dislike for being in the cellblocks, he said, "You stay here with Coop. I'll be back in a sec."

A-Block was running smoothly, so José told T.K. to carry on and rejoined Beth in the central corridor.

"How's T.K. doing?" Coop asked.

Ignoring the question, José pushed past Coop and guided Beth to the access gate for the other cellblocks. The door clicked open at the appropriate moment, activated by José's ostensibly obedient helpers in the control room.

"I'll go in with you this time," Beth said when they reached B-Block. José was shocked. *Why the sudden change?* He began to suspect that Beth had some ulterior motive. It felt like a hole was forming in the pit of his stomach. But he would let her come into the cellblock with him, and he'd see where this went.

All four bodyguards accompanied them inside. Only Squeeze, his soldiers, and a few worker bees roamed around on the first level while the rest of the prisoners remained locked in their cells. B-Block was a model of efficiency, and he was glad Beth had chosen to see this one.

Squeeze welcomed them with a smile and sauntered over. His slick, black hair was more greasy than shiny now, and the guard's uniform he was wearing was a mess. His appearance reminded José that the revolution had already lasted several days. Even the prisoners who supported him and were free from their cells, must be getting tired of the monotony and craving a shower and change of clothes.

Squeeze stopped a few feet away from them. He spun around, put one hand on his hip, and extended the other in the air in some kind of disco pose. José rolled his eyes. Their reunion was interrupted by screaming from a cell on the upper tier.

"What the hell are you doing here? Are you crazy, bitch? Get me the hell out of here!"

José and his crew turned toward the noise. A man on the upper level had his chest pressed against the bars of a cell and was reaching his arms through. He wore the standard blue prisoner clothes, but José recognized him as a guard. Monroe was his name.

José knew the guard well. He was infamous in the prison for being the most cruel and dirty. He could be paid off with money or favors to look the other way while a prisoner was beaten, and he sometimes delivered his own brutal punishments whenever he felt the need. He brought drugs and other contraband into the prison, but the administration never did anything to stop him. Despite his reputation, Monroe had kept his job and continued to harass and abuse the men he was supposed to be watching over. This irked José to no end.

"Wow. That's Monroe, isn't it?" Coop said. "He's one lucky sonofabitch to have ended up in here with you, Squeeze. In any of the other blocks, he'd be dead already."

"Oh. He's dead already," José declared. "Squeeze, call the control room and tell them to open that cell."

This needed to be done. José didn't care that Beth would see it either. He wanted her support almost more than anything else, but he needed respect. That was the only way he could maintain control. Beth would have to accept that this was a form of justice. Monroe had hurt many people, and he deserved this. This was the type of justice that prisoners had the power—the duty even—to dispense.

"Open cell B-42, loves," Squeeze crooned into the radio.

The inmates in their cells strained their necks to see, and everyone waited in silence for the cell door to open. Monroe began shouting again. "What? No! Do something, bitch! No!" When the cell door slid open and clicked into place, the guard leapt out and scrambled along the walkway toward the stairs.

José pointed to Krueger and his other bodyguards. Weapons in hand, they rushed to the staircase. At the sight of them, Monroe halted in his tracks. But his legs stopped first, and the momentum caused his upper body to continue downward. He managed to catch himself by grasping tightly to the handrails, and he spun around to clamber back up. But there was no way for him to escape and nowhere for him to hide, and José's men caught up with him before he reached the open cell he'd emerged from moments before.

The G's pushed him down and took turns kicking him. They stopped only briefly to lift him from the floor and prop him against the metal railing. His legs folded under him, and his head fell forward only to roll back again. Coop stood a few feet away and didn't help at all. Krueger set aside his studded club, his usual weapon of choice, in favor of a knife he borrowed from one of his fellow attackers.

From José's viewpoint, the knife looked solid, with a shiny tip and a thick handle fastened with tape or cloth or a combination of both. Still, the blade was small, maybe only three inches in length. It wouldn't be easy to kill with that weapon, but José guessed that this was exactly Krueger's intention. He stabbed the guard in the chest, arms, and stomach again and again and again, blood pouring in a steady stream through the grates and onto the floor below. Krueger continued to gore the guard long after he was dead.

The other inmates hooted and hollered, cheering on the attackers. When it was over, José's men abandoned the guard's body on the grated walkway and came down the stairs. The men wiped the blood from their hands and returned to their posts.

Beth leaned over and vomited. José acknowledged that this may have been too much for her, and he felt regret for putting her through it. Purposely avoiding eye contact with her, he motioned for the group to exit the cellblock.

Coop placed his hand on the small of Beth's back and steered her toward the exit, but Beth grabbed hold of the door jamb and halted their progress. She switched direction and dashed past José, heading straight for Squeeze. She pulled something out of her pocket, shoved it into Squeeze's hand, turned around, and exited the cellblock. José shared a confused look with Coop, but Coop just shrugged his shoulders and followed Beth out the door.

What the hell? José thought. He had to know what Beth had given to Squeeze. He went over to him and spoke quietly. "What you got there?"

The other prisoners hushed, no doubt trying to listen in on the conversation.

Squeeze held up a tube of lipstick. "It's my favorite color," he said, his eyes welling with tears.

This was why José cared so much about Beth. He had needed this reminder. Beth was the most caring person he had ever met. She had gone out of her way to bring that lipstick to Squeeze—not because she had to or because anyone asked her to. She did it because she knew that it was important to him.

This gesture showed how much Beth cared for all of them. Just being there in the prison with him now meant that she valued and supported them. José knew that she was just as invested as he was in getting justice. She had promised to help him in every way possible. Likewise, he had made a commitment to her to stay true to the ideals she had taught him. No matter what, he would see this through.

CHAPTER THIRTY-FIVE

Inside

Beth replayed the gruesome murder scene through her mind and wondered if she might have been able to stop it. If she hadn't returned to the prison that day, Monroe might not have drawn attention to himself, and he might still be alive. If she had been braver, she could have pleaded with José to spare the guard's life. But, would he have listened? Would it have made a difference?

It doesn't matter. You should have done something. She berated herself over and over again in her mind.

But the prison was still full of inmates and hostages. Would their fate be the same as Monroe's? Beth forced herself to focus on the living rather than the dead. But she worried that the revolution was nearing its end, whether José realized it or not.

Beth waited in the hallway while José visited the remaining cellblocks. She was left under the protection of one bodyguard, and she was thankful that it was Coop and not Krueger. Although Coop's crimes on the outside had resulted in a long prison term, on the inside he was a model of good behavior. He showed civility to his fellow inmates and the staff, and from what Beth had observed during the

234

prison revolution, he continued to conduct himself ethically while remaining loyal to José.

"How's everything going?" she asked after the others had disappeared into C-Block.

"I'm not worried. It's under control in there," Coop said, although his body language suggested otherwise as he peered through the tiny window in the door.

"That's not...I mean, that's great. But, what I'm asking is how is *everything going*?" Beth said, drawing a circle in the air. "How are all of you holding up?"

"Oh, we're all good," he said, glancing back at her but still distracted by the activity in the block. Finally, he let out a breath that Beth hadn't realized he was holding. Whatever had concerned Coop in C-Block must have been resolved. He relaxed with his back against the wall and addressed Beth again. "To answer your question, though, things are definitely heating up in here. José's still in charge, but it's not rock solid anymore. H-Block is totally empty, and we're not sure where all the protective custody bitches went. Some are still doing their worker bee jobs, but the rest are just missing. They're probably dead or getting beat up in the blocks, or maybe they're hiding out somewhere. We just don't know."

Oh no, Beth thought. *More people dead.*

"We had a lot of trouble last night. Some guys from D-Block got out." Coop raised his eyebrows and pursed his lips. "They were fighting and causing trouble. José decided to lock up D-Block for good. Nobody's allowed in or out for any reason, and the door's jammed shut. José probably doesn't want you to know all the details, so let's just say we almost lost control of the whole prison last night."

"That's really scary," Beth said. "Do you think you can last another night? What if there's another raid by the police? Is there a plan for that? Do you have a plan to fight them off this time?"

Before Coop responded, José and his bodyguards reemerged. The sounds of inmates shouting followed them through the open door into the hallway.

"Everything okay?" José said, looking from Beth to Coop and back to Beth again.

"All good," Coop replied, a flush creeping over his face.

Nearly two hours had passed since Beth had entered the prison, and she was overdue on her promise to contact the warden with information about the hostages' welfare. Any chance for continued negotiation slipped further away with every passing minute. By nightfall, the authorities would have no choice but to raid again. She needed to convince José to provide food and water to the hostages in the chapel, and she had to communicate that development to the warden. There was no time to lose.

When José completed his inspection of the cellblocks, they left Mateo to watch over things in the control room and headed to the warden's office. Beth readily consented to accompany José. This could be her best chance to talk to him alone and convince him to concede this point.

"It's really important that the hostages are being cared for, José," Beth said when they arrived in the lobby. "If I can just check in on the ones in the chapel, then I can send the warden a message that they're doing okay. Maybe that will be enough to satisfy him."

"Go ahead and look if it makes you feel better," José replied dismissively. "But I don't need to satisfy the warden. He's the one who owes me."

Coop took Beth to the chapel and opened the door. The stench entered the hallway before the door was fully open, and Beth could not bring herself to step foot inside. When she peered in, the sight that greeted her was far worse than the smell. The guards were lying on the floor with their hands tied behind their backs. Their glazed-over eyes stared back at her, but they seemed too weak to raise their heads. Only the sentries sat upright on the long wooden pew. They acknowledged her with halfhearted waves.

Beth turned away and went back to José. She knew he would not appreciate another appeal for the hostages, and he might react poorly to a perceived scolding. She was walking a fine line between ally and enemy, but she decided that this issue was critical enough to justify the risk.

"José, they don't look healthy at all," she began. "You really have to take care of them. They need fresh water. I can't tell you how important this is. The whole negotiation hinges on this. It really does. Please."

"Enough, Beth. Seriously. Enough," José snapped. "When I get what I want, then the warden can start asking for what he wants."

José's tone confirmed Beth's suspicion that his patience was nearing its end. She was supposed to contact the warden as soon as possible to communicate the status of the hostages. But if she revealed their condition, the police raid would happen sooner rather than later. She couldn't tell the warden that the hostages were fine either. It would be wrong and, in this case, it might actually be criminal for her to misrepresent the facts. Of course, she would not let the hostages die. But if she waited just a little longer before making contact, she might be able to convince José to make this one concession and tend to the hostages. If she did nothing, there was still a chance for a peaceful resolution.

Mateo burst into the lobby. Out of breath and leaning over with one hand on his knee, he held the radio out for José. "You better talk to them," he said between gasps. "This isn't good."

José took the radio and pressed the talk button. "Unless you've met my demands, there is nothing to talk about."

"This is Warden Hayward," a voice responded. "Your list of demands is in the hands of the governor now. There is nothing you or I can do about that. There is something else though, so please don't disconnect. The state police have arrested your mother. She's been charged with several crimes, including aiding and abetting, bringing contraband into a state prison, breach of peace, inciting a riot, and conspiracy to commit murder. Several of these are felonies, and obviously they carry severe sentences."

José's jaw dropped, his shoulders hunched, and he stood inches shorter than he had only moments before. He stared down at the radio, which had dropped from his hand.

Here it comes, Beth thought. *They had finally found José's mother.*

The voice continued from the radio on the floor. "We know everything about your mother's role in instigating this riot, and the state attorney's office will prosecute her to the fullest extent of the law. That said, I am willing to intercede on your behalf, Mr. Ayala. If you cooperate with us to bring this riot to a peaceful end, I will have the charges against your mother dropped. Your decision now will determine your mother's fate. You either release the hostages and facilitate the peaceful turnover of the prison to us, or your mother suffers. If you don't cooperate, I will make sure she spends this night and every future night in the custody of the state. She will live out the rest of her life in a correctional institution, and eventually she will die there. The way I see it, unless you want your mother, who obviously cares deeply for you, to be punished for your actions, you have no choice but to surrender."

Beth had warned the authorities about what would happen if they threatened José's mother, and they had still chosen to do it while Beth was inside the prison. She was alarmed by their obvious disregard for her safety.

"This is how we will proceed," the warden continued. "You will send the hostages out in an orderly manner, starting within the hour. Then, you will surrender yourself and your co-conspirators and walk through the front door unarmed and with your hands over your head. You will face prosecution for the actions you've taken during the riot, but your mother will not. If you do this, Mr. Ayala, you have my personal assurance that your mother will receive leniency."

Coop bent over to the pick up the radio, and José lashed out at him. He pushed Coop to his knees and unleashed a half dozen kicks to his chest, stomach, and arms, growling like a wild animal as he did so. Mateo and the others, eyes wide, stood by and watched the attack.

Beth finally found her voice. "José stop! Please!" she begged. "Coop isn't the one doing this. Please stop!"

He stopped and, panting from exertion, picked up the radio that Coop had unsuccessfully tried to retrieve for him.

"Don't mess with my mother, you fucker!" José screamed into the radio. "You just crossed the line, pig. I tried to negotiate with you, but all this time you've been planning this? If that's the way you want this to go, then I can play that game, and I can do it a hell of a lot better than you."

José dropped the radio and headed for the door to the central corridor. The forsaken device emitted a new voice, this one gentler and higher pitched.

"Pepito? Pepito? Soy tu madre. Por favor, Pepito. Respóndeme."

José slowly reversed direction and, again, bent over to pick up the radio. "Sí, mamá," he said. "Are you okay?"

"No," she replied. "The police found me, even though I stayed inside tía's house, like you told me. They broke her door down, and they're gonna put me in jail. I don't want to go to jail, Pepito." Her sobbing was audible, but she continued. "They want me to tell you to give up too, or else they'll kill you. Mi hijo, I don't want you to die. Promise me you will live."

"I will, mamá. And I will take care of you like I always do. I promise."

"This is the warden." The voice came again. "You must release the hostages—all of them, unharmed—and surrender yourself to the authorities. This is the only way that your mother will be spared a lifetime in prison. I will give you one hour to comply, but you must promise that no one will be hurt before then. What is your answer?"

"I won't let you use my mother against me," José said. "This fight for justice is bigger than any one of us. I won't let you change my plans. Like I said in my letter, you got until five o'clock today to meet my demands, or I kill hostages. That's my answer." José switched the radio off and handed it to Mateo. He leaned over and offered his hand to Coop, helping him to his feet. He patted Coop on the back but offered no apology for his assault.

Beth knew that José's reputation as a fierce leader would be weakened by the broadcast of the conversation with his mother, her use of his childhood nickname, and her pleas for him to surrender. Beth heard noises coming from the central corridor at a volume unsurpassed by any she had heard in the prison before. It frightened her. Neither she nor José uttered a word, not that they would have heard each other anyway, until Mateo walked over and slammed the door shut.

José was first to speak, and he leveled an accusatory stare at Beth. "Did you know about this?"

"No! This is the first I've heard of it," she said in defense. "The warden told me to make sure the hostages in the chapel were fed, and that was my only assignment for today. They said they were working on some other strategy, but I had no idea they were planning to arrest your mother. And I didn't know they were going to send her to jail." The last part, at least, was true.

"As much as I want you to stay here, Beth—" José motioned for the other inmates to give them privacy and, taking Beth by the arm, walked her a few steps away from the others before continuing. "As much as I want you in here with me, I need to you to stand up for me with the warden. This is wrong what he's doing to my mother. I know you think so too. She's totally innocent. I want you to go out there and tell the warden to leave my mother out of this. I need you to make sure she's safe." His voice lowered to a whisper. "Tell him that if the governor pardons her, reinstates parole, and puts it in writing that she will at least consider the rest of my demands, then I'll give myself up and the warden can have his prison back. Nobody else will die if he does this. But," he said, raising his voice enough for the others to hear, "if he doesn't do as I say, he'll regret it. I'll turn this place inside out, and he'll never clean up all the blood. You tell him that. Then you come back in here and let me know what he decides. The radios will be off from now on. I'm going to get all of them out of the blocks and smash them, so he can't threaten me again. You come back and let me know if I'm going to be remembered as the one who brought justice to my brothers or the one who brought death to his."

Beth agreed with José that using his mother as a pawn was morally wrong. Still, he was asking her to threaten the murder of innocent people. And if the warden refused to grant his requests, she was supposed to deliver that news to him and initiate a slaughter. That, she would not do. But at this point she couldn't tell what José might do—even what he might do to her—if she refused. She had no choice but to agree. Whether she carried out his instructions in the end was a decision she would make later.

"I'll tell him," Beth breathed her reply. José nodded, and Beth managed a stilted nod in return.

Coop hobbled forward to escort her to the exit and removed the metal rod that spanned the pull-handle of the door. He pushed the door open and whispered, "Don't come back, Beth. I don't think—" he sighed, "I don't think it'll be safe for you to come back. Bad things are going down, and it's gonna happen fast. I can feel it."

Chapter Thirty-Six

Outside

DAY FOUR
1:01 PM

Beth's thoughts wandered as she made the trek to the perimeter fence. José was clearly losing his hold of the prison. But what could she do, without betraying either her duty to the law or her mission to preserve life? It no longer seemed plausible that both sides could succeed simultaneously. By leaving the prison now, was she abandoning her responsibilities to help José and the other inmates?

No, she decided. There was still a chance to bring the revolution to a peaceful end. That belief was the only thing keeping her upright. But she needed to act quickly.

Beth rushed into the command center. "We don't have a lot of time," she began. "José's losing—" She was cut off suddenly by a constricting and unwelcome embrace.

"Oh, you must be Mary Beth! My Pepito told me all about you. Let me look at you," the woman gushed, releasing Beth from the bear hug but still gripping her arms. "You are beautiful."

Beth shook her head, not in disagreement but in disbelief, and finally took notice of her surroundings. The woman whom she assumed was José's mother was still holding onto her, and everyone else was watching with almost as much surprise as Beth felt. She locked eyes uncomfortably with the warden.

"That was a warm welcome," Captain Sullivan said, disapproval raging in every word. "It took an hour before she would even talk to us. We had to get an interpreter in here," he said, pointing to a diminutive man whose services were no longer needed but who had not yet been dismissed. "But apparently she can speak English just fine when she wants to, and it seems like you two are good friends."

The woman ignored Captain Sullivan, as well as Beth's attempts to respond. "I just want to thank you for helping my son. He's a good boy—a really good boy. And I know he depends on you. You are his inspiración. But José always takes care of his mamá first. These men are treating me bad, but José can't stop them because he's locked up. You'll help me, right? You'll make them let me go."

Beth sensed the anger emanating from Captain Sullivan and the warden. The men in the command center did not know what to do with this woman, and they hadn't predicted José's initial response to their threat to punish her. To Beth, this was a painfully clear example of how people on both sides misjudged the other.

José had mistakenly expected the warden to be sympathetic to his protests and be swayed, as he was, by the lessons of Frederick Douglass and others. He had expected that the administrators would acknowledge the truths as he presented them—that inmates were people who had value and that everyone, even the guards, should face the same justice. José had thought that negotiations would have a foundation built on the same set of facts. And he had thought that the governor would be concerned with justice rather than simply regaining control.

Likewise, the warden and his colleagues had failed to understand that the inmates were complex human beings with mixed allegiances. José was indeed the mastermind of a deadly prison riot, but he was at the same time a devoted son, a loyal member of the Los Solidos gang, and an engaged student who enjoyed reading poetry and discussing profound ideas. The warden only wanted the riot to be over. He cared nothing about the injustice José was fighting against, and he didn't grasp the inmates' level of commitment to the cause. Beth reluctantly admitted that any negotiation between these people, who were unable to recognize each other's multifaceted humanity, was doomed to failure.

"I don't know if I can help you," Beth spoke softly to José's mother, gently pulling out of her grasp. She turned to the warden next. "That's what I was trying to say—José is willing to deal for his mother's safety, but he has specific terms."

"What do you mean?" the warden asked. "That isn't what he said over the radio. I don't know if you heard, but he seemed quite unwilling to cooperate."

"I heard." Beth let out a breath, remembering José's rage. "But think about it—the other inmates were listening in on their own radios. What else could he have said? He's already losing control of the prison. If he'd agreed over the radio, it would have been all over right then. The hostages would be dead, and I might not have made it out alive."

"Then how do you know he'll deal?" Agent Dean didn't sound upset, just confused.

"He told me in private right before I left, so his men wouldn't hear. He wants a full pardon for his mother, as well as a return of parole and assurances that the rest of his demands will be considered," Beth explained. "He will surrender himself and turn over control of the prison if those conditions are met." She paused. "Surely we can grant those requests if it means a peaceful end."

"My staff is working on a document that addresses each of the inmates' demands," Fitzroy added. "It doesn't grant them by any means, but it acknowledges them. I'll check on that."

"We haven't heard anything more on the radios. We've tried to contact the inmates again, but there's been no response. Do you know why that is?" Agent Dean addressed this question to Beth.

"Yes." She knew. "José won't communicate further except for an answer to his demands delivered by me. When I left, he said he was going to find and destroy all the radios, so you won't be able to threaten him again."

"So, José isn't listening anymore?" Colonel Mitchell was suddenly interested. "But, certainly he won't find all of the radios. There must be others that are hidden. Maybe some guards managed to keep theirs? Plus, I assume that there are inmates who aren't one hundred percent on board with José's plan. Isn't that right?" Beth nodded. She thought about Angel in D-Block and how José had barred that cellblock door. He wouldn't get the radios from in there.

"Good. Good." Colonel Mitchell clapped his hands together. "We'll give him some time to destroy all the radios he knows about, and then we'll have a way to talk with the inmates who don't support him."

"There's more you should know," Beth began, but she was interrupted by commotion near the door.

Captain Sullivan was having a heated conversation with José's mother. "You don't need to be here anymore," he yelled. "You should sit in a jail cell until we know what the outcome is." He turned his fierce gaze at the police interpreter. "You, get out of here, and take her with you."

The officer complied, taking hold of her arm.

"Cuff her," Captain Sullivan ordered.

"What? No!" the woman shouted. "Stop pushing me!"

"Lydia Henry," the warden said. "You entered my home under false pretenses and took advantage of my sick wife. You helped the leader of a riot get a weapon that he used to kill an innocent person. That's why you're leaving here in handcuffs, and that's why you're going directly to jail." For the first time ever, Beth noted malice in the warden's words and behavior.

José's mother abandoned all restraint. She lashed out against the officer who had yet to fasten a handcuff to one of her wrists, knocking him into Andrew and sending papers flying. Colonel Mitchell came to the officer's aid, pinning the thrashing woman with his knee on her back and struggling to affix the handcuffs. Once restrained, the two officers lifted her by the arms and dragged her out of the command center. All the while, she screamed, "Ay! Get off me! Bastardo! Cabrón!"

Beth wanted to scream as well. She thought of how José would react if he knew his mother was being treated this way.

The command center was quiet after the woman's forcible eviction.

Captain Sullivan was the first to break the silence. "Have the hostages been fed yet?"

There it was. Beth braced herself. "No," she admitted. "I tried to convince him, but he said 'no.' The guards in the cellblocks are okay, I think, but not the ones in the chapel." She remembered the incident in B-Block. *Most of the guards in the cellblocks.* She would tell them about Monroe soon. She just had to build up the courage.

The warden simply shook his head. Fitzroy lifted his cell phone to his ear and left the room.

"You were supposed to tell us that right away!" Captain Sullivan shouted. "Those were your orders. This changes everything! What else haven't you told us? We heard someone on the radio order a cell door opened in B-Block. What was that for?"

Beth's throat caught, and she let out a ragged breath.

"What? Tell me what happened!" Captain Sullivan demanded.

"They killed a guard," Beth confessed. "It was Officer Monroe." Her voice grew quiet, the words sticking in her throat. "They stabbed him to death."

"Son of a bitch! How could you let that happen?" Captain Sullivan shouted. He lunged at her, but Colonel Mitchell caught him and twisted his arm behind his back. Captain Sullivan cried out. Agent Dean scrambled to help drag him toward the door, and this time it was Captain Sullivan's turn to be forcibly removed from the command center.

"If we don't respond soon," Beth warned, "at least to acknowledge the inmates' demands, the whole place could go up in smoke. We'll lose a lot of the hostages for sure."

"This riot ends now, Ms. Sharpe," the warden replied. "Since another guard has been killed, we must assume that the others are in imminent danger. We can't leave them in there—not for another minute. More could die if we don't act. There is no other choice. Plus, in case you haven't heard, riots have started in several other prisons. If this goes on much longer, we're going to lose control of the entire state correctional system."

Beth hadn't heard. But this explained some of the urgency in the decision-making.

"As much as I wanted to negotiate, this has to be finished now, one way or the other. It's the only option left," the warden concluded.

Colonel Mitchell took his cue. "Governor Webb told us to wait until dark, but I'm ready to go any time. Our forces are assembled over the hill, out of sight from inside the prison. It will be a surprise attack with enough force to overpower any resistance. At a moment's notice, I can have the assault vehicles through the fence and pulled right up to the building. We'll deliver 300 heavily armed officers to the front door. They'll be inside within minutes, and they'll have no problem putting down the leaders and regaining control of the facility."

Panic threatened to overtake Beth, but she wouldn't give up yet. "No. It's not the only option." Beth looked to the warden, to Colonel Mitchell, and back to the warden again. "You want this over now. I get it, but it doesn't mean that everyone has to die in the process. You don't need to attack. All we have to do is give José's mother immunity and promise to bring back parole and seriously consider the rest of his demands. That's all he's asking for now. That isn't too much. Let me go back in. I'll convince José to surrender. Give me one more chance. I can do it."

"You've had enough chances," Colonel Mitchell said. "And you've accomplished nothing. Why should this time be any different?"

"The governor's office is in favor of allowing Ms. Sharpe another opportunity," Fitzroy stated as a matter of fact. Beth hadn't noticed him return after leaving to make a call. "We are willing to grant immunity to Lydia Henry, and I have a letter stating that the governor has heard the inmates' complaints. If Ms. Sharpe can convince the leader to surrender, that would be the best case scenario. If not, and Ms. Sharpe remains inside, she could provide the diversion we need to ensure that the police raid is a success. The inmates will not expect an assault while she is inside, so we can launch the attack without them realizing it." Fitzroy handed the letter to Beth, and she put it in her pocket.

"I must point out that Ms. Sharpe will be at significant risk if she is present during the raid," Colonel Mitchell said. "I cannot guarantee her safety. She might be killed in the crossfire."

"I'm aware of that," Fitzroy admitted, "as is the governor. But Ms. Sharpe has made her own bed, as they say, and if she is asking to lie in it, we are quite willing to let her do so if it increases our chances for success."

No one in the command center objected to Fitzroy's logic or to his conclusion. Beth didn't even care that the governor was willing to sacrifice her for a chance at a more efficient assault on the prison. If she survived the day, perhaps she would eventually feel offended by their low valuation of her life. At the moment, however, she was willing to do whatever they asked if it meant she had another opportunity to save her friends.

"Surely, we can wait until nightfall. Right, colonel?" The warden was making one last attempt to save her. "Ms. Sharpe, try to get Ayala to surrender, if you're willing to take that risk. But do it quickly and get out of there. There is no need for you to die today."

"That's the plan then," Fitzroy decided.

"But we need to be ready just in case," Agent Dean said. "I've seen enough hostage situations to know that this could go downhill fast. Believe me. I've been in this exact position before. We don't want to be caught off guard if we have to rush in there."

Colonel Mitchell nodded. "I understand. My men will be ready. But I have another idea." He paused a moment.

Spit it out, Beth thought. She was eager to get out of there and back to the prison.

Colonel Mitchell spoke into a radio, which was tuned to the frequency used inside the prison, "To any inmates or prison personnel who can hear my voice, the police are retaking the prison. If you want to survive, you must remain in your cells. Stay calm and surrender yourself to the police. Do not fight. We are coming in soon."

"What are you doing?" the warden protested. "You're tipping them off?"

"We know the leaders destroyed their radios," Colonel Mitchell explained. "But there's no way they got all of them. Some of the guards might be listening. Giving them the heads-up could save your men's lives."

"I understand," the warden nodded, turning toward the information specialists. "Andrew, keep broadcasting that message while we prepare the raid."

"I'm ready," Beth declared. She pushed past the others to exit the command center.

The men caught up with her as she reached the outer gate. She passed through, and an officer closed it behind her. Before proceeding, Beth turned and spoke to Colonel Mitchell. "The cafeteria door is clear now," she told him. "The debris that was blocking it is gone. There's only one prisoner guarding it, as far as I know. You can access the central corridor and the rest of the prison easily from there."

"What? Why are you telling me this now?"

Beth perceived doubt, as well as shock, in his eyes. "I'm telling you the truth, colonel. I swear. The back entrance is your best way in." She hoped that telling Colonel Mitchell about the unsecured cafeteria entrance would increase the effectiveness of the impending raid. If the police met less resistance when they entered the prison, fewer people would die in the process. While she couldn't save everyone, she might at least lower the death toll if the raid happened.

Colonel Mitchell rushed off, barking orders into his radio, and Beth walked as fast as she could toward the prison. She needed to make José understand that this was his last chance. He could choose to live and to fight for his beliefs another day, or—and she knew this was more likely—he could choose to fight.

A burning smell nudged Beth out of her thoughts. She looked up to see a spiraling column of black smoke billowing from somewhere inside the prison. Her comment earlier about the prison going up in smoke came back to her. She hadn't meant it literally. She pushed the accidentally prophetic comment out of her mind. She was still going in.

Chapter Thirty-Seven

Inside

DAY FOUR
4:05 PM

Beth let herself in. No one had replaced the metal rod that had secured the front door for the past four days. Perhaps Coop had forgotten when he had let her out earlier, or maybe he had done it on purpose. The silence that had greeted her every other time she entered the prison lobby was replaced by sounds of shouting and the slamming of doors. She spotted a figure in light blue run past the propped-open door to the central corridor. The pattering sound of running feet faded as he ran toward the cafeteria, then it disappeared entirely as the door slammed shut behind him. Was it one of the head cases that had been released to help fight against the first SWAT raid? Or was it someone who had recently escaped from one of the cellblocks? Maybe it was one of José's men who had abandoned his post. In any case, José's control of the prison was unraveling. Beth knew this with certainty. Fear wrenched her body, temporarily paralyzing her, as she began to fully recognize the danger she was in.

She heard a thud behind her, and she held her breath but did not move. It was the defense of a helpless creature against a motion-sensitive predator, but it would be utterly ineffective against a human attacker. Fortunately for Beth, the sound was Mateo emerging from the warden's office. He rushed to her side. "Beth! Are you alright? Talk to me. Come on."

Beth recovered somewhat as the result of Mateo's concerned attention, and she agreed to accompany him to the control room where she would be safe. The two didn't make it that far, however, before José spotted them in the central corridor and motioned for them to go back to the lobby.

José and his entourage followed, and they assembled together facing Beth. Coop fidgeted and glanced repeatedly over his shoulder toward the central corridor. Big G shifted his weight from one leg to the other, a wooden club grasped tightly in his hand. He was standing so close to his little brother that they could have been holding hands.

"You came back!" José said enthusiastically. "What did the warden say about my mother? Will he pardon her and give us back parole?"

Beth ignored his question. Hers were more pressing. "Where's the smoke coming from? What's happening?"

"You saw smoke? I didn't know if the fire was big enough yet. It's Angel and his guys in D-Block, of course. They must've started a fire. They're trying to smoke us out, I guess. Or else it's just for fun. I don't fucking know. They've been trouble from the start," José said. "That was my only mistake in all this—putting Angel in charge of one of the blocks."

"*That* was your only mistake?" Beth had finally reached the limits of both her empathy and her patience. She was angry and frustrated, and she'd had enough. She clenched her fists by her side and tightened her whole body. "What about starting this whole thing in the first place? Don't you think that was a mistake? And outright refusing to feed the hostages? That one thing would've given you some leverage. I'll tell you what. That was a huge mistake. And then you killed Monroe right in front of me yesterday. I had to tell them. Captain Sullivan nearly lost his mind, and the police can't trust that the hostages are safe anymore. I've been trying to save you, José. I've been trying to get you to cooperate because that's the only way you could succeed, but you just wouldn't listen! The governor has a response to your demands," she said, taking Fitzroy's letter out of her pocket and waving it in front of him. "But now you're out of time, José.

"My mother?"

"Well, I just watched the police wrestle her to the ground and drag her away in handcuffs. They'll pardon her if you give yourself up right now. If not, she's going to prison, and it's because of your stubbornness. Everyone wants this over now, and the police are going to raid at dark. You have to surrender before that happens. It's the only chance you have to survive."

José simply shook his head. He seemed lost for a response.

Mateo gasped, his eyes wide with alarm. "José. You hear that, man?"

They listened. Beth's first thought was that it was raining. But then she saw José's face go pale. The sound was the drumming of hundreds of rampaging footsteps. Howls and cries from the central corridor echoed into the lobby.

They had no time to escape. No time to prepare for a fight. No time to decide which of those was the best option. Krueger appeared in the doorway, and Angel walked in behind them. They both started toward José.

"Run, Beth. Get out of here!" José yelled.

Beth's gaze met José's, and she suffered with him through a quick succession of anguish, regret, and finally surrender. Krueger reached José in an instant and seized him by the throat. Angel punched Mateo in the face and wrestled him to the floor.

José did not attempt to free himself from Krueger's grasp. In fact, he did nothing at all to resist. Beth realized, to her horror, that José had given up. He would have none of the justice he so desperately wanted, and he was sacrificing himself because his cause was lost.

There was nothing she could do to save him, and her urge for self-preservation took over. She pivoted toward the exit, but with her hand on the door, she stopped. José was beyond salvation now, but the others were not. "Coop, come with me! Baby G! Hurry!" Beth shouted.

Inmates pushed through the door from the central corridor. So many were trying to enter at once that they created a temporary blockage, but the force of their bodies finally broke through the log-jam, and they swarmed in.

Beth ran out of the prison, leaving behind their collective hopes for justice.

But all were not lost. Coop and Baby G ran out with her. Big G made it out too, but he walked from the prison, rather than ran.

CHAPTER THIRTY-EIGHT

Outside

DAY FOUR
4:12 PM

Beth stopped running and waved her arms above her. Then she pointed toward the prison. She alternated between these two gestures in the hope that Colonel Mitchell would start the raid. Now that the inmates were actually rioting inside, the police raid might save lives.

Army National Guard soldiers and police began entering through the front gate. Beth was amazed at how quickly they were reacting, but she remembered Agent Dean's warning about how the situation might unravel and Colonel Mitchell's promise to be ready.

Beth remained standing halfway between the prison and the fence, forcing the soldiers to go around her as they jogged toward the entrance. When she looked into the soldiers' faces, she saw terrified young men who had been trained for combat but were inexperienced fighters and loathed to play any role in this attack. She presumed that they knew about the previous failed raid and the casualties that had resulted. These young men had likely never before grappled with violent criminals, and they had never faced the kind of danger that they would confront inside the prison walls. Their predicament was no less desperate than her own. She watched helplessly as the police tackled Coop and the others who had run out with her.

Beth walked slowly out the gate, passing several military vehicles, their parted camouflage canvas releasing more soldiers. She did not bother to ask about the level of force the soldiers would use against the inmates. She already knew the answer.

She also knew that José would not survive the raid. She had deserted him—just as she had rejected and abandoned her father when he was most vulnerable. Her actions had caused the two people she loved most to take their own lives. Her father had done so several years before, leaving behind a note that apologized for his uselessness and explained that his choice was no one else's fault. But Beth knew the truth. She had driven him to despair.

José would die at the hands of his fellow inmates, but the end result was the same. The people she cared for most had both decided that leaving this world was their best option. And, once again, Beth was alone.

More inmates ran out of the prison and surrendered to the police who restrained them and rushed them toward the many vehicles lined up to hold them.

The soldiers entered the prison, and the sound of gunshots followed. A wearingly long time passed before the radio cackled to life. "We have the building secured. Repeat. The building is secured."

CHAPTER THIRTY-NINE

Outside

The police raid was a success. At least that was what they were calling it. Beth wasn't sure if she agreed. Either way, the warden was back in charge of the Arnone State Correctional Institution, at least for the time being. Even if the prison reopened in the future, Ronald Hayward was unlikely to be appointed to the leadership position. Beth doubted that the prison would ever return to operation again anyway. The building itself was unrecognizable from the one she had known. There was a large hole in the wall of D-Block that the fire department had made to access the flames. The fire had also created a hole in the roof, leaving the interior saturated with water and wholly exposed to the elements.

With the raid over, the first priority for the government was to rescue the hostages. Beth and the others watched from outside the perimeter fence as those who were able to do so walked out of the prison. Medical personnel waited outside to escort the injured hostages to the many ambulances lined up along the road.

The media had taken advantage of the distractions to sneak closer to the action, positioning themselves in the crowd of spectators.

Beth noted the television crews pressed up against the fence, focusing their cameras on the haggard hostages trudging toward the gate. She felt a perverse pleasure in the fact that the governor had not been granted her wish for the raid to happen after dark. The whole world would see, in the full light of day, the reality of the prison riot and the aftermath of the government raid to end it by force.

The dramatic reactions of bystanders and family members provided additional fodder for the cameras. A woman offered one such spectacle, shrieking and sobbing, when she caught sight of her wife, a guard, hobbling toward the gate. Others boisterously lamented the absence of their loved ones. As was always true for the media and witnesses, the displays of emotional distress were far more captivating than those of relief.

Captain Sullivan helped one guard hobble toward the fence. It seemed that every one of the guard's heavy footsteps was causing him pain. When they passed through the gate, Captain Sullivan shouted, "Is Mrs. Palmer here?"

Some in the crowd scrambled to locate her. "I know she was here," one guard said. "Aubrey Palmer!" another yelled. "I'll go find her."

A few moments later, a woman came running, pushing people aside as she made her way to the gate. "I'm here!" she cried, grabbing him in a tight hug.

The battered guard did not return her embrace. His arms hung by his sides, his shoulders hunched, and he started crying. Beth wondered what kind of trauma he had suffered inside. It must have been something terrible. His wife stepped back, held his face in her hands, and tried to lift his head. But he would not allow it. He would not meet her eyes. He continued to weep, and it was such a sorrowful cry that everyone who heard it and witnessed the reunion was crying as well. Captain Sullivan guided the Palmers toward an awaiting ambulance.

The evacuation of hostages continued throughout the evening. Beth remained outside the fence, watching the prison door and hoping to see many more people walk through it. Once the cellblocks were locked down, ambulances drove up to the building, and the seriously injured hostages were carried out on stretchers. Only after the prison employees were rescued did attention turn to the welfare of the inmates. A second wave of ambulances carried the gravely wounded to area hospitals. Everyone else, including those with less serious injuries, remained locked inside through the night.

Chapter Forty

Outside

DAY FIVE
6:10 AM

Beth remained on the prison grounds all night. She managed to get an hour of sleep, lying in the field with her blazer rolled up under her head. Dawn broke, and buses arrived to transport the inmates out of Arnone and deliver them to other prisons throughout the state. Warden Hayward was overseeing the proceedings with a clipboard in hand. Captain Sullivan followed silently behind him, seeming to be more of a shadow than an assistant.

Beth squinted through the fence links in an attempt to identify the survivors from afar. She glimpsed a handcuffed Angel as he boarded a bus, flanked as always by members of his Latin Kings crew. Beth was not at all surprised by Angel's survival, but she questioned why he should live when so many others had not. Angel had deliberately sought to undermine José's authority, despite his pledge to support him. He was the least worthy of a second chance at life.

Hours later, as the last buses drove away, another type of vehicle took their place—a white sedan with the state crest and the words, "medical examiner," emblazoned on its doors. A van of the same color and markings followed. Beth realized that anyone who would leave the prison alive had already done so. The rest would be carried out in body bags, and that was precisely what happened next.

The medical examiner's staff began carrying bodies out of the prison and laying them in a neat line in front of the building. Again, Beth's thoughts went to the governor and how she must be reacting to this scene being broadcast by the media. She no doubt regretted her decision to spend taxpayer money to replace the prison's old bronze dedication plaques with new ones that prominently displayed her name. Beth almost smiled and then caught herself, disturbed by her own secret thoughts.

The body bags multiplied, numbering in the dozens, by the time a tractor trailer truck arrived to haul them away. The warden and Captain Sullivan stepped between the black lumps, stopping to peer into each one as the medical examiner's staff unzipped the bags. Based on their shrugs and gestures, it was obvious, even from where Beth stood many yards away, that the two men were unable to identify the occupants of the bags. The warden looked up from his futile efforts and pointed to Beth. Captain Sullivan nodded, lumbered toward the main gate, and motioned for her to approach. Beth thought she knew what he was going to ask. She steeled herself, but she was ready to agree.

"Come with me," Captain Sullivan demanded. Beth's preparation proved unnecessary, since no question came. She followed the captain regardless.

As usual, the warden was more considerate than his colleague. "I'm sorry to ask this of you," he said, leading her toward the first in the long row of body bags. "I thought you might help identify the bodies. Since you're familiar with the inmates, maybe you will recognize some of them. It'll certainly make the medical examiner's job easier."

"I'll do my best," Beth promised.

The medical examiner stood by with a clipboard and pen in her hand, while her white-suited assistant unzipped the first bag. Warden Hayward, Captain Sullivan, and Beth all leaned over to peer inside, and their simultaneous movements resulted in a near collision of their heads. The medical examiner motioned for the men to step back. "Give her some space."

Beth leaned over the bag again and examined the face in it. She shook her head and shrugged her shoulders. "I'm sorry," she said, "I don't know who this is."

"Well, you're no use at all are you?" Captain Sullivan looked like he had more to say, but the warden stopped him.

"Calm down, captain," the warden said wearily. "Why don't you try the next one, Ms. Sharpe?"

Beth nodded, and they moved to the next body in the line. This time, Beth recognized the face inside. It was contorted, with one eye partially opened and the other pinched shut. The jaw jutted to one side, and the open mouth revealed a broken canine tooth. "I know this man. It's Mateo Ray. He is," she corrected herself, "he was José's best friend."

Captain Sullivan grunted, whether in acknowledgement for her help or in satisfaction that Mateo was dead, Beth did not know. She suspected it was the latter. The medical examiner scribbled on her papers and instructed her assistant to zip the body bag closed and move to the next one in the line.

Beth was unable to identify the next body, but since the word "rata" had been carved into the man's forehead, she surmised that he had been assigned to the prison's protective custody unit. That detail would narrow the list of possible names to those housed in H-Block.

The assistant unzipped the next body bag, and Beth peeked inside. She gasped and covered her mouth with her hand, immediately recognizing Squeeze's black, slicked back hair and his shiny chest peeking through the open collar of the uniform he had taken from a guard in B-Block. The perfectly-applied red lipstick on the left side of his mouth was smeared across the other half and beyond, leaving red clumps in a line across his right cheek. It looked as if he were in the act of applying it at the moment he was killed. Beth clenched her fists and willed her tears not to fall.

After Squeeze, Beth identified the next body as Krueger. She was surprised that Krueger was dead, but she was equally shocked by her feelings about it. She felt satisfied—even glad—that Krueger had not survived. Krueger had quietly defied José, solely to allow himself more opportunities to satisfy his sadistic urges. She wondered which inmate, or more likely inmates, had finally gotten him. Before today, she had believed that every person's life had the same value. But now she was questioning even that simplest idea. Somehow, Krueger's killing seemed justified.

Beth looked into yet another body bag. "Oh," she stammered. "I'm sorry, Captain Sullivan, but this is one of your men—the guard I told you about—Monroe. He was murdered."

Captain Sullivan growled and bared his teeth. "Goddammit!" he roared. "I didn't recognize him. Why the hell is he wearing an inmate's clothes? Help me lift him. He doesn't deserve to be lying here with these pieces of shit." One of the medical examiner's assistants helped him drag the body bag away from the others, disrupting the orderly pattern they'd formed. Captain Sullivan ambled to the gate to arrange for transportation of the body and notification of his family.

To Beth, Captain Sullivan's reaction was proof of the validity of José's complaints. Monroe was just as mean as Krueger and as criminal as any of the inmates. But Monroe had power and was protected by his position. He was "too good," according to the captain, to even lie beside the inmates.

Beth sighed and resumed her duties, peering into the next body bag.

Her breath caught in her throat. The moment she'd dreaded, but accepted as inevitable, had arrived. José's empty eyes stared past her. His face was not contorted or mutilated like many of the others. In fact, he looked almost exactly the same as when she last saw him, although his blood-soaked shirt hinted at the location of his mortal injuries. She was grateful that Captain Sullivan was busy elsewhere. She wasn't sure if she could handle his ridicule in this moment.

Beth did not cry or lament or even avert her eyes. Instead, she announced, "This is José Ayala. He was the leader of the Arnone Prison Revolution. He died fighting against the injustice of the prison system, and he sacrificed himself for that cause."

Beth hoped that she was honoring José with this declaration. She yearned for some formal acknowledgement of his dignity and of her fidelity, but she received neither. The warden made no reply, and the medical examiner simply scribbled on her papers.

Beth continued to scrutinize the faces of the dead inmates. Some she recognized, including Hacker and T.K. Others she did not. The absence of some from this ill-fated group was notable. Angel and Fido were still alive, likely because they had abandoned José. Just like Beth. Most of those who'd been devoted to his cause were zipped into body bags. But she was still alive, cataloguing their remains.

By midday, all of the bodies had been taken away and the survivors moved to different facilities. Beth's responsibilities were fulfilled, and she, along with the others who had stood vigil throughout the ordeal, would finally leave the prison grounds.

The riot was over, but Beth wondered if she could ever recover. She had lost so much, and she was not the only one. The loved ones of those who died would suffer through grief for their losses. The hostages would process their experiences and deal with post-traumatic stresses, as would many of the inmates who had been caught up in or witnessed the brutality inside. Even the soldiers and police officers who had participated in the raids would likely be tormented by memories of the horrors they saw inside. The lives of all the survivors would be forever changed.

Governor Webb would be dealing with the fallout from this mess for a long time to come. Beth took some consolation in the knowledge that the government would be forced to deal with José's demands, even though the riot was over. The contents of José's letter had already been disseminated to the media, and the governor was promising to conduct a full investigation into the allegations of mistreatment and abuse in the prison system. The television news channels were discussing the injustice of eliminating the possibility of parole for inmates who clearly deserved a chance at freedom. The public was finally being forced to recognize the reality of the hopelessness that inmates faced. Surely, some progress toward justice would come from José's sacrifice, even though he would never see it.

Beth walked past Warden Hayward, who was speaking with Commissioner Holmes near the mobile command center. His shoulders were more rounded than they had been before the riot started, his head tipped forward as if it were too heavy for his neck, and his face sagged. This five-day ordeal had added ten years to his appearance. His reputation in the community was forever tarnished, and his otherwise illustrious career would be eclipsed by this one terrible event.

Dan was waiting for her by the road, and he smiled as she approached. She knew their relationship would not last, and her conscience was screaming for her to stop taking advantage of him, since his feelings for her went well beyond her own. There was only so much guilt one person could bear, and Beth had reached her limit. But he was exactly what she needed right now, so she would go home with Dan that night and allow herself the familiar comfort of his embrace. But she would end the relationship soon—for both of their sakes.

Beth had learned her lesson. But she had learned it in the hardest possible way. She had been naïve, as her colleagues had pointed out all along. She had taught José and the other inmates about the principles of justice without considering how their life experiences would influence their understanding of it. She had focused on empowering them and wanting to make a difference, but she hadn't realized they would interpret the ideas—and even her own words—as a call to revolution. She had overlooked the impact that their backgrounds of poverty, violence, and systematic injustice would have on their analyses of everything. She wished she could have learned this lesson by some other means. But how else could she do life except the hard way?

Her mistakes had caused tragedy. And it wasn't the first time. What she felt now was something beyond pain. There was a pressure on her chest that threatened to suffocate her. She could not breathe deeply enough to weep, but she felt a tear roll gently down her cheek.

Though Beth found herself doubting whether her own life still had value, she would not—could not—allow herself to crumble into despair. She had to persevere through her anguish. She had saved Coop, Big G, and Baby G. That was something—a small accomplishment, to be sure, but something.

Perhaps that was what she needed to do going forward—focus on smaller steps that lead toward the ultimate goal. She would not cower in the face of the community's judgement of her. She could help Coop by providing testimony about how he had tried to minimize the violence during the revolution. She would continue to speak out.

The struggle within the criminal justice system would continue, as it should, until the inequities were acknowledged and addressed. So too would the struggle within the individuals who suffered with the consequences of their own poor choices in a system that was stacked against them. José's struggle was over, but Beth's was not. She would continue to work for justice. She would carry on the struggle within.

THE END